IRON TONGUE OF MIDNIGHT

◆ The Forge & Fracture Saga ◆

IRON TONGUE OF MIDNIGHT

◆ The Forge & Fracture Saga ◆

BRITTANY N. WILLIAMS

AMULET BOOKS • NEW YORK

PUBLISHER'S NOTE: This is a work of fiction. Names, characters, places, and incidents are either the product of the author's imagination or used fictitiously, and any resemblance to actual persons, living or dead, business establishments, events, or locales is entirely coincidental.

Cataloging-in-Publication Data has been applied for and may be obtained from the Library of Congress.

ISBN 978-1-4197-5868-3
eISBN 978-1-64700-525-2

Text © 2025 Brittany N. Williams
Book design by Chelsea Hunter
Sword artwork courtesy Ezepov Dmitry/Shutterstock.com
Maps on pages vi–vii by Jaime Zollars

Published in 2025 by Amulet Books, an imprint of ABRAMS. All rights reserved. No portion of this book may be reproduced, stored in a retrieval system, or transmitted in any form or by any means, mechanical, electronic, photocopying, recording, or otherwise, without written permission from the publisher.

Printed and bound in the United States
10 9 8 7 6 5 4 3 2 1

Amulet Books are available at special discounts when purchased in quantity for premiums and promotions as well as fundraising or educational use. Special editions can also be created to specification. For details, contact specialsales@abramsbooks.com or the address below.

Amulet Books® is a registered trademark of Harry N. Abrams, Inc.

ABRAMS The Art of Books
195 Broadway, New York, NY 10007
abramsbooks.com

Whitehall Palace

Thames river

The Globe
London

DRAMATIS PERSONAE

The Sands Family
Joan—a teenage swordswoman blessed by Ogun
James—her twin brother & an actor blessed by Oya
Bess—her mother blessed by Elegua
Thomas—her father blessed by Yemoja
Nan—their maid

The Shakespeare Family
William—playwright & actor blessed by Oshun
Mary—his mother blessed by Obatala
Anne—his wife blessed by Oya
Susanna—his oldest daughter blessed by Shango
Judith—his youngest daughter blessed by Ochoosi

The King's Men
William Shakespeare—playwright & actor blessed by Oshun
Richard Burbage—actor
Nicholas "Nick" Tooley—actor
Robert Armin—actor
Rob Gough—actor

The Fae
Titanea—queen of the fae disguised as Queen Anne
Robin Goodfellow—a powerful fae
Rose—their half-mortal daughter
Herne the Hunter—leader of the Wild Hunt
Various sirens, red caps, jacks-in-irons, goblins, hags, grim, and the like

The Children of the Orisha
Sir Oscar Pearce—a knight blessed by Aganju
Tobias—a young man blessed by Elegua
Avalee—a young woman blessed by Oshun
Martin—a man blessed by Ochoosi
Roger—a man blessed by Ochoosi

The Royal Court in Exile
King James I—king of England
Philip Herbert—Earl of Montgomery & the king's favorite
William Cecil—Robert Cecil's son
Frances Cecil—Robert Cecil's daughter
Grace—a palace servant

IRON TONGUE OF MIDNIGHT

◆ The Forge & Fracture Saga ◆

CHAPTER ONE
All the Devils Are Here

hree months ago, the Pact protecting the mortal realm shattered. Ten days ago, assassins murdered its custodian, Benjamin Wick, in his cell in the Tower of London. Eight days ago, the Fae and their queen conquered Whitehall Palace as the children of the Orisha fled.

Augustine Phillips shoved Joan through the magical doorway into Stratford-upon-Avon as fingers burst through his chest in a spray of blood that splattered across her skin.

Seven days ago, Joan Sands decided she was done losing.

"Close it," Phillips whispered, crimson dripping from his lips.

Joan stood before the forge in her father's workshop, their abandoned house creaking and groaning around her. Wind buffeted the front windows. They shook violently in their frames as January's chill claimed the air inside. The hollow sounds thundered in the stark absence of the home's inhabitants.

Of her family.

She shivered beneath her heavy wool cloak and rubbed at her icy nose. Her brother's clothes offered less of a shield from the cold than her usual gowns, but she hadn't borrowed them for comfort. Maybe the discomfort was payment for her deception.

Joan could accept that, if this gambit succeeded. And it must succeed.

Blood gushed down Phillips' doublet as another set of fingers shoved through his chest.

"Close the doorway," Joan rasped, her voice tight with tears. *"Close it."*

The old man seemed to smile before the hands impaling him rent his body in two. The bloody remains fell away to reveal Goodfellow, cold-eyed and covered in gore. They stared at Joan as the portal between London and Stratford-upon-Avon slammed closed between them.

Bile rose in her throat as she swiped at the wetness splattered across her face. She looked down, expecting her palm to be smeared with blood again but found it clean, the phantom droplets nothing but a memory. She clenched her fist. That moment refused to leave her. The sudden spray of red, the horrific sound of rending flesh and bone, the sharp ache of betrayal.

Bia's warm metal pressed against the skin of her wrist, a stark contrast to the air around her. The shrunken sword hummed gently, offering comfort.

Enough.

Joan huffed out a breath and strode toward the cold forge, shifting her heavy cloak back over her shoulders. Her feet squelched over the spoilt rushes strewn across the floor, the damp stink of rot wafting up with each step. Shadows stretched long against the orange light of the setting sun as the few candles she'd lit made them twist and dance at the edges of her vision. The neglected hearth gaped like an open mouth. A breeze shot down the chimney, puffing old soot into Joan's face. She sneezed and shivered again.

They'd only been gone a week, yet her family's home felt foreign and hostile.

Another injury she'd pay back to Titanea, perhaps soon. Joan had placed herself in the middle of the Fae's territory, and their queen would take notice.

She *had* to take notice, for the sake of the others. This audacious gamble would prove worthless otherwise, and the consequences of failure were unacceptable. She refused to lose anyone else.

Joan grabbed the spade from the rack leaned against the stone base and raked it along the grate to sweep the old ashes away. Each loud scrape vibrated in her chest, drawing her back to the present. A fine dust kicked up into the air as she worked. It sparkled in the fading sunlight. She'd allowed the uncanny emptiness of her home and the seductive pull of painful memories to distract her, but this, this familiar, repetitive movement, this action, settled her mind.

This felt right.

She cleaned until she was satisfied, then hauled up an armful of wood in one scoop, the bulky weight nothing against her supernatural strength. She tossed the logs into the forge, and they clattered into a messy pile. The sound echoed around her, devouring the silence greedily. Joan threw one more in for good measure.

At this moment, Joan's mother and Master Shakespeare were with Master Burbage and Nick retrieving the families they'd been forced to leave behind after Titanea's victory.

This was why Joan snuck to London today. She'd draw Titanea to this house and distract her while the Burbages and Tooleys were rescued. She'd only have to evade Titanea until James revealed that Joan had come to London in his place and sent their mother to retrieve her.

The plan was far from perfect and quite dangerous, but Joan would do anything to cure Master Burbage of the melancholy that shrank his great presence and the misery that hung round Nick's neck like a loadstone. Besides, she could handle the risk. As a child of Ogun, she was the only one who could now that her godfather was dead.

Joan tried to swallow around the lump in her throat and turned back to lighting the forge. She snatched up the kindling, shoving it furiously into the gaps between the firewood. She flinched, hissing as the splinter buried itself beneath her skin. The tiny point of pain grounded her in the present. She wiped away the blood and let possibilities of the far future flow from her mind.

Anger made her sloppy. She need only focus on lighting the fire and preparing for Titanea to find her here. Any other worries left her vulnerable.

She lifted the flint and steel, tilted it at an angle, and struck. The spark caught the kindling on the first hit. She leaned forward, blowing gently against the tiny flame.

"James?"

Joan spun at the sound of her brother's name, flicking Bia into her hand as it grew to its full size. A wide-eyed Henry stumbled backward, his hands raised placatingly as he looked down at her blade. His light brown skin paled.

"Joan? How did you . . ." His gaze darted from her face to her sword, then back again. "Why are you . . ."

She scowled at the older boy but didn't lower Bia. "What are you doing here?"

"What am *I* doing here? I'm your father's apprentice." He gripped his curly black hair, his voice raising in pitch as he spoke. "Was I to ignore the fact that my master and his whole family had disappeared without a word? That the house and the shop and all our work had just been abandoned?"

She took a deep breath and lowered her sword. She couldn't blame Henry for his prying. Her father should have told him something instead of leaving behind an empty goldsmith's shop and an apprentice with no direction.

Henry ran his hands down his face and shook his head. "What happened at the palace, Joan? Why are you here dressed like your brother?"

"You shouldn't be here," Joan blurted. She discreetly touched her handkerchief, shifting it to secure the sword to her belt.

No, Henry wasn't wrong for coming to check on the Sands family, but it didn't mean he could stay. It was far too dangerous for that.

She grabbed the tall boy's shoulders, turning him quickly and shoving him toward the door. She felt it then, the slightest shift in the air. Bia shook at her hip, the blade itching for a fight. Not that she'd needed the warning. She laid her hand over its hilt. The hair at the back of her neck lifted, drawing all of her attention to the space near the worktable to her right.

She's here, Ogun whispered the words inside her head as his burning energy filled her chest. Titanea had come.

Henry glanced over his shoulder, his eyes widening.

Joan nudged him forward again, catching his gaze when he looked down at her. "Hide," she whispered, putting the urgency she wouldn't let her body show into the word.

He obeyed her terse command with an uncharacteristic quickness, and Joan watched him disappear behind the wall that separated the work area from the shop. The fire crackled in the forge, flames devouring the wood in snapping licks. Heat rolled against her back. She touched the handkerchief, letting Bia slip into her grip as the fabric went slack. A drip of sweat slid down her spine. Finally, Joan turned.

The Fae queen sat atop the worktable; her legs delicately crossed one over the other. The growing flames cast a golden glow over the rich brown skin of her true form. She wore a crimson velvet doublet embroidered with swirling gold thread and a set of black hose and boots—King James's clothes, Joan realized.

The true king was safely in Stratford along with his courtier Philip Herbert, whisked there on the night of Titanea's attack. That the Fae queen now wore his clothes meant that she'd likely abandoned her guise of Queen Anne for one with far more power. None of it boded well.

Titanea stared at Joan, her gaze sharp and predatory.

"You shouldn't be here," she echoed, her tone mocking. She jerked her head toward Bia. "But since you are, give us the sword."

Joan subtly shifted her stance to balance her weight on her toes, ready to dodge or attack if Titanea so much as twitched. "No," she said defiantly.

"You cannot defeat us here, dear Joan," Titanea cooed, wrapping Joan's name in false affection. "But if you hand over that sword, you shall be greatly rewarded. Think carefully before you . . ."

"No."

Rage burst across Titanea's face before she wrestled her expression to calm benevolence. The table beneath her creaked as her hand clenched around it, the wood splintering under the force of her grip.

Steady, Joan thought. She sent iron flowing down Bia's blade.

The wind kicked up, shrieking against the windows and rattling the glass. It echoed through the house, amplified by the empty rooms until it seemed to roar around them.

Titanea pushed herself to her feet, the quiet menace in her movements in stark contrast to her soft expression. "Give up the sword and forswear that spirit who drives you against us and you shall be protected from all that is to come." She smiled. "And there is much to come."

Something in the distance yowled, deep and primal. Joan felt panic surge within her. She clutched Bia tighter, her sweat-slick palm sliding against the grip as she shoved the feeling down fiercely.

Titanea held out her hand, beckoning with her fingers.

Joan didn't move.

"Hand over that damned sword!" the Fae queen screamed. The house trembled with the force of her words. "We will not tell you again!"

Joan glared back at her, ignoring the fine tremors shaking her hands as she steadied Bia. "I said no."

Titanea dove at her. Joan dodged, scrambling across the floor as the Fae queen soared past her. She surged to her feet and swiped at Titanea's throat. Titanea shoved her arm away, jerking Joan backward by the collar. Joan stumbled at the sudden shift in weight and tried to regain her footing. Titanea twisted the fabric, tightening it around Joan's neck.. Joan gasped and thrust Bia under her arm in a desperate strike. Titanea hissed as the sword sliced across her skin. She threw Joan to the floor and danced out of the blade's reach.

Joan grunted as the back of her head cracked against the ground. Her vision went white but she scrambled to her feet. She had to keep moving or Titanea would . . .

Titanea appeared in Joan's face, snatching up both Joan's wrists before she could react and wrapping her other hand around Joan's throat. She squeezed.

"That offer wasn't a lie, Joan, but you know that," she said softly. She stretched Joan's arms so high her shoulders popped. "Our affection would've protected you had you been obedient." She glanced up to where Joan held Bia uselessly above them, and her lips twisted into a sneer. "You're so much like her."

Do not speak of her! Ogun's voice burst into Joan's mind as she struggled to breathe, the Orisha's anger burning fiercely in her chest.

If she could hit Titanea with some iron, she might...

Her head throbbed as her vision darkened around the edges. Every movement felt sluggish and impossible. She jerked her arms down, trying futilely to break Titanea's hold.

The Fae queen tugged them up again and leaned in close to whisper into Joan's ear. "But disobedience has its own reward. You can reap what she and your god sowed."

She slid her thumb along Joan's neck, slowly forcing her head to the side until it twisted unnaturally. Searing pain shot through Joan as her muscles threatened to tear under Titanea's supernatural strength and the world shifted into sudden, stark focus.

Titanea would snap her neck if she didn't move.

She kicked at Titanea's torso, her eyes tearing up as the Fae queen took every blow as if a feather's brush. Joan's chest burned for air. Something popped in her neck.

"Pity," Titanea said, her face dispassionate. "You truly were our favorite."

CLANG!

Titanea pitched to the side, brow furrowed with pain. Henry struck her again with the iron skillet, throwing all of his weight into the blow.

CLANG!

Titanea's eyes rolled up into her head as her body went slack.

Joan collapsed, her knees slamming into the wooden floor with a crack. She gasped and coughed and gulped in air as she tried to regain her senses and think beyond the joy of being able to breathe again. Her neck ached. Henry stood above her, staring at the spot where Titanea had fallen, his knuckles pale from how tightly he gripped his makeshift weapon in shaking hands. His gaze drifted to Joan.

He blinked rapidly and crouched down beside her. "Get up," he whispered, tugging at her arm, his grip tight enough to bruise, "before she comes for both of us."

Henry was right; they needed to escape. The Burbage house was nearby. Her mother was there, and she'd take them all safely back to Stratford-upon-Avon.

Titanea started to rise from the ground.

But for that, they needed time.

Joan held out her hand. Heat blazed in her chest as the tools hanging around the forge vibrated and swept into the air. The metal that sang back was more steel than iron, but she didn't care.

Any iron at all would hurt.

The tongs and hammer melted into a shimmering flow of liquified metal that danced into the air at Joan's command. She flicked her fingers in Titanea's direction. A set of cuffs slammed shut around the Fae queen's wrists as thick metal braids shot out from them and burst through the floor, pinning her to the foundation beneath the house. Titanea shrieked in fury. The sound echoed through the house. She glared up at Joan, naked betrayal cut across her face.

"You'll earn what you deserve, Iron Blade," Titanea said, her voice raspy and tight. The light caught a shimmer in her eyes that disappeared as she blinked rapidly. She grunted, tugging at the restraints holding her in place. The house groaned as it rattled beneath the force.

The cuffs wouldn't hold her for long. They needed to run.

"We'll pay it to you from our own hands." Titanea bared her teeth in a smile that sent a shiver down Joan's spine. "What you all deserve."

Henry dragged Joan to her feet, her rising panic allowing him to move her with ease. He swung the door open. The gust of frigid air buffeted them and seemed to find all the exposed skin between the folds of her cloak.

Titanea jerked her hands upward. Somewhere beneath her, wood splintered with a shriek. The house gave a violent shiver.

The sound might as well have been the boom of a canon. Fear shot through Joan as Henry gave a half-swallowed shriek. His nails cut into her arm through the fabric of her shirt. Bia slipped in her sweaty hands. She locked her fingers around the hilt as the sword vibrated in her grip.

Titanea scowled, her gaze shifting slowly to Joan. Their eyes locked. "Run, little girl."

Joan obeyed.

CHAPTER TWO
The Foul Fiend

oan's mind raced as she struggled to hold any thought beyond the panicked repeat of *Run, run, run, run*. It propelled her from the house, driving her through the streets of London with Henry at her side. She glanced at him. Sweat beaded on his face despite the cold January air, and his skin hadn't regained its color. He constantly looked over his shoulder, his longer legs keeping him from falling behind.

Between her magic and Titanea's... Joan knew his mind reeled from everything he'd seen tonight. Her grip on Bia tightened again. She'd wanted to forever keep her secrets from Henry and hoped he wouldn't question her until they were safe. The Burbage house wasn't far from here.

Her mother wasn't far from here.

The sun had nearly disappeared on the horizon, the sky above them indigo with inky darkness not far behind. Sodden earth sucked at her feet with every step as if the muddy roads sought to trap her in place. All around, people rushed toward their own homes seeking safety before nightfall. This wasn't unusual. Between the mandated curfew and the inconvenience of darkness, no one lingered on the streets after sunset. But an edge pervaded the air tonight. Joan could see it in the way eyes shifted over and away from them quickly, in the way everyone moved with their heads tucked low as they scurried from place to place.

This was London without the safety of the Pact. How much worse would it become if Joan didn't act soon? She touched trembling fingers to her aching throat, flinching as she put pressure on skin that was surely purpled with bruises.

She'd been so foolish . . .

"We need to get to Shoreditch," Joan said. She grabbed at Henry's hand and ran straight into a man walking in the opposite direction.

The man grunted as he stumbled back, his pale face turning a sudden sharp red. "Shite! Watch where you're going." He glared at her and swiped at his clothes. "No manners . . ."

"Apologies," Joan said quickly with a lowered voice.

She tried to shift around the man, but he caught sight of the sword clutched in her hand. His eyes widened. Joan tensed, bracing herself for his reaction. Would he call for a guard? Attempt to have her arrested?

They didn't have time for a confrontation.

Henry snatched her arm and bolted away down a side street. The man shouted behind them, his voice fading as they retreated. Henry tugged her across the next main throughway, then cut a sharp left into a narrow alleyway between rows of houses. He tucked her behind him in the shadows along the backside of some shop, turning to watch the street beyond. They stood together in the dark, Henry's breath rushing out in gasps as they both listened for the sounds of pursuit.

Nothing.

Joan sighed and leaned back against the building. She took a moment to orient herself. Everything looked foreign in the fading light, but as her panic subsided, the sign hanging from the building opposite the alley—a raven in flight with a tankard clutched in its talons—caught her attention. The Rook alehouse was near the Burbage house. Relief surged through her. They were still heading in the right direction. They needed to hurry if they hoped to catch her mother before she and the others made their way back to Stratford-upon-Avon, but they wouldn't have to retrace any steps.

Behind them, the lights inside the shop disappeared one by one as the owner closed down their business for the evening. The orange glow of the setting sun slanted across the white plaster walls. Bia thrummed hard enough to nearly jerk out of her grip. A warning.

Something was coming their way.

"We have to move. Now," Joan said.

She slipped out from behind Henry, heading toward the opposite end of the alley before beckoning him along. He sighed but followed as she led them back out on the main roadway. The crowds had cleared considerably as darkness claimed the streets. Any light from the houses around them glowed dimly, as if the people who lived there sought to hide their presence. It set Joan's senses further on edge. She felt too aware of everything: the scratch of her wool trousers against her legs, the heavy drag of her cloak on her shoulders, Henry's harsh breathing. A quick look over her shoulder showed that the same unease hung over the few who remained on the streets. She watched a man, his pale face half-obscured by the light behind him, squint at them from the doorway of his bakery before slamming the door as they passed.

Henry scoffed. "Small-minded people disgust me."

Joan hummed but didn't respond. It wasn't that she disagreed; petty prejudices enraged her too. But this . . . this was something different. Bia thrummed at her wrist again, shaking her arm.

Titanea had claimed her territory.

Joan didn't need Ogun's confirmation to know the truth of the thought. She could see it for herself.

Something small and dark skittered through the shadows, letting out a cackle like the rattling of bones as it moved. A man nearest the sound jerked to a stop and abruptly turned in the opposite direction, his head low and his eyes wide.

Another couple walking together noticed his movements and gave the area a wide berth; one woman staring into the dark as the other guided them along, her gaze determinedly forward. They clutched each other tightly before disappearing into the safety of a house, latches sliding into place almost as soon as the heavy wood door closed behind them.

Her clever plan of distraction felt more naive with each passing moment.

"We need to get inside before dark," Henry said suddenly. "Nothing good has been happening after dark." His eyes darted around before meeting hers, and he frowned. "But you already know that, don't you?"

Joan thought about ignoring the sharp comment but nodded instead. "I do."

Something comes.

Joan's feet were moving before Ogun's voice even settled in her head. Bia jerked in her hand, sending her arm swinging erratically. She was sure she made quite the sight hurrying through the streets near dark and openly carrying a sword, but she didn't dare shrink Bia back down. Not until they reached the Burbage house and her mother. If they moved quickly, they might be able to avoid the approaching threat.

She'd made it about ten paces before she realized Henry wasn't with her. She turned, ready to fight whatever held him, but he only stood there, that same sour look contorting his face. She scowled back and hissed his name.

"What is all this? Who was that woman back there?"

Joan shook her head, beckoning him toward her. "We need to meet my mother so she can get us out of here."

"No. Tell me what's going on, Joan," he said, crossing his arms stubbornly.

She gestured down the road. "There'll be time enough for that once we get to my mother."

He shook his head. Joan swallowed a curse and doubled back, reaching for his arm.

"No." He jerked away from her. "What trouble have you found? Is it because of that damned playhouse that enamors you so? I've told you nothing good will come of you working in that *place*."

She clenched her jaw around the scream that threatened to escape her. This was what she hated about Henry. Even when he was kind or helpful, it was only a matter of time before his sense of superiority won over his better nature. He always expected her to stand beneath him because she was a girl. As if he were her guardian and not an overconfident boy who worked for her father and stood to inherit everything despite Joan being the one to constantly repair his shite craftsmanship.

She couldn't believe she ever thought of marrying the clod. Not even keeping some hand in her father's goldsmith business was worth spending the rest of her days as Henry's wife.

She breathed deeply and tried to calm herself. Berating him wouldn't make him comply. She flexed her fingers around Bia's hilt. Cramps shot through her knuckles as she relaxed her tight grip.

Henry had saved her life earlier. She could scrounge up some modicum of patience for him with that fact in mind.

"I'll answer all your questions once we get to my mother," she said softly. "I swear it."

He stared at her for a long moment. "If it's not the playhouse, then it must be because of that strange magic you use in the shop."

The urge to deny his claim nearly pushed an explanation—a lie—out of her mouth, but she stamped it down. He'd already seen too much today to believe any excuses she might offer. She nodded.

"You're not half as subtle as you think," he said. "But your"—he flapped his hand at her—"made my work easier so I saw no need to mention it."

She rolled her eyes. "How generous of you . . ." She glanced down the alley, then back at him again. "Now can we get moving?"

It's close.

Ogun's voice sprang into her mind as a howl echoed in the distance once more, sounding much closer than it had when they'd been back at the house. Joan spun in its direction and searched the sky for its source. A dark shape soared overhead, blotting out the stars as it moved toward them.

Fear clawed at Joan's belly. She snatched hold of Henry's wrist and, without another word, dragged the taller boy down the street behind her.

"Joan—"

She shushed him and kept moving. She could hear the fear shaking his voice, knew he'd glimpsed the creature too. The thrum of beating wings and strange breezes kissing her face quickened her steps.

Only prey runs, child. Stay calm.

Henry slammed into Joan's back as she suddenly slowed down. Her hands shook as she fought hard against her instincts.

"Only prey runs," she whispered Ogun's words to Henry and kept a tight hold on his wrist. Up ahead was the turn that would lead to the last street before the Burbages' house, a narrow block only wide enough to pass on foot.

It might not stop the creature, but, based on Joan's glimpse of its size, it would slow the thing down and buy them some time. She heard a thud and the screech of claws on the stone roadway. Henry's arm jerked in her grip, and she squeezed harder.

"Don't look," she whispered. "Keep your eyes on the road." She tried to steady her voice even as the hair on the back of her neck stood on end and everything within her screamed to run.

The creature snorted, the sound thundering around them and blowing hard enough to ruffle both their cloaks.

Only prey runs, Joan thought, repeating the words in her head to beat down her instincts. *Only prey runs.*

A few more steps to the street, a few more steps to salvation.

"By God's grace!"

Joan turned toward the voice. A man had ridden out onto the wide street. The horse beneath him neighed frantically and bucked its rider, sprinting past Joan and Henry as the man tumbled to the ground. His eyes were wide as he scrambled back the way he'd come. A large reptilian head on a long, sleek neck swung in the man's direction. Joan clutched Bia in her grip and sprinted out into the road.

"Don't!"

Henry's hand slammed over her mouth as he wrapped his arm around her waist and jerked her backward. Joan had one more glimpse of the creature—tall enough to reach the second floor of the buildings around it. It leaned down over the poor man, swishing its long, whiplike tail like a cat on the hunt.

Henry's back hit the wall of a building on the tiny side street, his breath harsh in her ear. She squirmed against him as he used his whole body to keep her in their hiding place. Screams erupted behind them and then went suddenly silent, replaced with the wet crunch of the creature feeding.

"Do you want us to be next?" he whispered.

Joan went still as fear and rage battled in her gut.

He was right. She could've broken Henry's hold and attempted to save the stranger and made a target of herself, but then what? She'd have no chance against it alone, and only James knew she was here . . .

She shook her head and hated herself for it.

Henry let her go but stayed close enough to whisper. "Where are we going?"

"Holywell Stre—"

A leathery green tail slammed into the ground in front of them with a thud that rattled Joan's bones. It curled toward her. She scrambled out of reach, grabbing at Henry to drag him with her. He shoved her away. She hit the ground with a grunt, barely managing to keep hold of Bia. Tiny stones dug into her knees through her wool trousers as she pushed herself up. The creature's tail wrapped around Henry's waist. He beat against it, his face going red with the effort.

Joan's heart thudded in her chest. "Henry!" She lifted Bia, the iron-coated blade glinting in the moonlight, and slashed at the tail. The sword cut through in one clean blow. The creature screeched in pain as the blade burned through its flesh. The useless appendage dropped to the ground, and Henry stumbled forward into her arms.

"Let's go," Joan said as she pulled him down the street with her.

A deep grumble vibrated the road beneath her, and Henry jerked back against her hand. She turned, locking eyes with him, terror spread across his face. His gaze shifted down to the talons wrapped around his ankle. Over his shoulder, Joan met the slitted gaze of the creature. The narrow street barely gave it space to stretch its wing out to them, but it was enough. The single eye narrowed at her before it yanked Henry toward itself. He screamed as it pulled him up into the air. Joan locked her hand around his wrist and dug her heels into the ground. The creature dragged them both back down the road.

"Hold on!" Joan shouted. She dropped Bia and grabbed hold of a dark wooden beam, grunting as the force of halting their movement popped her shoulder. "I've got you."

The creature let out another rumbling growl. Joan gritted her teeth and held fast. She scrambled to stay upright and keep her grip. Henry watched her with wide eyes. Her fingers ached. Her feet slipped in the mud. Henry grunted as the creature yanked at him again before he clenched his jaw. His gaze hardened.

Joan's heart thudded in her chest. "Don't . . ." she ground out. "I've got you."

He twisted his arm and broke free at the weakest part of her grip. Joan grabbed at him, her battered fingers leaving bloody trails on his white sleeve as he was jerked up and out of sight. He screamed again before the sound was muffled by a wet crunch.

Joan snatched Bia up with shaking hands and slipped back into the shadows of the tiny street, out of the creature's sight. The bell at St. Paul's clanged in the distance, marking a new hour. She jerked as the sound seemed to rattle through her head. A sob built in her throat. Her eyes burned and her nose clogged, but she swallowed it down.

A rush of foul, hot air washed over her—the creature's breath—as it tried to shove its head between the street's close-set buildings. Joan froze as it sniffed the air, the tip of its snout just beyond her hiding place. It snorted again and pulled back, scraping plaster off the buildings its head dragged against.

The next toll of St. Paul's bell launched her into motion. She bolted down the street, everything around her blurring with her speed and the hot burn of tears in her eyes. She didn't stop; she trusted her feet to remember the familiar path as she desperately listened. She clutched Bia in her hand and, by the sixth knell, found herself on the doorstep of the Burbage household, breathless and heartbroken.

CHAPTER THREE
Trust Not the Air

he Burbage family lived in Shoreditch at the center of Holywell Street, in two connected houses that rose up in three floors of white plaster and dark wood beams. Master Burbage and his wife, Winifred, resided on one side while his mother and brother, Mr. Cuthbert, occupied the other. Though at least three windows spread across each floor, light glowed only from a single one on the first floor of Master Burbage's side, the shadowy forms moving about the only evidence that someone was inside and awake.

Joan stood on the stone front step and tried to remember the secret knock pattern James had taught her. She could barely focus. Sweat and blood mingled together, stinging every tiny cut on her hands. Still, she clung to Bia's hilt. She struggled not to drop the sword as it shook and twitched in her grip. Her ears listened desperately for the sounds of the creature's approach.

She had no idea what she would do if it had followed her here; only that she refused to lose another person tonight. She screwed her eyes closed. The image of Henry's horrified face as he was yanked into the darkness appeared in her mind as clearly as if she was watching it happen again, details she hadn't noticed before bursting forth. The beads of sweat spread across his hairline, the sheen of tears glossing his resolved gaze. How he'd grabbed at her outstretched hand for the briefest moment and pulled back before she could reach him again.

Smaller noises, the scurrying footfalls of something with legs too numerous to be human, drifted out of the shadows along the road. Her eyes popped open, breaths rushing out of her in quick pants. She glanced over her shoulder and saw the slightest reflection of light off of something that might've been a bit of glass. Or an eye . . .

She needed to get inside. She needed to get back to Stratford.

She never should've come in the first place.

Bia twitched in her grip again. Joan wrapped both hands around the sword and focused on its vibrations. It settled her mind. She took a steadying breath and finally pulled the pattern from her memory: one long hit, a pause, then four short raps. Her knocking sounded like rifle shots in the quiet. The movements she'd been hearing went suddenly silent.

She braced herself to be attacked.

The heavy wooden door creaked open, and Master Shakespeare peeked around its side. "What are you doing? You shouldn't be here!" He noticed her trousers and shook his head. "The curse of twins . . ." he muttered.

Master Shakespeare frowned at her, eyes widening in alarm as he took in her bloody, shaking hands. He pulled her inside with an arm around her shoulders, then tugged down one of his sleeves, using the fabric to wipe the tears from her face. "Come along, we're getting you back to Stratford immediately."

Joan nodded and followed him up the dimly lit stairs to the house's main floor, wood creaking loudly under their feet. She slipped Bia around her wrist discreetly as they moved. Her presence and ragged appearance would be alarming enough, a stark deviation from the careful plan they'd laid out the day before in the safety of Master Shakespeare's home. Her mother could get them all back to Stratford-upon-Avon before Joan would need to draw it again. Showing up with the sword in hand would only cause more panic.

Bia vibrated, and Joan tucked her arm behind her back as they reached the top of the staircase. The sitting room spread out before them, the wide open space large enough to fit most of the company of the King's Men at once—and often had. The fireplace took up most of the wall directly opposite the stairs, plush rugs woven through with dusky green and cream covered the wood floors—they gave gently under Joan's feet. She flinched as she tracked muddy footprints across them. A long brown and emerald settee surrounded by four matching high-backed chairs sat around a low table of ash gray wood. Two matching benches pressed against the opposite wall, thick knit blankets folded and placed on them in two neat stacks.

Usually, the arrangement felt warm and welcoming, the space obviously meant for fellowship, but a miasma of fear permeated the room now. It lurked in the dark corners, seeming to send the shadows creeping out to swallow any bit of candlelight. A chill raced down Joan's spine. She clenched her fist against it and flinched as she agitated the cuts on her hand. She wiped it along her trousers and hoped the blood wouldn't show against the dark wool.

Master Burbage stood near the fireplace. He clung to his wife, whispering tenderly to her and the baby in her arms as he stroked his wife's hair. Mrs. Burbage gripped him back just as tightly. Her blond braid hung over her shoulder, brushing against the blanket-wrapped bundle she held close to her pale face. A tiny, chubby hand of the same complexion reached up to pat at her cheek. The baby cooed and wiggled sleepily but seemed content enough not to cry.

Joan's mother walked over to the settee where Mother Burbage, her pale face tired beneath her cap, and Master Burbage's brother, Mr. Cuthbert, both huddled. Mrs. Sands tucked a heavy wool cloak around the old woman's shoulders as Cuthbert looked on, shifting nervously from side to side. Several bags lay on the floor around their feet.

Bia shook again at Joan's wrist, and Ogun's presence burned hot in her chest.

There's danger here.

She almost blurted out the words but held them in her head. The three Burbages were already frightened enough without hearing Ogun's warning.

She grabbed Shakespeare's arm and whispered, "Ogun says there's something here with us."

Shakespeare frowned, glancing back down the stairs before quickly moving across the room to Joan's mother.

"Bess," he said, his voice quiet but enough to catch everyone's attention. "Make your doorway."

Her mother caught sight of her, jerking in alarm. "Joan? What are you—" She clamped her mouth shut and scowled pointedly at Joan before she sprang into action.

Shakespeare came over to help Mother Burbage stand as Joan's mother traced the shape of a door in the empty air. Joan hung behind, shifting her attention from the dark stairway to the rooms around them. If there was danger here, she'd find it.

"I'm glad you've come for us," Mr. Cuthbert said. He'd walked across the room to stand close by her, wringing his hands and glancing between his brother, sister-in-law, and mother. He towered over Joan, tall and thin where his brother was more broadly built. His coppery brown hair hung around his slightly tanned face and ears in a short cut that defied modern fashion. His bushy mustache twitched as he smiled, the skin around his impossibly blue eyes crinkling in deep wrinkles.

Joan forced an answering turn to her lips. She didn't want to risk fraying the man's nerves any further by revealing her own nervousness. It seemed to work, as his shoulders dropped a bit and he relaxed.

Hinges creaked as Mrs. Sands opened her magical doorway. On the other side, Joan could see the neat white facade of New Place, Master Shakespeare's house in the countryside, windows lit brightly and shining like a beacon in the night.

Mrs. Sands waved her hand at Burbage and his wife, letting the two of them cross through to safety with their baby. Shakespeare approached more slowly with Mother Burbage, the old woman's steps sluggish with the aches of age. Joan turned to tell Mr. Cuthbert to follow.

"Thank you," he said, taking her hand in both of his. His fingers trembled with fear even as he held hers firmly. "Thank all of you." He brushed against the sword at Joan's wrist and tore away from her with a sharp hiss.

Her eyes widened as their gazes met. Cuthbert stared back at her, calm confusion on his face. Joan grabbed his arm, iron flowing across her palm as she moved. He dodged her touch with a screech, his mouth opening wide enough to split his face. He lashed out. Too-sharp nails scratched across Joan's cheek as he twisted out of her reach.

"Christ!" Shakespeare shouted. He tugged Mother Burbage back as the creature pretending to be Cuthbert shoved his way toward the open doorway into Stratford.

Shite!

Mother Burbage screamed and reached for the creature. "My boy! What's happened to my boy?"

Joan dove after the false Cuthbert, catching it around the waist and dragging it to the floor. Her breath whooshed out of her as the Fae landed fully on top of her but threaded her arms around its shoulders and tightened her grip to hold it in place. Just beyond them, Shakespeare held on to Mother Burbage, pulling her toward the doorway. Their already slow progress nearly stopped as she reached desperately for the creature she still thought was her son.

"My boy! Cuthbert!"

The creature thrashed in Joan's hold. She tried to get her fingertips to Bia without losing her grip. It nearly broke free before she jerked it back.

"Go," Joan shouted, "while I'm holding it."

Her mother placed her hands on either side of the doorway and pulled it toward herself. The magical opening seemed to shiver before easing across the floor.

The creature screeched and flipped the two of them over onto their sides. It bucked against her, trying to shake her off, but Joan locked her legs around its waist. She slammed her iron-coated palm into its face. It shrieked again and stilled. Joan fortified her hold and glanced up at the others. Shakespeare was attempting to carry Mother Burbage through the doorway as the old woman found every possible way to thwart his efforts. They'd barely made it beyond the settee, and the safety of Stratford was still several paces away.

The false Cuthbert twitched suddenly and its shoulders seemed to pop out of their sockets and flip backward. Its head turned fully on its body, neck twisting unnaturally until its false blue eyes peered directly into Joan's.

She shoved herself back with a shout as it snapped at her, forced to let go or be bitten. It grinned, smile too wide and feet still turned in the wrong direction, before bounding over her head.

"No!" Joan scrambled after it but could already see she wouldn't catch up in time.

She reached out a hand, calling to the metal candlesticks from the mantle to her left. They sang in response as the silver dissolved into liquid and swept toward her. Joan twisted her fingers. The metal shaped itself into a rope that wrapped around the creature's shoulders before flowing back into Joan's grip. She pulled it taught. The creature jerked to a stop just as it reached the doorway. She planted her feet as it threatened to drag her along with it and wound the rope's slack around her hand. She hauled the creature back.

Her mother looked up, scowling in exertion as she struggled to shift the doorway toward the center of the room. Her eyes widened as she saw the creature straining against Joan's hold. Joan grunted and pulled the creature backward two more steps.

"Go," Joan ground out, her voice strained, "I can't hold it much longer."

Her mother scowled over at Shakespeare, who still wrestled with an uncooperative Mother Burbage. Mrs. Sands screamed in frustration and pulled the door with all her might. The magic shivered, whining like stressed wood before shooting past the creature and sweeping the three of them safely into Stratford-upon-Avon.

Joan looped the metal rope around her arm as the creature attempted to follow the doorway. She jerked it back again and met her mother's gaze through the opening. With the creature positioned between Joan and the doorway, she couldn't follow the others through. She nodded to her mother.

"I'm coming back for you," Mrs. Sands said fiercely.

Joan forced a smile through the strain of holding the creature. "I know." The metal rope slipped a little as fresh blood leaked out over her fingers, but she held fast.

Her mother slammed the doorway closed, leaving Joan alone in London once again.

CHAPTER FOUR
Some Monster in Thy Thought

oan let the silver rope slip from her grasp as the doorway slammed closed. The creature stumbled forward as she released it, crashing into the velvet settee. She flexed her hand, unfastening the metal clasp that held her cloak without touching it. The heavy wool slipped from her shoulders and pooled on the floor at her feet. Her throat ached from Titanea's throttling earlier and her fingers stung from struggling to hold on to Henry. The pain settled in her mind. It narrowed her focus.

The two of them were alone in the house now, the others safely out of reach. There was no one to be cautious of as she fought.

Not when there was only her and her enemy.

Joan twisted her fingers, calling the silver rope to her hand and threading iron through it. The settee thudded against the floor as the false Cuthbert pushed itself to its feet. Its bones cracked and crunched as it twisted its head and arms back to the front of its body. Joan scowled and swallowed down the bile that rose in her throat. Some things just shouldn't be witnessed in this world . . .

The creature grunted, leveling its gaze on Joan. "All alone now, Iron Blade?" It hadn't dropped Cuthbert Burbage's form, and now that its head and limbs had been righted, nothing marked it as different than the real man. The creature grinned, showing the dimple in Cuthbert's left cheek.

Joan's hands went cold as a terrifying reality struck her.

This Fae did not glow.

Until now, nearly every Fae she'd encountered bore that supernatural light beneath their skin visible to all the children of the Orisha. Titanea and Goodfellow were the only exceptions, a sign of their great power. If this particular creature could match the strength of those two, that boded ill for all of them.

"You should've left this family alone," she said, even as she could feel her heart racing in her chest.

Calm, child. Fear distracts.

Joan breathed deeply and tried to take Ogun's words to heart as Bia vibrated at her wrist. Her Orisha was right; whether this creature was stronger than her or not, letting fear drive her was a sure path to death.

The creature leapt at her. Joan twisted, slipping out of its reach, and tossed her coil of silver and iron into the air. It swirled around the creature's torso as it thundered past. She yanked at the slack with both hands and pulled the creature to the ground.

Joan squeezed, and the remaining rope flattened over the creature in a wide band. She clenched her hands again, and the metal buried itself deeply into the floor. The creature contorted its elbows to tug and thrash at the restraint. It hissed as the iron-infused silver seared its skin, but the wooden floor held firmly.

No, this creature was nowhere near the Fae queen's strength.

Joan breathed deeply again, her heart calming. She stepped close enough to look the creature in the eye. It sneered at her. She scowled back.

"The queen won't let you bind us again," the creature said, spreading Cuthbert's mouth in that gruesome, too-wide smile. "I see the fear in your eyes. She'll kill you, Iron Blade, and let us bathe in your blood."

Panic surged through her at the mention of Titanea. She tried to ignore it, but the throbbing along her neck wouldn't be put out of her mind.

Think only on this enemy, child. Focus.

Joan shook her head, her fingers a breath away from touching her bruised throat. She exhaled and turned her mind to the heat of her Orisha's presence burning in her chest. She let it bolster her.

She flicked her hand forward, and Bia leapt from her wrist at its full size. She snatched it from the air, sending iron flowing down the blade.

"Is Mr. Cuthbert dead?" She sharpened the sword's edge.

The creature laughed, a high-pitched cackle overlaid with Cuthbert's deeper voice. "You will be soon, Iron Blade."

It hadn't answered her question, which likely meant that a yes would be a lie. The Fae could not lie, but they'd twist words to distort the truth. She guessed the real Cuthbert lived and might still be in the house. That was all she needed to know for now.

"You're dead, Iron Blade! Dea—"

Joan lopped the creature's head off in one stroke. It was a quick death. Merciful.

Bia absorbed the blood, leaving the blade clean as Joan stabbed it into the floor. She swiped her hands over her face and sent a mental apology to Master Burbage, although it'd be far easier to fix the small cut than clean the Fae's blood staining the rugs.

Well done, child, Ogun whispered.

Joan took several deep breaths as the night's events threatened to overwhelm her. She crouched down, face still buried in her hands and screamed. The sound echoed in the empty house, ringing in Joan's ears.

Foolish, she thought. *Reckless and foolish.*

She swiped the tears from her eyes, then stood to take up Bia again, wrapping it around her wrist. The sword's vibrations had calmed now that the danger was gone. Ogun's presence remained as a comforting simmer in her chest.

Joan clenched her fists and tried to stop the shaking in her hands. She couldn't pretend the mention of Titanea hadn't scared her, especially after their earlier encounter.

Once the Pact was restored, all this trouble would end. She'd make sure of it.

She cast one last glance at the severed head on the floor, the false face of Cuthbert Burbage staring up at her with unseeing blue eyes clouded by death. She frowned and headed up the stairs that led to the house's second floor. She needed to find the real Cuthbert and get them both out of here.

She couldn't bear to stay in London another moment.

Joan found the man just as the bell at St. Paul's tolled seven. She'd had to venture into the second Burbage house, which was thankfully connected by a long hallway.

Cuthbert had been stuffed underneath his own bed, the downy mattress muffling his moans of pain. He was battered and bloodied but alive and alert enough to respond when she called his name. Joan used all her strength to heave the heavy bedframe off him. The tall ebony wood posts closest to her scraped against the ceiling as she lifted and the gauzy curtains that draped across it tickled her face. She sneezed and nearly dropped the whole thing.

She grunted and fortified her grip to pull it clear of his shoulders. She held it up with one hand, wrapping her other arm around his chest and tugging him free. He scooted himself across the floor as best he could, but Joan still found herself doing most of the work. Once he was free, she dropped the bed with a heavy thud and collapsed to the floor beside him, both struggling to catch their breath.

"Thank you," he panted.

Joan gave him a tiny half smile. "We're not safe yet."

They couldn't remain in this house, not when the Fae knew they were here. She didn't dare go back to her own house, and Cuthbert couldn't make the trek all the way to the Globe. They needed somewhere close and familiar so that her mother could reach them with her doorway. Joan's mind raced.

Baba's house . . .

If nowhere was safe, maybe going to the most obvious place would buy them enough time to be retrieved. With her godfather already dead, there'd be no reason to turn eyes there. It was brazen and incredibly risky, but what other choice did they have?

She'd take Cuthbert to Baba Ben's house. She pressed her shaking hands against her legs and stood.

"Can you stand?" She looked down at Cuthbert. "Can you walk?"

He flopped over onto his belly and stumbled up with painstaking slowness. Joan rushed to help him, wrapping his arm around her shoulders and tucking herself close to bear most of his weight. He stumbled, but was able to walk to the hall without collapsing. The top of the stairs seemed impossibly far. The dark corridor extending before them looked much longer than it had when Joan had taken it alone. She adjusted Cuthbert to take on more of his weight and half dragged him along. The deep shadows set her on edge, her ears strained against the silence of the house, and she did her best to keep her grip on Cuthbert light. They finally reached the stairs and took them one at a time, their pace slow.

The wood floor groaned behind them, like the shifting of a heavy weight. Cuthbert jerked to a stop. Bia vibrated at Joan's wrist.

One approaches, Ogun whispered to her.

Joan clenched her jaw and braced Cuthbert's hands on the banister as she slipped out from beneath his arm. His head whipped toward her, eyes wide enough to show the whites all around.

"Keep going," she said, gently. "I'll take care of it."

She let Bia slither into her hand like a serpent, wrapping her hand around the hilt as it grew to its full size. That seemed to comfort the older man. He nodded and continued down the stairs without a question.

No doubt Master Burbage had mentioned her magic to his family. The brothers shared everything, even going so far as to connect the two houses they'd bought.

Joan felt her shoulders relax slightly at that. She had no desire to soothe that man if her abilities frightened him. Not when a physical threat lurked so nearby. She turned and headed back up the stairs. She'd make quick work of this creature, then they'd be safe to escape to Baba Ben's. At least for now.

CHAPTER FIVE
INTERLUDE: Ghouls at the Grave

hey'd searched for so long at their queen's command, forsaking all other sustenance, that they might roam this world uninhibited. The Pact that had barred their most powerful from this realm could be breached only if they forwent harming the mortals who inhabited it. It meant nearly two millennia without food, but for their queen, they'd starve. For their queen, they'd search until they wasted into oblivion. For their queen, they'd suffer. So many of their clan had already succumbed to the hunger.

In those old days, a gathering of ghouls resembled a great cloud, a roiling mass of flowing cloaks and bodies like fresh death bloated with the souls and bones of mortals. They moved in a mighty storm that engulfed towns until time and hunger shrank their number. Now only a few remained, a cluster of twenty in tattered shrouds with bodies emaciated to skin stretched taut over bones. But they'd felt the shattering of the magic that threatened to drag them back through the veil between realms. The enticing hope of full bellies nearly lured them from their duty. A temptation that tugged at hungry, bare frames, that wafted up from graves fresh and ancient and ensnared their senses.

Feed. Feed and be free . . .

But they would not, could not, defy their queen. As *she* commanded, so they obeyed. They'd remain steadfast until they succeeded.

For none rooted out things long dead and buried as masterfully as a ghoul.

But their desperate fast would end today at their queen's pleasure. Here, in the center of this mortal city, surrounded by the lure of all the most delicious fare—flesh, and life, and the human souls and bones they'd craved with the devastation of near two thousand years of lack—they found the corpse Titanea had ordered them to hunt.

The final resting place of The Traitor.

They knew by the corpse's smell, one they'd passed through their collective memory since the sealing of the Pact. That stink of betrayal and forsaken vows laid buried beneath centuries of earth in a tomb long forgotten by the living who walked the streets above it.

But the ghouls couldn't forget because their queen wouldn't forget, and soon she'd reward them with freedom to feast.

Soon.

Triumphantly, they clawed at the ground. Hands meant for rending spirits from flesh scraped at dirt, grasping and burrowing until their nails screeched against the marble tile of the ancient tomb.

A stone slab barred their entry, an unmovable obstacle in their current weakened state, but no such thing could keep out their queen. The strongest and fastest of them all broke from the clan and flew off to find their mistress. It swooped off into the night sky, a fluttering shroud draping a body made of the things left behind after death. The rest waited. They tugged at the stone fruitlessly, the nearness of success—of freedom—after all this time driving them.

Titanea appeared suddenly, stepping out into the air above the tomb. Their messenger curled around her shoulders affectionately before it drifted back into the safety of the clan. The other ghouls guided the queen down to the tomb's entrance with reverent touches. She accepted them with the benevolence that kept them obedient through their suffering.

The ghouls would never betray their queen.

Finally, Titanea stood before the stone slab, the ghouls a curious swirling cloud at her back. She ran her fingertips across the inscription carved into the rock. The ghouls knew them to be words but could not glean their meaning; they'd forgotten the language centuries ago, its fleeting existence worthless in lives so long-lived.

The queen remembered everything about The Traitor.

"Well done, children," she said, her voice a raw whisper.

Pain, deep and ancient, spread over her face as she caressed the carvings tenderly like wounds in the stone. Her expression shifted, a smile tilting her lips. Then she drove her fist into the stone, shattering it in a single blow.

The ghouls shrieked joyously as dust and grit rained down on them, the savory taste of death clinging to the crushed rocks that they licked clean. The debris cleared away to reveal a skeleton, poised with its arms crossed and hands clasped together as though they'd once held something. Treated with more reverence than a breaker of vows deserved.

Beneath the stink of the traitor lay the irresistible aroma of bones. And they were so very hungry...

The queen held up her hand, halting their frenzy.

"This one is not food," she said. Her eyes roved over the skeleton. "Not yet." She reached forward and yanked the skull away from the body, the rest of the bones rattling before settling into place again.

She stared into the empty eye sockets, caught up in some memory. The ghouls waited and hoped.

She turned to smile at them, her eyes shining in the moonlight. "This spirit has been at rest for so long." Her expression darkened. "Wake her up."

They surged forward as she put the skull back into its place and stepped away. The ghouls grabbed at the skeleton, the multitude of hands settling wherever they could touch. As one, the clan turned their senses beyond, reaching into the land of the dead to call forth the soul once tied to these bones.

Come back, they sang. *Return to this world. Come back.*

The spirit answered quickly. It swept in not from the land of souls at peace but from the space between life and death, a place for the restless ones who were held in purgatory by regret. The skeleton jerked as its soul returned. Fleshless fingers grasped. Teeth clacked together. Its jaw dropped open as a howling moan poured forth from a baren mouth.

They'd dragged the Traitor back to this world. Victoriously, the ghouls swirled around their queen, awaiting her praise. She smiled at the newly animated skeleton and the soul now trapped within it.

"Come," she cooed. "You can pay your betrayal back on your people."

The skeleton lurched forward. "Forgive . . ." The word hissed out of its mouth. "Forgive . . ."

The queen swayed as if she'd been struck, her face twisting in misery, then rage. Her lip curled, and she raised her hand to strike. The Traitor's corpse stared back at her though empty eyes.

Titanea's fist clenched and unclenched before dropping back to her side. "Do our bidding and you may earn it."

The Traitor moaned and nodded in a clatter of bones. It jerked forward to lumber after the queen. The ghouls made to follow, but their mistress dismissed them.

"Go, children, you may feed on the rest." She curled her fingers under the chin of one of the swarm, but the release from her command shivered through the whole clan.

Freedom . . .

"Sate your hunger," Titanea said. Then she was gone, the skeleton along with her.

Freedom . . .

Joyously, they burst from the open tomb, swooping off through the rest of the uncovered burial ground, howling with the anticipation of the meal here and in the mortal world above.

It had been so long since they'd fed. Centuries without cutting their teeth on bones, sucking the sweet marrow. Centuries without forcing a new soul to join their number. Now, free of both the Pact and their queen's orders, the swarm would follow the nature they'd suppressed for millennia.

"Sate your hunger."

Ghastly laughter echoed through the dark as for the first time in more than fifteen hundred years, the ghouls feasted.

CHAPTER SIX
Fortune's Buffets & Rewards

oan knocked on the door to Baba Ben's shop as the bell tolled eight, her attention split between Cuthbert leaning heavily on her shoulder and the dark street around them. She'd handled the second threat at the Burbage house easily, but something else had been following them for the last few streets. She hadn't dared let go of Cuthbert to face it directly. So long as it kept its distance, Joan was fine leaving it be.

The light of a single candle flickered behind the curtains drawn across the windows before Pearl swung the door open. Relief flooded through Joan at the sight of the brownie who'd been Baba Ben's assistant. She looked like a normal old woman, her brown skin creased with wrinkles and her curly white hair covered in a blue and green patterned scarf. As she shifted against one side of the door, Joan noticed Pearl no longer glowed the inner light that marked her as Fae.

"Hurry, hurry." She gestured them inside, her strong hands helping take Cuthbert's stumbling weight.

Warmth engulfed them as soon as they crossed the threshold, but Joan felt as if she'd been punched in the gut. She was sure now. It hadn't been that the two at the Burbage house were powerful. None of the Fae glowed any longer, and Pearl proved it. And with nothing to reveal the truth behind their glamour, every Fae deception was impenetrable. The children of the Orisha's best defense was gone.

What did that mean for this fight?

Pearl helped Cuthbert sit in one of the front room's chairs, usually reserved for waiting customers. "I have a few things to patch you up, young man."

"Thank you," he replied. He winced and clutched a hand to his chest.

Pearl shifted the curtain aside to slip into Baba's workshop. Joan got a glimpse of the room, fabrics tossed across tables in disorderly stacks that her godfather never would've allowed and a ruined gold and steel mirror frame leaned against the wall. Evidence of her battle with the goblin and Baba Ben's absence.

His now-permanent absence...

Joan looked away, her throat tight. She'd done this, and being in Baba's home now felt like an invasion. Joan destroyed his workshop in that fight with a goblin. Robert Cecil sent the murderers to the Tower that night to punish Joan, not because of anything her godfather had done.

What right did she have to stand in this place now?

She swiped the tears from her eyes as Pearl returned from the back room carrying a basket full of bandages and bottles.

The brownie paused near Joan and leaned close to whisper, "What are you doing here? You know it's not safe."

"It was our only option..." Joan trailed off, fighting the panic that she had indeed been wrong in choosing this place. That she'd made another foolish decision that might cost someone their life.

She looked down at her hands, scratched but no longer bleeding and too weak to hold onto the life of one boy.

"Things must be dire indeed." Pearl smiled softly at Joan. "It's good you've come. You should go upstairs." She gave Joan one last pointed look before heading over to tend to Cuthbert.

Joan glanced toward the stairway, where Baba kept his office. He kept meticulous notes on everything, from his business ventures to the private inventory of his home. He'd always encouraged her to write down the details he shared about the practices to honor Ogun, so surely he'd done the same.

She'd cursed herself every day for not seeking Baba's counsel when he'd been alive, but maybe there was hope. She only needed to find his notes.

She glanced back at Pearl and Cuthbert one last time before snagging a candle and hurrying up to her godfather's private study, Pearl's soft voice fading behind her.

The heavy wood door screeched as Joan swung it open, announcing her intrusion into the abandoned room. Panic, then shame settled in her gut like a stone at the thought of being in this space when Baba wasn't . . .

When he was no longer . . .

When her godfather was dead.

Joan rubbed at her eyes and stepped inside. Pearl clearly hadn't entered this room since Baba Ben's arrest last October. Joan couldn't blame her. She felt her chest tighten as she moved through it.

Baba Ben's study was always unnaturally neat, but now a thick layer of dust coated every surface. She kicked some up as she strode across the neglected rugs, sneezing hard enough to stumble. The room's bergamot aroma had long faded, replaced by that damned smell of moldy reeds.

She shook herself and moved farther in, blinking back tears. She touched her candle to a few of the tapers along the wall as she passed before setting it down on Baba's desk. A book lay open on its center, it's pages just as dusty as every surface around it. Joan's heart beat hard in her chest.

Baba had an immense collection of notebooks. They lined the low bookshelf behind the desk, their faded leather covers showing their age. Most of them were ledgers that tracked customer clothing orders all the way back to his days as an apprentice tailor, but some were his personal journals.

She prayed this open book was one of the latter.

Joan shifted Baba's chair out of the way and brushed the pages clean. The tidy handwriting was different from the scrawled way Baba wrote now. If she checked one of the ledgers from his apprenticeship, she knew the neat print here would be an exact match. Her heart raced even as her skin seemed to itch with the reality of what she prepared to do. She would never have dared to read her godfather's journals when he was alive. She wouldn't have needed to. He'd never been secretive with his thoughts, and she'd always felt free to ask him nearly any question. Except this—she'd been too afraid to talk to him about the Orisha they shared. How foolish she'd been then, and now she'd never have the chance to talk to him again ...

But these journals were better than nothing. She wiped her sweaty hands on her trousers and leaned close to the open page.

The ritual must be performed before a newly crowned monarch prior to the passing of the next celebration of the dead.

She snatched the whole book up. Dust burst into the air around her. She sneezed again, staring at the page with watery eyes. Laid before her were the instructions for fortifying the Pact with a new king or queen, a ritual that would have prevented all of this from happening if it had been completed. But Baba had never gotten the chance.

This was why he'd been in the palace last October and why Titanea had orchestrated his arrest and subsequent imprisonment. Joan swallowed and forced her hands to release her tight grip on the book. The paper crackled.

Perhaps there'd be some clue here that could help her restore the Pact from nothing, some detail that Baba had written down and forgotten.

She flipped through the journal, her eyes roving over the writing. The distant clang of the bell at St. Paul's marked another hour gone, but Joan couldn't be bothered to count the peals.

The hair at the back of her neck raised as the sensation of being watched overcame her. She glanced up slowly, hoping to see Pearl in the doorway, but a stranger peered back at her.

The woman stood near one corner of the desk, her form faint in the candlelight. An ornate metal pin held the fabric of her dress at one shoulder while the rest draped her body in luxurious folds. Her thick black hair was braided and pinned tightly to her head in neat loops. The woman stared at Joan, her expression curious.

Bia leapt against Joan's wrist as Ogun's familiar presence pulsed in her chest, then faded. She flipped the journal closed with one hand, pressing her palm against the strange feeling. Ogun's warmth had never appeared and departed so suddenly.

Who was this woman?

The apparition's eyes narrowed. She surged forward to touch incorporeal fingers to the sword at Joan's wrist. Bia pulsed, the vibrations rattling through Joan's bones and shaking everything in the room. Joan gasped and tugged her arm away. Realization shot through her.

"It's you..."

The ghost scowled at Joan, then was gone. Joan blinked rapidly, clenching her teeth against the vibrations that still raced through her body.

That was her, wasn't it? Joan thought, though she already felt the answer deep within herself.

Ogun's voice eased into her mind, a strange melancholy coloring the word. *Yes.*

This ghost was the ancestor Ogun had mentioned that night in the tower, the woman who'd sealed the first Pact and held the method to forge it anew.

What is her name? She prayed Ogun would answer, the erratic burn of the Orisha's presence earlier drawing fear within her.

"Joan."

Joan yelped, her whole body jerking at the sound of her name. She scrambled to keep hold of the journal and turned to see Rose standing in the center of the room looking harried and relieved.

"What are you doing—" Joan shook her head. "How did you—" She slumped against the desk and tried to steady her racing heart.

Rose frowned. "You didn't return with the others." She flinched as she moved toward Joan, pressing a hand against her side.

Joan hurried to steady the other girl with a hand at her elbow. A sheen of sweat covered Rose's face, and pain pinched the corner of her eyes. Joan started to guide her toward Baba's chair but Rose shook her head.

"I need to get you back." Her gaze darted to the room's single window as she took a shuddering breath. "Now."

Joan gestured toward the door. "There are two others downstairs, and you're in no shape to transport three of us." She looked pointedly at the place where Rose had been stabbed only a week prior. "Not yet."

Something heavy slammed into the roof directly above their heads, sending dust raining down from the rafters. Both girls dropped to a crouch and clutched each other. The beams strained under the immense weight of something as claws raked along the roof.

A chill raced down Joan's spine. She knew what this was.

She turned wide eyes to Rose. "Get my mother."

"I'm not leaving you," Rose whispered back.

"And I can't leave them. You know I can't."

Rose looked ready to protest, so Joan surged forward to kiss her quickly. A foul trick but an effective one.

"Please, Rose," Joan said, still close enough for their breath to mingle. "I'll be fine, I promise."

Rose scowled but nodded. The beams above them went silent as the weight they strained against disappeared. They both looked up.

"Go," Joan whispered, squeezing Rose's hand.

Rose pressed a quick kiss against Joan's lips, then disappeared into thin air. Joan scrambled to her feet, clutching Baba's journal to her chest as she bounded back down the stairs two at a time.

Cuthbert slumped in the chair, bandaged and gulping desperately from a cup Pearl had given him. They glanced over as Joan hit the ground floor landing.

"We have to—"

Blam!

Something lage slammed into the front of the shop, spraying shattered glass across the room. Joan scrambled toward Cuthbert, urging him up and away from the broken windows as shards fell around them. He groaned as she moved him too forcefully but tried to keep up. Pearl grabbed him on the other side, supporting the weight Joan couldn't.

Blam!

Joan could hear wood splintering. She glanced back. The dark shape of an enormous lizard-like head on a serpentine neck swept past the broken windows. A chill raced through her.

It was the creature from earlier. The one that had killed Henry.

"A wyvern," Pearl whispered, her voice shaking.

The foreign word seemed to flutter in Joan's gut, sending an icy rush of fear out through her body. Her hands shook but she didn't dare take her eyes off the creature or stop moving. It reared back, about to strike the building again.

"Here!" Her mother's voice sounded in the room suddenly, and Joan tore her eyes away from the thing—the wyvern—to see a magical doorway opened directly to salvation. Her mother straddled it, one foot in the shop, the other in Stratford-upon-Avon. She waved them over, her eyes widening as she caught sight of the beast tearing apart Baba's home.

Blam!

The front door buckled and shattered in a spray of wood, the noise loud enough that they all screamed. Bia shook at Joan's wrist. She touched the sword, drawing it to its full size as she slipped out from under Cuthbert's arm.

"Get him through," she shouted to Pearl and turned to the door. "I'll distract it."

Blam!

The wyvern didn't pull back this time, pressing its head against the compromised wall. The foundation whined under the pressure, and the whole house seemed to groan.

It's going to bring the whole place down on us, Joan thought with alarm. *But the others will be fine if I just hold it here.* She braced herself.

"Not this time," her mother said in her ear.

Joan's stomach lurched as her mother yanked her backward through the doorway. Magic shivered over her skin, then the bright, earthy smell of the countryside filled her nose.

Blam!

The front wall buckled completely, crushing everything in its path as it crashed to the floor. The wyvern huffed and swung its head through the hole. Joan got her second glimpse of deep green skin and slitted yellow eyes before her mother slammed the doorway closed.

CHAPTER SEVEN
More Than Kin, Less Than Kind

J oan, her mother, and Pearl carried a stumbling Cuthbert directly to the drawing room at New Place and settled him on one of the couches.

"Your father's with Iya Mary." Joan's mother nodded toward the door. "Hurry and get them both." She turned back to Cuthbert without looking at Joan, her posture tense.

Joan almost spoke, the half insincere apology she knew she should give at the tip of her tongue. Instead, she slipped out of the room, pausing outside the closed door to stuff Baba's journal into a dark corner between two close beams. She hesitated for a moment longer, then hurried up the stairs.

The large house rumbled with life, people settling in for the night or helping with those who'd just arrived, but all children of the Orisha. Master Shakespeare owned the second-largest building in Stratford-upon-Avon, but even New Place's thirty-odd rooms strained with the presence of fifty extra bodies. And when King James demanded four for himself if they wanted him to stoop so low as to even consider staying here instead of Warwick Castle—it was the most prudent course, but what was that to a king—most of the Orisha folks found themselves sharing the rooms left between two or more people.

A door swung open as she reached the top of the stairs, and James came barreling toward her, still wearing her blue gown.

"Joan!" He grabbed her arms and shook her. "We're in so much trouble."

She nodded, unsure of how to begin recounting the evening's events to her brother. Some movement over his shoulder caught her attention, and she looked up to see Nick guiding his parents and two younger siblings into one of the rooms. The Tooleys had all made it safely to Stratford-upon-Avon.

Some of the tension within her relaxed at that. As if he felt her gaze, Nick turned, and their eyes met.

"You're bleeding," James said suddenly.

Joan hissed as he grabbed her hand. James' eyes narrowed as he finally noticed the bruises circling her neck. She pulled free, shifting her injured fingers out of her brother's view. When she looked for Nick again, he had disappeared into the room. She cleared her throat.

"Mr. Cuthbert needs Father to treat him," she said.

James frowned but jerked his head down the hall. Joan mumbled her thanks and slipped around him. He grabbed her arm as she passed, careful to avoid her injured hand. His gaze told her he expected a full explanation later. She owed him that for assisting with her deception even though recalling the events of the night in her mind alone filled her with panic.

She needed a moment to collect her thoughts before she . . .

Henry's frightened gaze as he was snatched into the darkness. The crunch of teeth on bones. The smell of that beast's foul breath . . .

Joan blinked rapidly but nodded at James. He let her continue down the long hallway with narrowed eyes. She heard his footsteps retreat in the opposite direction and fought the urge to call him back to accompany her. The walls pressed in on either side of her, the honey-colored wood feeling too narrow in the dim candlelight. Had Iya Mary's room always been this far from the main stairwell or did the dread of another confrontation distort Joan's perception?

She finally reached the door marked with an ornate white snail, its shell painted in intricate, monochrome swirls. Joan stood with her hand poised before the door, her heart racing wildly in her chest.

The community matriarch had made her displeasure with Joan known from the moment they'd arrived, and Joan was sure this incident would do nothing to raise her in the old woman's esteem.

She sighed and knocked.

"One moment," Iya Mary's voice called from within.

Joan waited, tapping her fingers against the sword at her wrist as hurried footsteps approached on the other side. She spotted a smudge of red blood along the wood from where she'd knocked and swiped it away with her sleeve just as the door swung open. Her father blinked down at her.

"Joan," he said, sweeping her into his arms. "God . . ." He squeezed her until she could scarcely breathe.

Every bit of bravery that had held her steady this night seemed to seep out of her all at once as she pressed her face against father's shoulder. She wouldn't refuse his fierce embrace, hadn't realized how much she needed to be held until this moment.

She'd been so foolish, and her mother had been rightfully furious, and if not for Joan, Henry would bealive.

She didn't deserve this comfort.

Joan swallowed around the lump in her throat and let her arms drop to her sides.

51

"We . . ." Her voice cracked. She coughed and tried again. "We need you and Iya Mary downstairs."

He pulled away and frowned as he took in Joan's expression. "I'll get my things." He released her with one last pat to her shoulders before leaning back into the room. "Iya—"

"So, she's returned," the old woman said. Her thin fingers wrapped around the door as she shooed Mr. Sands away. "Go get what you need and meet me downstairs."

He nodded and, with a quick glance at Joan, disappeared down the hallway toward his own room.

Iya Mary emerged from her room, a thick wool shawl clutched around her slim shoulders and her silver hair braided neatly around her head. Silver eyebrows furrowed on her wrinkled brown forehead, her tan skin blemish free but for those marks of age. Joan felt every muscle within her tense as the old woman looked her over. It was obvious that Shakespeare got his height from his mother. She was slim, but she still towered over Joan. It didn't help her feel less intimidated.

She slipped past Joan and strode to the stairs. "What foolish notion sent you running directly into the lion's den?"

"I . . ." Joan swallowed thickly. "I wanted to ensure they'd make it back."

The old woman hummed, the sound dripping with skepticism.

"I went there to protect them, and I did," Joan blurted, some of that bravado slipping back in the face of Iya Mary's disdain. She jogged around to stand directly in front of the woman. "Everyone made it here thanks to me."

Iya Mary paused, raising an eyebrow. "Did they?"

"I . . ." Joan cleared her throat again as Henry's face filled her mind, the fear in his eyes as he was dragged into the darkness by the wyvern.

She stared Joan down as if she could see the memory too. Despite her hopes, she'd only managed to fuel Iya Mary's distaste. The choice to go to London had been foolish—that became obvious as soon as Joan came face-to-face with Titanea—but she couldn't bear to sit here waiting and hoping, not when staying her hand had already cost her so much.

"And where would we be if *you* hadn't come back?" Iya Mary said. "Where would the Pact be if you'd died on this little *excursion*?"

Joan looked away, eyes burning. The old woman shook her head and left Joan alone in the empty hallway.

Joan clenched her fists, the tiny cuts along her palm burning with the pressure as her throat ached. Tonight's haste cost her far more than her mother's disappointment and Iya Mary's admonishment.

Henry's final moments invaded her mind again, his screams ringing in her ears.

"Are you coming down?" Her father strode down the hallway and gestured toward the stairs.

Joan started. "Yes, but I . . ." She cleared her throat. "I have to tell you . . ." That damned lump in her throat refused to move. She could hardly speak through its thick suffocation. "Henry . . ." She swiped at her eyes with the back of her fist and looked up at her father. "Henry's dead." Her voice broke over the hoarse words.

He jerked as if she'd slapped him, his expression horrified. "Henry? How did he . . ." He shook his head. "That poor boy . . . He wasn't involved in any of this."

"He found me at the house," she blurted, knowing the confession wouldn't come at all if she stopped. "I tried to bring him back here, but we were . . ." Her voice cracked again. "I couldn't protect him. I'm sorry."

Joan held his gaze, sniffling against the burn of tears. She had no right to cry over this, not when it had been her fault.

Baba Ben, Master Phillips, and now Henry had all died shielding her; it was her duty to carry the guilt of their losses without breaking. She needed to be strong enough to at least manage that in the face of her failures.

His eyes shifted over her face, as if he could read her every thought. Joan flinched, twisting her fingers around each other. She braced herself for his rage. Her hand throbbed as she agitated her wounds further.

"Oh, my love—" Her father swept her into his embrace. "I'm so sorry you had to face that alone."

Joan clung to his back as tears sprang to her eyes.

She needed to take responsibility for her mistakes, not cry like a child. She needed be stronger than this.

She needed . . .

Joan buried her face in the thick wool of her father's jacket and let herself be weak.

Her father made her sit at the top of the stairs as he rubbed salve on her bruised neck and wrapped her hand in clean bandages. She sniffled, murmuring her thanks. He hugged her and kissed the top of her head before going down to the drawing room.

Joan took a moment to collect herself when she was alone again. She flexed her fingers. The pain from her injuries had subsided, and she knew they all would be healed completely by morning. Such was her father's power as a child of Yemoja.

Tomorrow, only the memories would remain, though those marked her much more deeply.

She took another steadying breath, then pulled herself to her feet and headed down the stairs. As she reached the drawing room, the door swung open. She leapt back, and Rose burst out into the hallway, her face red and her eyes shiny with tears. She exhaled as she saw Joan, her whole body relaxing as she pulled Joan into her arms. She leaned into Rose's embrace as the scent of lavender surrounded them. She touched a hand to the still-healing wound at Rose's side. Rose flinched and hugged Joan tighter.

"Thank you for finding me," Joan whispered. She let her hands glide along Rose's back. "Are you all right?"

Rose took a shuddering breath. "Don't do that again." She stepped back, tears threatening to spill over her lashes. "Not without telling me. Please." She caressed Joan's cheek.

"Are you going in?"

They both turned to see Susanna, Shakespeare's oldest daughter, standing in the open doorway, her body positioned to block the view of anyone inside the room. Her spiraling curls of thick blond hair hung loose around her shoulders, the strands frizzing out like a mane as if she'd been running her fingers through them.

Judging from her pinched expression, she probably had.

Joan always felt intimidated, impressed, and half-infatuated around Susanna—just like everyone else who laid eyes on her. Her commanding presence could be attributed to the fact that she'd been blessed by Shango, the king and Orisha of lightning, rain, and truth, but Joan suspected much of it existed within her innately.

Rose pressed a firm kiss to Joan's forehead, then slipped around her to head upstairs. Joan watched her disappear at the first landing before looking back to Susanna.

"I'll go talk to her," Susanna said gently. She glanced up the stairs and sighed. "You know how my grandmother can be."

She stepped aside, and Joan caught a glimpse of Iya Mary seated inside the room. She hesitated.

"Do you want me to stay?" Susanna glanced back through the doorway. "You know I can manage my grandmother if you need."

She watched Joan, the eagerness on her face promising to antagonize Iya Mary further than Joan could ever hope to and with far fewer consequences.

Well, fewer consequences for Susanna. Joan doubted she'd escape Iya Mary's increased ire.

Besides, she was in trouble enough already.

"Thank you, but I'll be fine." She smiled at Susanna. "I behaved foolishly tonight."

Susanna shook her head. "You did, but you needn't deal with Grandmother's"—She waved her hand in the air, her face going sour—"for it." She waited until Joan cracked a smile, then squeezed Joan's shoulder and headed up after Rose.

Joan shot a quick glance at the corner where she'd hidden Baba's journal. She caught sight of one worn edge in the dark. Satisfied, she took a steadying breath and stepped into the drawing room.

Mother Burbage sat next to Cuthbert, clutching her son's hands as Mr. Sands patiently wrapped the wounds along his arms. His case of magical ointments and salves was open beside him, the unlabeled bottles and jars placed meticulously in a pattern only he could decipher. Joan knew having to contort himself around the weeping woman's clinging frustrated her father to no end, though he made no show of it. With his care and Yemoja's blessings, Cuthbert's injuries would be healed in a day or less.

Master Shakespeare's wife, Iya Anne, spoke softly to Mrs. Burbage, who trembled and hugged herself while Joan's mother rubbed gentle circles on her back. Burbage rocked their sleeping baby as he stood near the hearth with Shakespeare. He caught Joan's eye as she entered the room, a grateful smile sliding over his face as he nodded to her.

Iya Mary sat in a high-backed chair to the other side of the hearth, speaking intently to an old man with curly white hair pulled back into a low ponytail—Sir Oscar Pearce, another elder in the Orisha community. Joan knew he was a child of Aganju, the spirit of the volcano and the wilderness. He'd been knighted in his younger days by Queen Elizabeth herself and now served as Iya Mary's closest council. Neither of them looked up as Joan entered.

But one person was missing.

"Where's Pearl?" Joan said, her voice sounding too loud in the somber room.

Her father's focus remained on his work, although his jaw clenched as he heard her question. Joan narrowed her eyes and looked to Iya Mary.

"We can't be safe with one of the Fae in this house," the old woman said. "It's enough to have that girl under our roof."

Joan scowled. "Her name is Rose."

Iya Mary rolled her eyes at Joan, then turned to continue speaking to Sir Pearce.

Joan bristled. "Pearl is family. You can't just turn her out like some—"

"I can and I have," Iya Mary said, her words cutting across Joan's as she turned to glare at her. "How many more must die before you learn that your desires do not outweigh the safety of the collective?"

Joan flinched. The room's temperature seemed to drop at Iya Mary's glare. Joan's retort turned to ash on her tongue as the memories of Samuel, of Baba, of Phillips, of Henry flooded her mind, each death as vivid as the moment they'd happened. Her chest tightened, breaths coming too short. Her head felt as if it was on fire, and she knew if she spoke now, only the most vile things would spring forth from her lips. She clenched her fists and bolted from the room. She faintly heard someone call her name but ignored it, bursting through the front door and out into the frigid night air.

Up ahead, the small form of a woman walked away from the house, her cloak drawn tightly over her shoulders.

"Pearl," Joan called.

The woman turned and waited patiently as Joan sprinted toward her.

"It's far too cold to be running around out of doors, Joan," she said softly.

Joan frowned and grabbed Pearl's hand. "She can't turn you away."

"Let it go, Joan."

"No. I won't let her—"

"Joan—" Pearl patted Joan's hand before pulling away. "Let it go." She smiled, her expression calm. "I'll be fine, I'm stronger than I look. We *all* are. You must know that now."

Her emphasis struck Joan immediately, the confirmation of the things she'd known but hoped weren't true. All of the Fae had grown even stronger since their desperate battle at the palace. She'd felt Titanea's strength first hand, had only escaped by luck.

And this wyvern was something else, something new and ferocious that she feared she couldn't handle. The thought of facing the creature again filled her with dread.

Joan pressed her shaking hands against her trousers and looked to Pearl. "Come back if you need to. I don't care what anyone says, I'll always protect you."

"You're so much like Ben." Pearl's eyes suddenly shone with tears. "He'd be so proud of you."

Would he?

The question burst into Joan's mind before she could silence it.

She pressed her lips into a rough approximation of a smile and felt the cold settling into her bones. She shivered but stayed, watching as Pearl's short form disappeared into the dark streets of Stratford-upon-Avon.

She wished she could believe her godfather wouldn't share Iya Mary's opinions of her, not when she'd faced his exasperation and frustration so often when he'd been alive. He hated when she behaved recklessly in small instances. Things now held far more weight.

Feet approached behind her, and someone slipped a heavy wool cloak around her shoulders. She glanced up to see Master Shakespeare standing over her, his expression soft. He gently guided her toward the door where she could see Master Burbage haloed by the light from within the house. Joan glanced back one last time, but only the thick shadows of night gazed back. Pearl was long gone.

CHAPTER EIGHT
Saucy Lictors

hen they slipped back into the house, Shakespeare led Joan right past the drawing room, to her great relief. Burbage fell into step beside them, the hallway wide enough for the three of them to walk down shoulder to shoulder.

"I need to talk to Iya Mary," Joan said.

Shakespeare hummed, his expression hesitant. "It's probably best to save that for tomorrow. Besides—" He gave her a little shake and caught her gaze. "I have my own words for you, Mistress Sands."

Joan felt dread pooling in her stomach but stamped it down. Whatever Master Shakespeare had to say, his mother's words would be far sharper and harder to face. She was fine skipping that confrontation for now but there was something she didn't want to leave behind. She doubled back to snatch Baba Ben's journal out of the corner where she'd hidden it, clutching it to her chest. The leather was soft under her fingers, and a small sense of comfort flowed through her as she slipped back between Shakespeare and Burbage and the three of them continued toward the large banquet room on the opposite side of the house.

"Far be it from me to look down upon a blessing," Shakespeare said idly, "but I was sure we explicitly told you not to come to London."

Joan blinked and glanced up at him. He stared back, one eyebrow raised as he waited for her response.

Joan pursed her lips and hummed. Shakespeare narrowed his eyes.

"I thought it best to give you a decoy." She braced for his judgment as soon as the words left her lips.

Shakespeare jerked to a stop, his gaze still locked on her. She heard Burbage do the same but didn't dare look to the other man. The hallway suddenly felt far too small.

"You thought . . ." Shakespeare took a deep breath, eyes closed as he tugged at his beard. "You came to London to purposely draw Titanea's attention while none of us knew—"

"James knew," Joan blurted. She clamped her mouth shut when Shakespeare glared at her.

"You went to face Titanea alone while disguised as your brother, who we all thought was helping Nick and the Tooleys."

Burbage shook his head. "Was he in on your plot as well?"

"No! Nick didn't know. James told him he'd . . ." She glanced over at Burbage, who watched her with his arms crossed. "We told him that James would be with you."

Shakespeare sputtered as laughter exploded from Burbage's mouth.

"The audacity you children have." Burbage shook his head and rubbed his hand over his mustache as if to wipe away his smile. "Chastise her later, Will. The others are waiting." He patted Joan's head and started down the hallway again.

Shakespeare groaned. "I thought my nerves were safe once Judith came of age. More the fool me." He glared at Burbage's retreating form. "Enjoy these early years, Richard, you'll see these struggles soon enough."

Burbage laughed harder, gripping his sides as he gasped for air. Shakespeare caught up to him and elbowed him out of the way even though he had plenty of room. Shakespeare turned back after a few steps, his gaze exhausted and affectionate.

"Well, come along. The company's waiting."

Joan felt her shoulders relax at his words. If Iya Mary did nothing but put her on edge, the King's Men—her beloved family of actors—set her heart at ease. Seeing them now would do her good.

The banquet room sat at the back of New Place, enormous and spacious, and befitting the second-largest building in the tiny town. As the three of them strode in, Joan could see the other players who'd joined them on their flight from London perched around the room's sizable hearth. James stared at her. She smiled, mouthing back "Later" before her gaze sought out another face she desperately wanted to see.

Nick Tooley stood beside the fire, his dark eyes intense and already locked on her. She stumbled as heat sprang to her cheeks. She caught herself awkwardly, and he lurched forward as if to leap across the room to catch her. A smile slid over her face, an answering one curling his lips. She was sure he was angry with her and she owed him an apology, but he wouldn't refuse her approach. She headed toward him.

Shakespeare grabbed her arm. "No, no distractions." He looked pointedly between the two of them and tugged her toward a pair of chairs on the opposite side of the hearth. "You'll stay beside me."

"Will the Puritan," Armin sang out, his bright red hair almost glowing in the dancing firelight and his pale cheeks pink with drinking. "Never thought I'd see the day, you old cat."

Shakespeare shook his head as Burbage guffawed again. He gestured for Joan to sit. She obeyed. He took in their group again before his gaze landed on James.

"You too." He crooked a finger at the boy, who reluctantly stood from where he'd been sitting near Rob.

James dropped into the chair beside Joan, a pair of her earrings still dangling from his ears. He'd changed back into his own clothes after their meeting on the stairs even though she remained in his. He grabbed her hand immediately.

"We can't do that again," he whispered, his voice strained. "Please don't ask me to do that again."

Any number of witty replies died on her lips as he squeezed so tightly Joan could feel her bones rub together. Shame settled in her belly like a stone.

She twisted her hand so she could interlace their fingers. "I won't."

"Is it done?" Shakespeare said suddenly to someone behind them.

Joan spun in her seat to see Rose approaching slowly, her palm pressed to her side. She caught Joan's gaze and let her hand fall as a soft smile slid over her lips.

Rose turned back to Shakespeare. "Yes. Pearl is safely out of Stratford with explicit orders to return should she find any trouble." Here she smiled pointedly at Joan. "She promised to return should she need."

"Thank you," Joan said first to Rose, then Shakespeare. A wide grin spread over her face, so broad it made her cheeks ache but she couldn't stop it. They'd protected Pearl because she was someone important to Joan. Warmth flowed through her.

Shakespeare nodded and gestured Rose toward Nick. "You sit over near him. I don't need you causing *mischief* either."

His implicit meaning had Joan covering her hot face with her hands as Burbage and Armin fell into each other laughing. She never expected Shakespeare of all people to quail at the thought of anyone showing physical affection. She glanced up to see Nick helping Rose into the chair nearest him, his hand gentle at her elbow. The touch lingered, and they smiled at each other.

Joan took in their expressions as her heart raced. She knew that soft tilt to Nick's lips, that flutter of Rose's eyelashes. She'd seen each directed at her but never at each other. Joan waited for jealousy to flood through her at seeing her two lovers engage with such intimacy.

She waited but felt no such emotion. Only curiosity and the slightest burst of excitement.

How might their dynamic shift—*grow*—should Nick and Rose . . .

Nick stepped away, both he and Rose turning to Joan. Their gazes pinned her to her seat, so perfectly timed she swore they'd heard her thoughts. Blood roared in her ears and she felt her face grow hotter. This all felt precarious and exciting, and Joan wanted to press—

"Excellent."

Shakespeare's voice burst into Joan's mind. She looked away, that thin line of possibility flowing between the three of them broken.

"Armin, Burbage, and I had planned this before certain unexpected events took place . . ." Shakespeare looked pointedly at Joan and James before shaking his head. "But we still wanted to do something to honor Augustine's memory."

The air in the room suddenly seemed too heavy, too thick at the mention of Master Phillips. Shakespeare picked up the lute sitting near his chair and strummed a distorted set of chords. The rising sparrow painted across its belly marked it as Phillips's own instrument. Joan wondered how they'd gotten hold of it when they'd been forced to leave so much behind when they'd fled London.

Hot blood seared her skin, the droplets splattered across her face as Goodfellow's hand shoved through Phillips's chest. The old man's wide eyes stared at her.

"Close it," he said, then Goodfellow tore him in two.

Joan jerked back into the present as James tugged at her arm. He stared at her curiously, concern spread across his face. She tried to catch her breath. Tried to smile at him. He squeezed her hand again, and she knew she'd failed.

The memory of Phillips's death burned too clearly in her mind. Her throat felt tight and her hands trembled.

Shakespeare struggled to play the familiar song. The strings clanged, clumsy and discordant, but no one stepped in to take the instrument from him.

That had been Master Phillips's office. His gift for playing the lute was far stronger than any actor in the company. Even when he'd no desire to exert his skill, all Shakespeare had to do was attempt and Phillips would snatch the instrument from him in frustration. It was a dynamic born of years of friendship, and they were all unsure how to proceed now that he was dead.

Shakespeare hit a particularly dissonant chord and his hands stilled. He cleared his throat, positioning himself to start again, but his fingers couldn't find the right notes. None of them dared ask him to stop.

This was their way of mourning. They all needed it, even when it felt like the most difficult thing in the world.

"May I try, Master Shakespeare?" Rose said suddenly. She glanced quickly at Joan before standing and crossing to take the abused lute from Shakespeare. She held the instrument gently and carefully positioned her fingers. They glided across the strings. A perfectly hamonius chord flowed forth. "You wanted 'Blow, blow, thou winter wind'?"

Shakespeare blinked at her, both startled and grateful. "You know it?"

"It was Cristobell's favorite." Here her smile shifted, taking on a familiar melancholy. "She forced me to learn it."

Joan remembered the name from what felt like ages ago but had only been a few months. When they'd fought the red cap chieftain, she'd been using the form of one of Rose's friends, Cristobell. Rose hadn't mentioned the woman since, and, shamefully, Joan had never thought the to ask about Rose's loss. And now Rose navigated that alone as she helped the King's Men through their own.

Joan wanted to rush across the room and gather Rose up in her arms, to surround her with love as they mourned their fallen friends together. Rose glanced up, catching her eye. She shook her head and turned her focus back to the lute. She seemed to close herself off, not with the sharp sting of loneliness but as one who found comfort in solitude. Joan sighed. Rose's reaction made sense. The King's Men might be Joan's secondary family but they were still mostly strangers to Rose.

If she needed space in the moment, Joan wouldn't push.

Rose strummed through the chorus with practiced ease before turning back to the chords of the verse. "*Freeze, freeze, thou bitter sky,*" Nick sang, "*That does not bite so nigh as benefits forgot—*"

His graceful tenor swept through the room, blending perfectly with Rose's playing. Joan felt that curious heat again even as something within her relaxed at the combined sound. She let it wash over her and leaned her shoulder against her brother's. He rested his head on top of hers before joining in on the chorus.

"*Heigh-ho, sing, heigh-ho unto the green holly—*"

James's bright voice matched with Nick's, the two of them falling into an intricate improvised harmony. It happened without effort, they'd worked together for so long. Rose smiled played a quick flourish of notes that sent Armin into a burst of applause before he added his own voice. His low, resonant tones rumbled pleasantly in Joan's chest.

She chanced a look at Shakespeare. The tall man watched it all with a small smile, unshed tears sparkling in the firelight. Burbage stood and drew him into a tight hug. Shakespeare tucked his face into the other man's shoulder as a shudder passed through his body. His shoulders shook.

Joan turned away to give him the privacy to fall apart.

CHAPTER NINE
What the Heart Thinks

At some point, Shakespeare, Burbage, and Armin had gotten hold of even stronger ale. The three had settled their chairs around the fire and were taking turns impersonating the late Augustine Phillips.

Burbage stood now, his neck stretched out ridiculously as he took dainty steps across the floor on the tips of his toes. Joan and James watched the whole affair from the chairs Shakespeare had assigned them.

"Master Phillips would *never*," James snorted in outrage. He shoved to his feet. "As his former apprentice, I can't let such a disgraceful performance stand." He shifted his stance and seemed to grow taller. He squinted, lowering his eyebrows and pursing his lips. The look he cast at Joan so perfectly captured Phillips's essence, she burst out laughing.

"Masters," he called, his voice deep and tinged with an air of affectionate exasperation. The resemblance was so uncanny that all three men immediately turned to James. "Must I show you how it's done?"

He strode over to them as they started whooping and cheering. Joan shook her head as she tried to calm her laughter.

Rob stood from the settee where he'd been lounging. "I'll go keep him out of trouble." He smiled at Joan, glanced at someone behind her, then headed over to James and the rest.

"Do the speech," Shakespeare demanded, his words slurring outrageously. "Do his speech!"

James immediately launched into King Claudius's lines from *Hamlet* as Shakespeare applauded in delight.

"Might I steal a moment of your time?" Nick whispered in her ear.

Joan shivered as his warm breath caressed her cheek. He must've crossed the room while her attention had been on James. She took his offered hand and, with one quick glance to ensure the others—particularly Shakespeare—were occupied, allowed him to lead her to a small anteroom tucked on the far side of the chamber.

He closed the door quietly behind them, wrapping his arms around her waist before she could turn to face him. She gasped as her back hit his firm chest.

"I should know by now not to worry so much about you"—his arms tightened around her as he buried his face in her hair—"but when we returned and you weren't here, I could barely stand the fear." He shuddered. "I know I'm a fool. Tell me I'm a fool."

Joan caressed his hands where they rested against her belly before interlocking their fingers. "You are a fool, Nicholas Tooley," she said, her voice soft in the dim room. "And I'll have you no other way." She slid her other palm along his shoulder and around the back of his neck, gently tugging him closer. She tickled the silky hair at his nape because she could. He gasped at the contact.

Joan's heart quickened as she felt him curl around her to run his nose along her neck.

"How can you smell so lovely after such a long night?" he whispered into her ear, urging her closer.

She pulled away and spun to face him. This close, she could see how the strains of his family's absence had worn at him. His rich brown complexion had taken on an ashen hue. Dark bruises marred the skin beneath his eyes, and even his beautiful black hair hung round his shoulders in melancholy clumps.

But they were safe now—he'd brought his mother, father, and siblings to New Place that night. He needn't bear that burden any longer.

Nick brushed his fingers across her lips, and every thought fled her mind. She speared her hands through his hair and yanked him down for a kiss. He went willingly, stumbling against the door with a thud. He released her just enough to rearrange his grip at her back.

Knock. Knock. Knock.

He tilted his head, urging her mouth open with his as he deepened the kiss.

Knock. Knock. Knock.

"Ignore it," Nick whispered against her lips.

Knock. Knock.

"Of course, this is how I find you two . . ."

Joan and Nick pulled back from their kiss, Nick yelping as he banged his head against the door in his haste. Rose stood in the middle of the anteroom where she'd suddenly appeared, arms crossed over her chest and eyebrow raised. She didn't look angry, just annoyed.

"The least you could do is answer when I knocked, Nicholas." She stretched his full name out as if reprimanding a child. "Then I wouldn't need to surprise you so." She looked at Joan, her expression shifting to a leer. "Or interrupt . . ."

Nick released Joan, dusting off her clothes. His hands touched only her arms and waist, carefully avoiding any more scandalous parts. "You might have waited."

"I might have . . ." Rose's gaze shifted away for a moment as a flush took over her cheeks. She seemed to steel herself before turning back to Joan. "But I was worried." She scowled suddenly. "Why did you go to London without telling me?"

Nick hummed. "Without telling *us*."

Joan opened her mouth, then closed it again. What could she say to them? That she'd feared they'd stop her had they known her plan? That she'd wanted to help rescue Nick's and Burbage's families as desperately as they had themselves? That she'd been chafing under Iya Mary's disdain and needed to prove to herself that she wasn't a failure?

That last seemed the most absurd of all. Her chest tightened at the thought of facing the disappointment of the two standing before her now.

Rose searched Joan's face, and her expression suddenly softened. She pulled Joan into her embrace. Joan sighed and let herself be held.

"Thank you for saving me," Joan said instead.

Rose's arms tightened around her. "I could do nothing else." She tickled along the side of Joan's neck, making her squeal and squirm away. "See that it doesn't happen again."

"I shall do my best," Joan gasped out between giggles.

Rose pressed closer, blowing a puff of air against the skin at the juncture of Joan's shoulder. Joan snorted and twisted out of Rose's grip. Joan lunged for Nick before Rose yanked her back. Nick grabbed her arms and tried to pull Joan toward him, but Rose held her by the waist and was stronger than them both. She jerked Joan back and Nick along with her. The three of them collided, stumbling deeper into the room as they all lost their footing. They slammed into the far wall and sent a basket of linens tumbling off a shelf. Rose grunted as Nick's weight crushed Joan against her.

"Sorry," Nick said as he leaned away.

Rose's hands shot out from beneath Joan's arm, and she pressed wiggling fingers into Nick's sides. He squeaked out a startled laugh. Joan grabbed the front of his jerkin, holding tight so he couldn't escape Rose's attack.

"Traitor," he gasped, everything else lost in the sudden rumble of his laughter.

He grabbed at Rose's hands, all three of them shaking with mirth as she dodged and tickled him mercilessly. He finally managed to catch her because she was cackling too hard to focus on her attack.

He pressed both Rose's wrists against the wall above her head, crushing their three bodies closer together. "Enough."

Joan felt Rose's breath hitch. Her own heart raced, and her grip on Nick's jerkin tightened. Nick licked his lips.

The door burst open, slamming against the wall with a loud thud.

"Not on my watch!" Shakespeare shouted, his foot still raised from kicking in the door. "Out! Everybody out!"

Nick immediately released Rose. She wrapped her arms around Nick and Joan at once and transported them out of the storeroom in a blink. They reappeared in the middle of the hall.

Shakespeare burst out of the storeroom. "Don't think your magic can save you!" He ran toward them on faltering steps.

Joan pressed her face against Nick's trembling chest to hide the mirthful tears sliding down her face. She could barely hear him and Rose laughing over her own gasps.

"What saucy children, all of them!" Armin shouted. He stood on his chair near the hearth, hands cupped around his mouth. "They'll make a bawd of you yet, Will! Look!"

He grinned at Joan before pointing directly at where James sat with Rob. The two boys pulled back from their tight embrace. James's hand flew to his lips, face turning red. Rob rolled his eyes as Shakespeare hurried over and shoved them apart.

"To bed, all of you!" Shakespeare pointed to the door, swaying on his feet for a moment but managing, barely, to stay upright.

Joan shook her head. She twisted so she could wrap her arms around both Nick and Rose. Rose drew her close for a deep kiss. Joan pulled away, trying to blink the world back into focus as Nick grinned down at her and gently touched his lips to her forehead. Her heart thudded in her chest.

"Go. To. Bed!" Shakespeare bellowed.

His hands clamped down on Joan's shoulders, tugging her from between Nick and Rose and turning her toward the door. She burst into laughter again, but let herself be marched off to her room.

· 21 JANUARY ·

CHAPTER TEN
INTERLUDE: The Stag

Caleb set out at first light, determined to make it as far from Oxford as his feet could take him before he was missed. School had been far from the great adventure his mother had promised; instead, its dull drudgery had plagued him endlessly. The need to keep up with lessons when he could be enjoying life and his family's money hung around him like a weight, anchoring him to this dreadful place with its dreadful teachers.

He'd never been one for rules. He'd tried for his mother's sake. For two whole years he'd tried, but enough was enough. He'd find his own way in the world . . . at least until the terror of his sudden disappearance from his university bed sent his parents into a regretful panic. He'd let them stew in their melancholy before returning to them. They'd let him do whatever he wanted after that.

He felt two weeks would be long enough to build appropriate contrition within them.

"Caleb, wait!"

Caleb groaned at the sound of his schoolmate's voice—well, former schoolmate—and turned to see the bespectacled boy running toward him, satchel slung over his back. He waited for Simon to catch up, dust flying around him with every step. A familiar annoyance flowed through Caleb as Simon reached him and doubled over to catch his breath. Caleb waved the dirt cloud away from his face.

"What are you doing, Simon?" He tried not to let his full exasperation enter his voice. "I told you not to follow."

Simon pulled himself up to his full height, towering over Caleb, and swiped a hand across his runny, red nose. "I couldn't let you go off alone when you can barely fend for yourself." He pointed back down the road. "You said you're heading toward Warwick, but the road you need to take is down the other fork." He tugged his wool cloak more tightly around his shoulders and smiled gently at Caleb. "You're not the best with directions."

Caleb felt his cheeks immediately redden at the other boy's words. Scowling, he shouldered past him to retrace his steps. He heard Simon follow close behind, still panting as he walked.

"Thank you," Caleb said as the boy caught up to him again, "but you can go back now." He felt Simon grab his arm and spun to face him. "I said you can go." He spat the words, letting every bit of his anger and frustration color them. Maybe then the other boy would understand. "I don't need you following me like a mother hen or some lovesick spaniel."

Simon flinched, his hand dropping away from Caleb's arm. He looked as if he'd been kicked in the face as he opened and closed his mouth without a word, cheeks bright red. Caleb shook his head and turned away again. Let Simon stand there like some mooncalf in his ill-fitting, dust-covered cloak. He'd be happy to be rid of the overbearing boy who thought his hovering was kindness. Caleb scowled again and squinted against the bright rising sun. Up ahead, he could see where he'd made his wrong turn, where the tree line split the road in two directions.

"I know," Simon called after him. "I know you say you don't need me, but I want to go with you. I want to help you. I—"

Caleb spun again, throwing his hands up. "Stop it, Simon. Enough." He waited until the boy's mouth had closed before speaking again. "I do not care for you, not as a friend and most assuredly not as a lover. If you want to make me happy, get out of my life." He saw Simon pale, his usually peachy skin going nearly white in the early morning light.

Good, maybe now he'd leave him be.

"Caleb..." Simon whispered, chin wavering and eyes wide.

Caleb rolled his eyes. "Go back to Oxford."

"Caleb..."

"No one wants you here!" The words echoed around them as Simon stared at him. Caleb turned back toward the crossroads and immediately realized that it wasn't his words that had shocked Simon so into silence.

A large white buck, its fur so stark in the sunlight that it seemed to glow, stood at the center of the road. Delicate gold chains hung with jewels dangled from antlers so wide that the buck seemed three times as large. The gems twinkled in the morning light. The stag turned toward Caleb, its eyes locking with his. A chill raced down his spine. Then its gaze slid past him to Simon. Caleb heard the other boy whimper as the stag pawed the ground. Dust floated into the air around it and sparkled in the sun's glow. It took a step toward them, jewels clanking together like the soft chiming of bells.

"What kind of..." Caleb let the words drift off as the animal strode past him. He'd never seen such a majestic creature, its movement as otherworldly as its appearance. This close, he could see an equally ornate saddle laid across the animal's back, seemingly calling out for a rider daring enough to claim its opulence.

Caleb's heart raced. He could be so daring.

The creature kept its focus on Simon, drawing Caleb's eyes back to the boy as well. Simon quaked with fear as it approached.

"Caleb," Simon whispered, his eyes glassy with tears. "Run now."

Caleb snorted. He hadn't expected Simon to be so duplicitous, hadn't believed the boy was capable of subterfuge at all, but here he was feigning fear just so he could claim the stag for himself. How easily this love he'd claimed to feel for Caleb faded when confronted with such treasure.

But such was "love" as Caleb had known from the start.

"I won't let you have it," he said sharply. "Its riches aren't meant for you."

He started toward the stag as Simon's eyes flew to his. Caleb paused, the naked pleading he saw there frightening him for a moment.

"For the love of God, Caleb"—Simon's lip quivered, a sob catching in his throat—"it's no treasure. Run and save yourself."

Caleb took a step back, something deep within him heeding the other boy's words before he could stop himself. The stag's head swung around, its gaze locking with Caleb's.

No. No. This was meant for him. He wouldn't let Simon claim this creature for himself. The jewels adorning one antler alone would be enough for him to survive for months on his own, and with all the jewels plus the saddle, he'd never need his father's money again.

He wouldn't let pitiful, whining Simon steal that from him.

"You want to be mine, don't you?" Caleb spoke directly to the stag, watching with joy as it moved closer. "That's it. Come to your new master."

From the corner of his eye, he could see Simon step toward him, hands outstretched.

"Stay where you are, Simon, or I swear I'll make you regret it." Caleb spat the words at him. "If you ruin this for me, you'll be lucky if you can crawl back to Oxford."

The buck's ears twitched, and Caleb flinched. He crouched lower, making himself less threatening as he beckoned and cooed at the animal. Its ears twitched again as Simon whimpered, swinging around toward the sound.

Rage surged through Caleb, as hot as any he'd ever felt. "I warned you! I warned you!" he shouted as he sprinted toward Simon, tackling him to the ground. "Why must you ruin everything for me?" He pinned Simon's arms to the ground with his knees, knowing that while he might be taller, Caleb was far stronger. His fist slammed into Simon's face, an explosion of blood bursting from his nose as he cried out.

Caleb didn't care. He had warned him, and now Simon would pay the price. He remembered every petty annoyance, every unwanted moment that Simon had inserted himself into Caleb's life. That rage and frustration powered his swings. He hit him again and again, joy rising in him that he could finally punish someone who displeased him without them fighting back.

He couldn't do this to his parents or the thrice-damned teachers at Oxford, but Simon? Simon was weak and would bear his rage with that infuriating patience he claimed came from love.

Caleb brought his fist up again, ready for his next strike, when a sudden pain stole his breath. He gasped, drawing his arm down to see blood gushing sluggishly from where his hand used to be. A scream burbled up from within him as his world erupted in agony. He threw himself off

Simon and collapsed in the dirt, clutching his bloody wrist to his chest. The white stag loomed over him. Crimson stained its mouth, stark against its blindingly white fur. It chewed something.

His hand...

The stag turned suddenly to Simon, the boy crying out as it leaned closer to him.

Hope cleared Caleb's mind for a moment. He could escape while the beast devoured Simon. Yes, he'd be forced to go back to Oxford, but he'd be blessedly alive. He'd gladly embrace his Latin lessons for the chance to live.

He scooted himself away from Simon and the stag, clenching his teeth against the searing pain in his wrist as he pressed his sleeve against the bleeding limb. He couldn't make a sound, not if he wanted to escape. The stag nuzzled Simon, wiping its bloody maw on his clothes as it sniffed at him. Simon sobbed and turned away, too afraid to face his death head on.

Typical...

The stag snorted and pushed its snout against Simon's chest, nudging the boy upright. Simon clamped his mouth shut, slowly easing to his feet, his eyes locked on the stag. It stepped around behind him and shoved him down the road in the direction of Oxford. Simon stumbled forward but caught himself. His eyes locked with Caleb's.

Caleb could see the damage he'd done to Simon in his anger. One of his eyes was swollen shut, blood dripping from his split lip and broken nose. The stag pressed Simon forward again, gentle but insistent. Then it turned to Caleb, revealing a mouth full of impossibly sharp teeth.

"No," Caleb whispered, the word catching in his throat. "No. You were supposed to eat him."

Heartbreak crossed Simon's face before he clenched his jaw and looked ahead, letting the stag's next nuzzle send him walking down the road. He strode past Caleb and, even though his eyes shone too bright in the morning light, he didn't spare the boy another glance.

The stag watched Simon for a couple steps. The jewels tinkled again, clashing together as it moved toward Caleb. He froze, locked in place by its stare.

It towered over him at its full height, the rising sun reflecting off its jewels and gold chains and pure white fur in blinding rays. He looked over at Simon, who'd stopped at the crossroads and turned back to watch Caleb and the stag. He was too far away for Caleb to make out his expression, but the cold detachment in his stance was obvious.

"Simon," Caleb cried, reaching out for him. "Simon, don't leave me here. Please."

The stag snorted at him and tossed its head. An emerald the size of a fist swung loose from its antlers, catching the light as it was flung through the air. It landed at Simon's feet. The stag watched, waiting to see how Simon would respond.

Simon glanced down at the shining thing in the dirt before him, then, with one last look at Caleb, turned to walk down the road that would lead him home to Oxford, leaving both the boy and jewel behind.

Caleb's heart pounded in his chest with every step the other boy took.

"Simon, don't leave me here!" he called. "Simon! Simon, don't leave me here!" He screamed, throat aching and voice rising as the other boy never even paused.

Simon turned down the road back to Oxford where it curved and disappeared behind the trees, hiding him from view, Caleb screaming his name. The stag bleated. The sound shifted and contorted until it sounded like human laughter.

"Simon! SIMON, DON'T LEAVE ME HERE!"

It shook its head again. The jewels on its antlers tinkled merrily as it stepped in front of Caleb. It snorted, blowing a hot, moist breath into Caleb's face that stank like a corpse in the sun.

"SIMON!"

The stag's mouth opened so impossibly wide, enough to swallow Caleb's body whole.

"SI—"

CHAPTER ELEVEN
Who Dares Say Jove Does III?

hree gold coins must be presented from the monarch's own stores—

The early morning sun just started to creep through the window as Joan poured through Baba's journal. The single candle next to her flickered, and she squinted as the words on the page disappeared in shadow for a moment. She shifted the curtain open slightly, light pouring into the room. She blinked as the steady brightness gave her eyes blessed relief.

She sat at a table by the window, a tall wardrobe and chest of drawers nestled along the wall to her right, and a cozy bed made of the same dark reddish wood behind her. Intricate tapestries depicting pastoral hunts lined the other walls, and a painting of two children running through fields of emerald grass hung over the large fireplace. The room was quite different from Joan's back in London, both in size and décor, but she was grateful that its owner had agreed to sharing.

*Three gold coins must be presented from the monarch's own stores along with the sealing blade *the blade is lost, use a pound of raw iron purified and placed with Ogun for three days**

Joan frowned at the note hastily scribbled alongside Baba's neat writing. Her eyes slid to Bia hanging around her wrist, quiet against her skin. The sword had found its way into her hands the day after Baba's arrest, as if it had known what was on the horizon. Beyond that, Ogun himself had confirmed that Bia was needed to reforge the Pact. It had to be the lost sealing blade his notes referenced.

She sighed and leaned back, rubbing at her tired eyes. She'd poured through Baba's journal all night in hopes of finding some clue. She'd discovered the method of fortifying the one that had been broken but nothing to build it anew.

Nothing she hadn't already known, anyway . . .

She turned back to the journal. Perhaps there was a way to use the ingredients listed to reforge the pact. The king resided under this very roof, which made retrieving some of his gold easy.

Well, slightly easy . . .

She'd have to ask Philip to get her an audience. The courtier would be willing to do her the favor, although Joan doubted she'd have any success. Every time she'd happened across King James's path here in New Place, the man had made his disgust clear.

He hated her more than Iya Mary did, which was quite the feat.

"Joan . . ." Judith groaned suddenly from the bed and rolled over. "Close the god forsaken curtain . . ." she mumbled—or at least that's what Joan thought she heard—and pulled the thick blanket over her head.

Joan pulled the heavy fabric across the window so that the table was lit but the bed was back in shadow. She wasn't used to sharing a bedroom and didn't want to offend the older girl. It was, after all, Judith's room.

Shakespeare and Joan's own mother denied her attempt to share a bed with Rose—as much as it annoyed Joan, she could understand why.

Instead, Rose was with Susanna and Joan found herself with Shakespeare's youngest daughter, Judith.

Joan had barely interacted with the two Shakespeare sisters before now. She'd seen them occasionally at Orisha ceremonies major enough to draw the communities spread across England together, though those barely happened once a year, and they'd always seemed unapproachable. Both were older and had more spiritual experience than Joan. She'd never had reason to think ill of Judith or Susanna, nor had she formed more than a surface opinion of either. In fact, she'd been as surprised to find out the two were Master Shakespeare's daughters as she'd been to discover Iya Mary was his mother. He'd never appeared at any ceremonies as far as Joan could recall, having turned his back on the religion and his Orisha after his son's death.

He'd proven to her that her connection to Ogun couldn't be broken easily in a moment when she'd felt beyond hope and his daughters had similarly reached their hands out to Joan in her time of need. She and the others had escaped to Stratford bloody and exhausted from their battle. In the face of Iya Mary's dismissal and insults, Susanna had immediately offered Joan her support and continued to stand between her grandmother and Joan whenever asked. Judith had offered up her room in a quieter show of support than her sister's but one no less meaningful.

Their aid felt like lifelines, and Joan found herself trusting them completely. Enough so that she didn't bother hiding the journal when she slipped out of the room.

She needed to talk to Iya Mary, and the earlier she found the old woman, the better.

The sounds of the rousing house were just starting to echo, and Joan could smell the delicious aroma of fresh bread. Her stomach growled but she ignored it. Up ahead, the door to Iya Mary's room loomed at the end of the hall, the white snail still far more menacing than such a creature had any right to be.

Joan grit her teeth, steeled herself, and strode up to the room. Bia slid against her wrist, the cool metal chilling her skin. Joan sighed and knocked.

The door swung open at her first rap. Iya Mary stared down at Joan, a frown spreading across her lips. She'd wrapped her hair in a fine white fabric that twisted around and through itself. It sat atop her head like a woven crown.

"Yes," she said.

Joan straightened and cleared her throat. "I—May I speak with you?"

"It must wait," the old woman said. She pushed past Joan, her steps steady but slow. "I've been summoned by His Majesty."

Joan stood awkwardly at the door, unsure how to proceed. She needed to see King James but doubted surprising him with a request for gold was prudent. Fierce admonishment would be the kindest reward for her impudence.

She could wait.

Iya Mary turned to consider Joan. "Come along and speak to me after." She walked off again. "I suppose it must be important if you sought me out at this hour."

Joan clamped her mouth shut against her retort and fell into step behind Iya Mary. They continued down another long, well-lit hall. Two thick tapers sat in each of the sconces lining the walls. The flames flickered merrily as they passed, illuminating the paintings and framed pages of text written in gilded ink. Joan squinted at one and glimpsed familiar lines from *Hamlet*. Another showed the opening speech from *Richard III*, and yet another held Rosalind's closing from *As You Like It*. The king had claimed Master Shakespeare's suite as his own, and these decorations were proof.

They finally reached the door at the end of the hall, a peacock and peafowl lovingly entwined painted across the waxed wood. Iya Mary knocked, her bony knuckles thudding loudly in the otherwise quiet hallway. The door swung open after a long moment, and Philip Herbert peered out at them, put together and as awake as if it had been noon instead of barely past sunrise. His blond hair hung loose around his shoulders, but his clothing hugged his form in clean lines worthy of a courtier who stood beside his king.

"Welcome, Madame Shakespeare," he said, inclining his head. "And you as well, Joan." He swung the door open to invite them inside, giving Joan a warm smile that she returned genuinely.

Though their acquaintance had been short, Joan counted him as a friend. She'd never forget the kindness Philip had shown her while she'd been under Titanea's thumb. In the midst of the Fae queen's attack, he'd protected King James and escaped with them to Stratford-upon-Avon. Even now, he remained a constant presence at the monarch's side, managing his moods with impressive skill. One might say his effort was the price of the king's favor, but Joan knew Philip's support was offered with a love beyond that of a subject of the crown.

And for her friend's sake, she hoped that affection was reciprocated.

Philip leaned close to Joan as she passed him. "I hadn't expected you to come as well, Joan," he whispered. "I fear this may worsen his mood."

Joan sighed, frustration and anxiety fluttering in her gut, but their small group stepped into the main part of the room before she could speak.

She and Iya Mary dropped into deep curtsies. Joan touched her knee to the floor as was proper before her king.

"Rise," King James said, his voice dripping with boredom. "I shall go hunting."

Joan pitched to the side at his blunt declaration. She blinked at the floor and tried to right herself.

He wanted to *hunt*?

"Gather me an appropriate party," he continued. "I expect you have such people, Madame Shakespeare."

Joan glanced quickly at Philip, who shrugged and mouthed an apology. She turned to Iya Mary, wondering what the woman would say. Her heart raced in her chest. It was only a matter of time before Titanea sent her forces to find them here. If the king wasn't within the safety of New Place when that happened . . .

Joan raised her head. "If it may please Your Majesty—"

"Deepest apologies, Your Majesty," Iya Mary interrupted, her voice careful and measured, "but I'm sure you're aware of the dangers we currently face. It is not—"

The king grunted. "I asked not for *permission*," he sneered the last word in disgust. "I am your king. Do not presume you may command me because you have the witch child's devilry at your disposal."

Joan flinched at his chosen name for her. After Robert Cecil had exposed her magic before the court, King James had watched her with disgust and fear. No one hated witches more than he; all of England knew of his determination to eradicate any within his kingdom. Thankfully, because of his early escape from Whitehall's Banqueting House and subsequent injury, he knew nothing of the magic the other children of the Orisha wielded. Thus, the king believed Joan was the only "witch" in their midst.

Joan was sure only the threat of the Fae stayed his order for her execution. She tried not to think of what would happen once that threat was gone or if he discovered the powers of the rest of her community.

Iya Mary bowed lower, dropping her knee to the floor. "I apologize for my impudence, my liege. I would never be so bold as to—"

"Send the witch child along with me." He flicked his hand in Joan's direction, his eyes pointedly looking anywhere but at her. "Assemble the other people I need along with your best horses and have them ready to depart on the hour. I will spend *some* portion of the morning outside this hovel." He lounged across the settee and leaned his head back against the arm. "You are dismissed."

Joan opened her mouth to speak, to protest, but Iya Mary jerked her down into another low curtsy. Her nails dug into Joan's skin through the thick fabric of her sleeve. Philip appeared in front of her when they stood. He took hold of her other arm, and before she could gather her wits, she found herself maneuvered out into the hallway again.

"Madam Shakespeare," Philip said, inclining his head to the woman, "might I have a word with Joan?"

Iya Mary frowned but stepped away to give them some privacy. Philip smiled politely before he leaned close to Joan again.

"He's afraid of you," he whispered, "and that wars with his gratitude for you saving his life."

Joan sighed. "You needn't make excuses for the king. His Majesty's behavior is above reproach as is his due."

"No, but I'd like my *friend* to understand that her mistreatment is unfair and not because any of her own actions." He grinned at her shocked look. "I want you to be sure of where I stand when it comes to you. Friend."

She clasped her hands around his, her chest feeling suddenly light. "Thank you, friend."

"Philip, I have need of you!" the king called from within.

Philip straightened. "I come anon!" He thanked Iya Mary and winked at Joan before he slipped back into the room. Some tension had left Joan at his reaffirmation of their friendship. Smiling, she looked to Iya Mary, who grabbed Joan's arm again and hurried her down the hallway.

"Must you always be at the center of foolishness?" Iya Mary dragged her along, her voice growing louder as they moved farther away from the room. "We cannot defy our king and must acquiesce to his every whim, however absurd."

They reached the top of the main staircase and Iya Mary dropped Joan's arm.

"I'll ready the others." She started down to the main floor but paused, turning back to Joan. "Be prepared to leave on the hour." Then she was gone, muttering angrily under her breath the whole while.

CHAPTER TWELVE
Those Strong Knots of Love

Joan couldn't quite gather her jumbled thoughts as she lingered at the top of the stairs. She hadn't gotten to speak with Iya Mary about her discovery in Baba's journal and she knew the opportunity wouldn't present itself again until after Joan played chaperone on the king's excursion. She sighed. looking down at the gown she'd dressed herself in this morning. She'd worn the repaired blue dress with orange sleeves to bolster her mood, now she couldn't help but feel that this particular ensemble was cursed.

She could fight in this attire—and had nearly lost her life to a goblin while wearing it last—but the heavy skirts made riding a horse difficult. She'd need to borrow James's trousers again. She headed toward her brother's room.

"Hist, Joan." Shakespeare leaned out from behind a slightly open door. His smile broadened when she turned to him. "Do you have some—of course you don't. Come here." He flapped his hand at her, the gesture becoming more urgent the longer she took to walk toward him. He sighed and dragged her inside the room once she was close enough for him to reach.

"Sit," he said, closing the door behind them.

Warm wood panels covered the walls, making it feel both private and comfortable. A large ebony desk took up most of the room, its surface strewn with papers and empty ink bottles. It faced away from a large window hung with cheery yellow curtains and framed by overflowing bookshelves on either side that reached to the ceiling. This was his office.

Joan sat in one of the damask chairs beside the large desk as he bustled into the room behind her. He snatched a single page from the chaos of his desk and handed it to her. His usually neat writing scrawled across it as if his hand had struggled to keep up with his mind.

"Read." He pointed to a chunk of words on the page. "That part there. I need to hear it in a woman's voice." He leaned back, grabbing the peacock feather quill to twist around his fingers as he watched her expectantly. "Aloud, please."

Aloud?

Joan looked down at the page. Her palms started to sweat. In all the time she'd known him, Master Shakespeare had only once asked her to speak his words, when she'd gone on as Hermia in *A Midsummer Night's Dream* instead of James, who'd been injured by the red cap chieftain.

She assumed he'd never ask her again. The play had ended in disaster because of Auberon's attack in the middle of it, not her performance—which had been going rather well as she remembered. Samuel's death and the melancholy aftermath had barely left room for congratulations or praise.

She peeked up at him from under her lashes. He tapped the desk with one hand and twirled his quill with the other. She turned back to the page and cleared her throat.

She wouldn't squander this moment.

"*Sir, I am made of that self-same metal as my sister / And prize me at her worth. In my true heart—*" The rest of the speech came more easily, drawing emotion from her as she read the lines.

His words were always like that. Just saying them aloud could turn anyone into a player, could stir up feelings with only their rhythm.

"Excellently done, Joan!" He clapped when she finished, his smile nearly splitting his face.

A thought sprang forth, one that she'd never allowed herself to consider before this moment. Even now, she felt the urge to shove it down into the abyss of her mind, but . . .

What harm was there in admitting to herself that she desired one more forbidden thing?

She'd read his speeches a thousand times if she could and feel that glorious rush of a crowd moved by her voice to weep, to laugh, to gasp.

"It already sounds wonderful." Joan handed him the page, her chest suddenly tight even as she matched Shakespeare's grin. "And while I'd love to hear more, I must be gone." She pushed herself to her feet. "The king has need of me."

Shakespeare frowned. "The king?" He straightened, his face going dark. "What need—"

"To protect him while he hunts," she said.

For a moment, it looked as if he would go give King James the denial that neither she nor Iya Mary had been brave enough to offer. As much as it warmed Joan's heart, she knew the disaster such a confrontation would bring.

"I plan to ride out dressed as a boy."

He nodded. "Excellent idea. James will have what we need. You two are of a size." He said the last with a pointed look that made Joan flush with shame.

He leapt from the desk and dragged her out of his office. They hurried down the hallway to the door painted with a blue bird in flight, the image rendered in brilliant cerulean paint. Shakespeare rapped his knuckles against the wood, then squinted down at her.

"I don't suppose we have enough time to braid down your hair," he said just as the door swung open.

James blinked at them blearily, a deep frown on his face. He still wore his nightshirt, and his hair was wrapped for sleep. The sound of laughter from within the room behind him let Joan know they likely hadn't been the ones to wake him.

"Who's that?" Nick's voice called out, sounding as alert as everyone besides James.

James scowled and rasped out, "It's Master Shakespeare and my sister." He grunted as two small bodies shoved past him on either side, giggling the whole while. He stumbled against the doorjamb with a curse.

Joan crouched down as Nick's twin siblings leapt into her arms.

"Joan," Margery exclaimed, "is it true you fought monsters?"

Matthew hugged her tightly. "I'll protect you from them next time, so make sure you call on me." He looked up at her, his face determined.

Joan couldn't stop the laugh that bubbled up in her as she embraced both children. The Tooley twins were only about eight years old and not quite the matched set that she and James were. Margery and Matthew shared Nick's beautiful dark complexion and long black hair, but where their older brother's features seemed to have been carved by a sculptor, the twins' faces held more softness. Matthew's lashes were longer, Margery's nose rounder. She was immensely grateful to see them safe here at New Place, although her worry could never compare to what Nick had felt.

She glanced up and caught his eye over James's shoulder. He smiled at her, the tension that had dogged him these several days finally releasing its hold fully.

"Did you need something?" James said, the early hour making him distempered.

Shakespeare laughed and ushered them all into the room with the ease of being the master of the house. "Your sister must be dressed to hunt with the king"—he gave James a look—"and not draw undue attention."

"To what?" James blinked at her for a long moment before springing into action. "Everyone out." He pointed Joan to the bed and turned toward the wardrobe.

Nick snatched up his siblings as he passed Joan, tucking one under each arm as they squealed and squirmed in protest. "Let's be off to find breakfast." He grinned at her and strode out of the room behind Shakespeare. The door swung shut behind them.

"Pull your hair back," James's muffled voice called from within the wardrobe. "I'll give you a cap."

Joan set to work unpinning her long twists and gathering them at the base of her head. James suddenly plopped a velvet cap on her head, the green so dark it was nearly black. It slipped down over her eyes. She pushed it up again to see him frowning at two doublets as he held them in front of her.

His gaze met hers and he raised an eyebrow. "You're lucky I work quickly. If we don't want you drawing attention . . ." He tossed the brown doublet to her and grabbed the matching trousers. "This is the only time I'll allow you this unflattering color, and I expect your show of appreciation to be appropriately effusive." He dodged out of the way of her swing. He'd never stop teasing her for preferring dull—in his opinion—colors.

Still, she could tell he felt her gratitude, and for now, that was enough.

CHAPTER THIRTEEN
Uncouple in the Western Valley

oan strode out of the garden gate in her brother's clothes at the first toll of seven. Wearing trousers still felt uncomfortable, but she appreciated not having to manage her skirts. She discreetly shifted her hips as she walked, trying to get the fabric to fall in a less irritating manner.

Predictably, it didn't work.

King James inspected one of the horses, a fine black mare with a braided mane and wavy tail, as Philip lingered behind him. Four men stood a respectful distance away, doing their best to disguise the stares directed at the monarch. She recognized three of them—Martin, Roger, and Tobias—though they'd never spoken directly. Martin's face was carefully blank until he turned to the others and his thick brows winged together in frustration over his golden brown forehead. Roger pressed his hand over his mouth even as his sharp cheekbones raised in a smile that seemed to make his deep brown skin glow. Both men were children of Ochossi—the Orisha of the hunt—and were close in age to Joan's parents. The other man standing with them seemed familiar, but she couldn't place him. He glanced Joan's way, and she caught a glimpse of a bushy blond mustache cutting across a pale face with the slightest tan beneath his wool cap. Joan frowned as he winked at her and turned back to the other two. The fourth, Tobias, was a child of Elegua—the Orisha of the crossroads. He could create doorways just like her mother and could get them back to New Place quickly should they need it. She admired Iya Mary's foresight in choosing this group.

Joan moved to join them when Shakespeare appeared and suddenly steered her aside.

"Keep your wits, Joan," he said, fiddling with the pin on her heavy wool cape, then her hat. He glanced over toward the king, then leaned close enough to her to whisper. "You'll have the others, but should anything seem amiss, come back directly."

His expression killed the smart remark on Joan's tongue, and she just nodded. Satisfied, he nudged her gently toward the rest before going to stand beside Iya Mary—who Joan was ashamed to realize had been watching them the whole time. The old woman glanced Joan's way before Shakespeare drew her into an intense conversation.

One of the Shakespeares' day servants had gathered the other horses on the edge of the field closest to the house. He held the reins of the black mare as King James swung himself into the saddle. Philip mounted his own horse, and the four others split up to claim the rest. Roger said something to the unknown man, who nodded, then waited, steadying a horse with both hands, until Joan approached.

"Thank you, sir." Joan grabbed the reins he offered.

The man grinned at her. "I suspect this shall be either thrilling," he said in Judith's familiar voice, "or breathtakingly boring."

Joan gasped out a laugh as Judith touched her false mustache as if to make sure it was still in place. Joan wondered how the older girl had convinced her grandmother to let her join the king's hunting party, but the way Judith deliberately kept her back to Iya Mary told Joan that the woman's consent likely wasn't involved.

"We'll watch out for each other," Judith said. She adjusted the crossbow and clutch of arrows attached to the saddle before mounting. "Can you ride?"

Joan nodded and swung herself up onto her own horse, a chestnut mare who danced obediently when she tugged the reins. From the corner of her eye, she noticed Tobias had yet to mount his horse and guided her mare over to his side. She knew the look of someone who'd never ridden.

"Having trouble?" She said the words lightly so as not to cause offense.

He glanced up at her, then frowned at his horse again. "I . . ." His pale brown skin was dusted with freckles, and his hazel eyes caught the sunlight, flickering between gray and brown as he shook his head. "I'm fine."

He reached for the saddle. The horse danced away from him, and he recoiled sharply. He caught Joan's eye again, his cheeks bright red. Joan swallowed down her laugh before reaching out a hand to him.

"Here, ride with me." She smiled and hoped it would soothe any wounded pride.

Tobias stared at her hand before taking it. She easily pulled him up into the saddle behind her. She settled his hands at her waist, then guided their horse over to the others. She caught Philip watching her with a wry smile on his lips.

"With me," King James crowed. He took off across the field at a gallop.

Philip sighed, and he raced after the king as Martin, Judith, and Roger followed.

"Hold on," Joan said. She jerked the reins, spurring her horse along.

Tobias yelped. His arms tightened around Joan's waist as they sped away from New Place. The icy morning air caressed her face, more refreshing than biting. It whipped under her cloak and chilled her skin.

This time, she let herself laugh.

The winter bare trees offered little cover from the sun or the harsh wind, but nothing dulled the excitement on King James's face. The party rode through to a clearing and he held up a hand. He said something to Philip as the rest of them cantered to a halt behind them. The king spoke too quietly for Joan to hear, but whatever he said made Judith tense in her saddle, exchanging pointed looks with Martin and Roger. Philip nodded and brought his horse about to address them.

"His Majesty shall have you three"—he pointed at Judith, Martin, and Roger—"dismount and follow us on foot."

Martin looked ready to complain, but Roger's quick head shake silenced him. He clamped his mouth shut. His jaw clenched and unclenched as he struggled to keep quiet. The three climbed off their horses and began unhooking their equipment, exchanging glances the entire while.

Philip watched them for a moment before turning to Joan. "While you are quite handsome in your hunting attire, Joan—" He grinned as she rolled her eyes. "—His Majesty has asked that you stay here with the horses and the boy who can't ride."

Joan felt Tobias flinch behind her and patted his hand where it still held on at her waist. "Don't you think I'd make a better protector if I stayed near—"

"I think it were best"—Philip cut across her, his voice lowering—"if you kept some distance, given past events." He gave her a pointed look that told all he couldn't speak aloud.

Joan glanced over to see the king glaring her way, disdain all over his face.

Yes, having some distance between her and his crossbow was the safer option.

"We'll await your return," she said, nodding to Philip. "But should you need us . . ."

Philip smiled apologetically. "Should we need you, we'll call."

Joan watched Philip ride back to the king, not even bothering to hide the frown on her face. She pressed the reins into Tobias's hands and slipped from the horse quickly. She hurried over to Judith and the others.

"Tobias and I will stay behind," she said loudly. She stood so her back concealed her movements from the king and flexed her fingers. Iron flowed forth from within her, twisting through the air and settling around the points of several crossbow bolts in the three packs. She heard the whisper of the metal as the horses' shoes attempted to heed her call and released the magic. She lowered her hand, fingers just barely trembling.

She clenched her fists.

"I've given you some iron, but if you meet danger . . ."

Roger laid a gentle hand on her shoulder. "We won't hesitate to return. Stay safe." He grinned, tapping his clutch of bolts with his other hand before striding past her.

Martin nodded to her, and Judith squeezed her arm quickly before leaving her behind. Joan watched them follow the king and Philip, then turned to help Tobias dismount.

She hated this plan. The king's prejudice left them all vulnerable, but none of them could deny his whims. He was the king after all.

That sense of powerlessness sat in Joan's belly, roiling like a lump of rotten meat.

CHAPTER FOURTEEN
A Fearful Summons

oan settled herself at the base of a tree once the hunting party moved out of sight. Bia hung quietly at her wrist, and Ogun's presence simmered warmly in her chest, neither hinting at any approaching danger. She needn't maintain a high level of vigilance.

The chill breeze flowed past her, welcome after their ride from New Place. It dried the sweat that had formed along her hairline and along her back. The bare branches above her swayed gently. Their shadows danced as the sun climbed overhead. The birds perched around the clearing resumed their songs, their bright trills and chirps the final layer of the forest's soothing symphony.

Being here amongst the trees gave her a sense of peace she'd only ever felt working at her father's hearth, the fire's heat against her face and metal singing through her. She breathed deeply and felt her whole body relax.

She gripped Henry's hand, straining to keep the wyvern from dragging him away.

With a sudden jerk, he twisted out of her grip and hit the ground. His terrified gaze met Joan's as he was pulled screaming into the darkness.

Joan jerked awake, her eyes wide. She clutched her chest, trying to calm her breathing against the memory. Her heart raced. When had she fallen asleep, and for how long? Where were the others?

She could hear Tobias wandering through the brush nearby, his steps unhurried. Nothing was amiss then. She let her head fall back against the tree and sighed.

It hadn't even been a day since the wyvern attack. It lurked fresh in her mind, ready to remind her of how she'd failed to protect Henry just as she'd failed Baba Ben and Master Phillips and Samuel. She pulled her legs up to rest her head on her knees and closed her eyes.

I'm sorry, she thought, swallowing back the tears that threatened to fall. She focused on the cool metal of the sword at her wrist, on the sounds of nature around her, on Tobias's distant presence. She took another deep breath and opened her eyes.

A ghostly figure stood before her, the same woman she'd seen in Baba's office. Ogun's presence blazed suddenly before disappearing just as quickly. Joan pressed a hand against her chest, the feeling unnerving. Bia gave a violent jerk.

The spirit looked down at Joan's wrist, disgust sweeping over her face at the sight of the sword. Bia vibrated again and sent a rush of melancholy through Joan. Realization struck her.

Without a doubt, this was the ancestor Ogun spoke of—both his and Bia's reactions were all the proof Joan needed. This ghost had sealed the first Pact nearly two centuries ago. She knew the method Joan needed to forge one anew and stop Titanea and her Fae. All Joan needed to do was ask.

"You . . ." she said, "I need to speak with you about the Pact."

The ghost flinched, and her rage-filled gaze shifted to Joan's face. She surged forward, hands grabbing at Joan, who yelped and rolled out of the way. The translucent body flew past past like an icy gust of wind. It slipped through the tree behind her. Joan scrambled out of reach and whirled around, her heart pounding in her chest. Bia pulsed quickly at her wrist as if sharing Joan's distress.

Carefully, Joan pushed herself to her feet, gaze fixed on the tree. Her instincts screamed at her to keep the ghost from touching the sword. She wasn't sure why but had no desire to find out. The hair at the back of her neck lifted in sudden awareness.

She turned just as the ghost lunged at her from behind, her wild eyes trained on Bia. The sword jerked on Joan's wrist, first toward the spirit, then frantically away.

"Don't!" Joan threw herself to the side, but the ghost snatched her arm. Spectral hands seemed to solidify as they touched Bia, their tight grasp on Joan's wrist feeling as real as any living being but icy cold. The sword pulsed, the pressure rattling Joan's bones and sending the trees bending away from them. The birds went silent as the forest creaked and swayed against the unnatural force. Tobias yelped and ran toward her through the underbrush. The ghost stared into Joan's eyes, her gaze full of rage.

"Die," she rasped.

Joan gasped and ripped herself free of the ghost's hold. She faded to nothing as the contact was lost. Joan's heart thudded in her chest as she tried desperately to collect herself.

Why did she attack me? She sent the thought directly to Ogun, praying the Orisha would answer. She couldn't feel the burn of his presence in her chest. The stark absence reminded her of when Auberon had taken James. She took a shuddering breath, and her hands shook.

Why did she attack me? she thought again.

Silence.

"What was that?" Tobias hissed as he finally reached her side. His eyes darted around wildly as he pulled her to her feet.

Joan shook her head and tried to fight against her rising panic. "I don't know."

Something has found you. Ogun's deep voice finally echoed through her mind.

She flinched as the heat of his presence bloomed in her chest again, stamping down on the frustrated anger that threatened to derail her thoughts. She couldn't give in, not when she needed to focus.

She checked the clearing around them for movement and caught a strange shift from the corner of her eye. She marked it but didn't look in its direction. The horses nearby snorted and pawed at the ground. Tobias rushed over to calm them, his shadow matching the movement a moment later. She turned to him, hand reaching for Bia. Her shadow stayed still.

Joan froze, the hair along her arms springing up as her heart beat wildly. That rush of power released by the ghost's touch had called the Fae here. At least three of them surrounded her and Tobias. The last time that ghost had touched Bia, a wyvern had set upon Baba's house. What terrible creatures might appear this time?

She didn't dare turn her gaze to the sky but listened for the thunderous beat of approaching wings. The woods around them lay blessedly silent but for the creaking of trees in the wind.

How far into the woods had the king led Judith and the others? With both Tobias and their horses here, the rest of the party would have no way to reach New Place if they were under attack. Wherever they were, she needed to get Tobias to them before they were outnumbered.

"Are you armed?" Joan touched her fingers to Bia, ready to release it to its full size.

Tobias nodded. He turned to her and yelped as his own shadow kept moving even though he'd stopped. "What is—"

"Is it iron?"

He shook his head.

Damnation.

Joan's shadow moved again, stretching along the length of the clearing as if the sun traveled across the sky above her.

"Draw it!" Joan shouted.

She flung Bia from her arm as Tobias drew his dagger with shaking hands. Joan flexed her fingers to send a rush of iron to wrap around it. Bia elongated as it flew through the air and she snatched it, sending iron down the blade when her hand closed around the hilt. The sword vibrated wildly in her grasp. "Keep yourself safe and prepare to make a doorway," she said to Tobias, keeping her eyes locked on her errant shadow. "We'll go retrieve the others."

"We're almost there, my boy." King James burst through the underbrush ahead of them. "Keep moving." Terror contorted his face as he dragged a mostly limp Philip into the clearing.

Blood flowed down the side of Philip's head but he struggled to keep pace with his king. Joan scanned the woods behind them for signs of the others, cold fear settling in her belly. She shoved it down to be dealt with later. Had Judith and the rest already—

She shook herself, cutting off the thought before it could send her into a panic. If they were still alive, they'd be fighting. She had to believe that. She'd only need a moment to help them. Once the king and Philip were safe, Joan would be free to find the others.

Joan's shadow lifted from the ground, a dark mirror of her own shape that stretched nearly as tall as the treetops. A sudden gust of wind swept through the brush, kicking up dust and fallen leaves.

A portion of her distorted shadow snapped off with a crack. It rolled across the ground, bulging and twisting until it solidified into a tall creature with the face of a woman. Six too-long limbs burst from its back, each tipped with dainty, human-like hands.

"Christ in heaven . . ." Philip whispered, too horrified to move.

The creature smiled gleefully and surged toward the king, clawed fingers carving deep gouges in the dirt as it laughed.

Shite!

CHAPTER FIFTEEN
The Game Is Up

oan sprinted toward the king and Philip, the sounds of their fright mingling with the clawing and panting of the Fae creature. Its claws caught the back of Philip's shirt and snatched him from the king's grip. Joan's heart leapt into her throat.

"Philip!" King James shouted.

They'd both be dead before she reached them.

"Joan!" Tobias called out to her. "Here!"

She turned just as Tobias opened a magical doorway beside himself. Its opposite appeared on the other side of the clearing just behind the king, Philip, and the creature..

Bless you, Tobias, and meferefun, Elegua, she thought.

Joan ran back toward Tobias, her gaze locked on the creature she could see through the magical doorway. The inferno of Ogun's power burned hot as iron flowed down her arm and poured from her palm. The creature jerked Philip's head back by his hair, sharp teeth bared at his exposed throat. Joan dove through the doorway, flinging an iron spike at the creature as she came out behind it on the opposite side of the clearing. The creature screeched and threw its hands up to block the attack.

Philip tried to wiggle out from beneath it, but the hands extending from the middle of its torso wrapped around his throat and held him still. It hissed at Joan as Tobias closed the doorway behind her. She could hear the distant sounds of him drawn into his own fight with some creatures and prayed he could hold his own for now.

No one's dying here.

A swirling current of iron surged from Joan's palm and swept around her. She pointed Bia at the Fae as the metal twisted like a living thing, crooning softly and awaiting her command.

"If you care to keep your life," she said, "let him go."

The creature hissed at her and squeezed Philip's throat. He gasped and tugged frantically at the hands. Joan scowled and flexed her fingers. The metal floating around her hardened into several long spikes. They all aimed at the creature.

"God shield me," King James whispered.

Her gaze shifted over to where he stood frozen in the clearing, his eyes wide and breathing erratic. His chin trembled as a clawed hand slid up along his shoulder. The unseen Fae's fingers clutched the fabric of the king's wool cloak and snatched him back toward the tree line.

Shite, shite, shite!

Joan sent her iron spikes flying at both creatures. Philip shouted as the Fae collapsed on top of him, dead.

"Stay where you are, Philip!" Joan sprinted toward where King James had fallen, Bia still held at the ready. She trusted Philip to do as she'd asked.

"Are you alive, Your Majesty?" she whispered as she stepped over to the king, praying for an answer.

He groaned then coughed. "Yes, I'm alive." His voice sounded strained, but it was steady.

The creature still gripped his shoulders, its body half buried beneath the king. One of its eye sockets sat empty, a bloody hole left where Joan's iron spike must have burst through it. King James's cloak fanned out around him like wings as he stared up at Joan, his face stark white. She knelt beside him. Bia vibrated hard enough to make her hand shake. The hair on Joan's arms stood on end.

Ah.

"Is it dead?" King James blinked rapidly but didn't take his eyes off hers.

Joan drove Bia through the king's chest. Betrayal shifted across his face as blood bubbled from his lips. He coughed, splattering crimson droplets across Joan's cheek.

His shape shivered like an illusion in the heat before the creature pretending to be King James shifted back to its true self, his skin flaking away to reveal a pale blue frog-like face and pure black eyes.

"Now it is," she said dispassionately. She jerked her sword free.

The Fae's magic shattered like a mirror and dissipated as the creature dropped back dead. There, just beside its body, lay the king, looking shaken but alive. Joan reached out to pull King James to his feet. He shied away from her touch and refused to meet her eyes. Joan let her hand fall back to her side.

"How—" He swallowed thickly, trying to speak around his fear. "How did you know that one was false?"

Joan pursed her lips as she shoved the corpse further away with her foot. "It didn't use your tone of voice, Your Majesty." The lie flowed easily from her tongue. She didn't dare admit that she'd guessed. "We must get you back to the house."

The king struggled to his feet as a dazed Philip tried to do the same. On the far side of the clearing, Tobias stood over a six-armed creature, brandishing his dagger at the dead Fae before him. Bia thrummed suddenly at Joan's wrist. She shoved the king toward Philip and spun, swinging her sword up. The goblin's sharp claws caught on her blade. It hissed and sprang over her head. She shouted as it rushed toward the others.

"No," Joan yelled, her haste sending her feet slipping across the dirt.

A hand snarled in Joan's hair and wrenched her head backward as claws dug into her scalp. She cried out, tears springing to her eyes. She grabbed the goblin's wrist and twisted until she heard the snap of bone. It shrieked, hand going limp. Joan flung it body away, taking no note of where it landed before leaping at the goblin yanking at the king's cloak. She caught the creature round the ankle, jerked it close. She slammed her elbow into the back of its head, smashing it face-first into the ground.

The goblin shoved Joan away as it scrambled up and spat out a mouthful of dirt. The one she'd thrown limped back toward her, one arm hanging uselessly at its side. Four more goblins skittered out into the clearing. Tobias shouted her name, but she held up a hand.

"Get Philip and the king out of here," she called back, "I'll be fine."

She heard a knock, then the creaking of hinges and knew Tobias did as she asked. The king rushed past her, Philip at his side. The goblins didn't follow. Their bulbous eyes locked on Joan as they slipped into a loose formation around her.

She was sorely outnumbered, but she'd fought worse.

"You can't take us all alone, Iron Blade," the goblin whose arm she'd broken sneered.

All six leapt toward her. Joan slashed one across the chest, then backhanded another into a tree. The other four swiped at her face, her back, her arm, her belly. She dodged again and again. A claw ripped into her hand. Joan hissed. Bia clattered to the ground. She scrambled for her fallen sword.

Thwip, thwip, thwip, thwip, thwip, thwip.

Three of the goblins dropped away from Joan, crossbow bolts protruding from their bodies. All dead. The fourth stumbled but didn't fall. It was enough for Joan to snatch up Bia again. She held the sword out in front of her and tried to ignore the throbbing pain in her hand.

Judith stepped out into the clearing, her blond curls flowing around her head like a halo. She'd lost her false mustache and blood poured down the side of her face from a wound at her temple. She held her crossbow at the ready, fierce determination spread across her face. Behind her, Martin stumbled forward with Roger draped across his back. One of Roger's sleeves had been tied at the elbow, and nothing of his arm remained below that, blood dying the fabric bright crimson.

A doorway opened behind them. Tobias leaned through, his face paling as he noticed Roger.

"Get him through," Judith said, "and he may yet survive this." She kept her eyes on the goblins near Joan, her crossbow held steady.

Martin nodded and backed through the doorway. The goblin Judith shot pulled the arrow from its chest with a whine. Blood gushed from the wound as it healed itself, leaving behind unblemished skin. A rasping chuckle floated through the air. Another six-limbed Fae crept down the trunk of a tree next to the magical doorway, a wide grin on its human face. Tobias's eyes went wide. He turned to Joan.

"Close it!" she and Judith shouted as one.

CHAPTER SIXTEEN
Genius Rebuked

obias slammed the doorway closed as a goblin dove at him. Judith shot it through the eye, loading another arrow before the creature hit the ground. It whined and lurched to its feet again. The bolt shoved out of its eye as the wound healed.

Judith had run out of iron-tipped arrows.

It was as good as being unarmed. Regular bolts couldn't take down the Fae.

Joan called out to her spikes and felt the iron sing back to her. She sent one flowing toward Judith. The quiver at her hip shook as liquid metal coated all the remaining bolts.

"You should've gone through too," Joan said. She held Bia out and kept her eyes on the six-legged creature as it crawled down the tree.

Judith snorted and loaded one of her new iron bolts. "As if I'd leave you to have all the fun."

The creature on the tree grinned; the expression contorting its human face made Joan's instincts scream to run. It glanced over her shoulder. Joan spun as another swung down to the ground behind her, landing upright and grabbing at her. An arrow struck it in the head. Joan swung at the creature. Bia sliced through its arm. The severed limb dropped to the ground. The creature screeched. Another arrow caught it in the shoulder.

The creature stumbled away from Joan's next strike. One of the goblins grabbed it by the throat and dragged it back into Bia's path. The blade cut through the creature's body and wedged into the trunk behind it.

Joan cursed and tugged at her sword. It didn't budge. Laughing, the goblin sprang off the tree, its feet slamming into Joan's chest. She grunted and fell hard. Bia slipped from her grip.. An arrow whistled past. A different goblin dropped to the ground dead as the first dropped down on Joan's chest, far heavier than its slight size suggested. The breath whooshed from her lungs, and she struggled to keep it from clawing out her eyes.

They grappled, Joan twisting her face out of its reach. It scratched her cheek and crowed victoriously. Joan shoved it away, punching it in the nose with an iron-covered fist as it reared back at her. It screeched and rolled off before snagging hold of Joan's hair as she tried to scramble back to Bia. Joan formed an iron blade at her elbow and drove it into the goblin's head.

It fell over dead. Another goblin landed on Joan's back. Her face slammed into the dirt as claws sank into her shoulder. She swung her elbow at it, its weight driving her into the ground as it dodged her blade. Dirt filled her mouth and nose as she struggled to breathe. Joan called iron to her palm and flicked it back desperately. The goblin screamed as the liquid metal splattered across its face. Its weight tumbled off Joan's body. She pushed herself up, panting and spitting. She clenched her fist and the liquid iron hardened. The goblin clawed at the metal, its fingers burning. Joan shoved herself to her feet as it twitched then lay still.

Judith shot another arrow at the six-legged creature in the tree. It speared through its hand as it dodged. She reached for another, but her quiver was nearly empty.

Hisses and giggles flowed out from the woods around them, hinting at the approach of many more creatures. Three more goblins crept out from the tree line.

They needed more iron weapons to stand a chance against these creatures. Joan could shape the metal they had, but that wasn't enough.

She reached within herself and pulled forth more. She swayed, suddenly weak, as the world seemed to pitch to the side. Joan steadied her feet and tried again. Her eyes lost focus, everything blurring for one terrifying moment before clearing. She dropped to the ground, hands pressed into the dirt.

No, she couldn't produce more from within herself, but there might be something else she could use. Joan reached out, commanding any metal that could hear her to obey. Their horses had long abandoned them, but if they were still close enough, their shoes would heed her call. She focused, stretching her senses as far as they could reach, desperately grasping for something, anything to aid them. A faint whisper of metal tickled her palms, the buzz of a song from deep in the earth. She pulled and felt it grow. Her heart thudded in her chest.

Keep calling, child, Ogun whispered to her. *Call and it shall heed.*

Joan obeyed, focusing on drawing that song toward herself. A sudden symphony of metal rumbled up from beneath her, louder than she expected as the element rushed to answer her. The ground rolled and shifted, the trees around her swaying. The metal's song rang in her ears, blocking any other sound. Ogun's searing heat blazed in her chest. She felt like she'd been engulfed by an inferno, but the intense heat prickled along her skin without pain.

She'd experienced this before, this burn that felt like an embrace, when she'd bent a sword to save Nick's life. She focused on it now as it rushed out along her limbs. It built and built until it seemed to explode out of her body.

Everything stilled. Joan felt panic rise within her before a rumbling groan shivered up from deep underground. Tiny particles of iron burst into the air in a silver mist. The motes shimmered in the light as they shifted through the clearing.

The goblin standing nearest Joan tried to shake the dust off as it burned through its flesh. Its mouth opened in a shriek Joan couldn't hear over the metal's singing, each speck crooning together in a symphony of thousands, the harmony rough but beautiful. Tears sprang to her eyes.

Well done, child.

Ogun's voice rang clearly in her head above all other noise. She looked around to see their remaining opponents being similarly dispatched, the metal mist drawn to them as if they were magnets. When the last of them stilled, the metal's song quieted as it lifted from the scorched bodies and swirled around her. It sparkled in the air, sending light flickering around the clearing like a thousand tiny stars. Joan turned up to see Judith staring at her in wonder.

"What is this?" Judith lowered her crossbow and waved a hand through the mist, and the iron curled harmlessly around her fingers.

Joan shook her head. "I . . ." This was something new, a power beyond any other she'd wielded. Her heart raced. "I called iron from the earth."

She focused, trying to force the flecks of metal together into a single shape. Ogun's presence blazed painfully, heat scorching the hand she pressed to her ribs. She grimaced and tried to breathe through it, determined to control this new power.

The iron dust shivered in the air. Refracted light flashed as the particles surged together in the rough shape of a machete as long as Joan's whole arm. Sweat poured down her face. She felt feverish despite the frigid winter air.

The blade formed before her, and she reached for it with a shaking hand. Her fingers brushed the icy cold metal and it exploded into a thousand tiny pieces. The force knocked Joan flat, breath whooshing from her body as she slammed into the ground. She groaned and rolled onto her side.

"I think that needs more practice," Judith said, leaning over Joan with a barely stifled grin.

Joan grunted as Judith pulled her to her feet. Around them, the soft birdsong had returned. She hadn't even noticed the sound's absence until now. Ogun's presence dispersed, the heat calming to a slight warmth. Judith's gaze shifted over her shoulder, her face turning a pale green as she caught sight of the charred bodies littering the clearing. She looked away from Joan and vomited. Joan felt her own stomach turn at the sound.

"Shall I . . ." Judith wiped her mouth, swallowing thickly as she cleared her throat, her voice raspy. "Shall I retrieve our horses?"

Joan nodded. She was still shaky on her feet, but she'd be fine until Judith returned.

She waited until Judith was out of sight before stumbling over to where Bia was still stuck in the tree. She shrunk the blade and pulled it free. She curled it back around her wrist. The corpses strewn about were already starting to fade and disintegrate into the earth beneath them. Soon there'd be no evidence left of their attack save for the claw marks gouged into the dirt. Bia gave a comforting pulse that did nothing to calm Joan.

There was no doubt Titanea knew that they hid in Stratford-upon-Avon. It wouldn't be long before she came for them herself.

Joan wanted to blame their compromised safety on the king and this thrice-damned hunting excursion, but she knew that hadn't been what revealed them.

That ghost . . .

Bia jerked against her wrist as the woman crossed Joan's mind. That spirit had twice now touched the sword with the Fae attacking immediately after, almost as if she'd called them. Joan couldn't make sense of it. Why would one of the Orisha-blessed and the originator of the Pact be able to summon the Fae? Why would they want to?

Joan pressed a hand to her chest, closed her eyes, and reached out to Ogun. She felt warmth beneath her palm and prayed he'd answer.

Tell me what happened, she thought, *please.*

Ogun's deep voice rumbled in her mind. *I know not. I can no longer reach that child, for she is mine no more.*

Joan flinched, her eyes flying open. An uncharacteristic sorrow infused the Orisha's words. What did Ogun mean that ancestor was no longer his? Had she somehow been pulled under Titanea's control in death and the bond she held with Ogun severed?

If that was true, Joan vowed to release the spirit from her imprisonment. She sent that thought to Ogun as she waited for Judith's return. What was one more step toward restoring the Pact if she could free her ancestor's spirit?

Shakespeare paced the yard behind New Place, Joan's mother standing just behind him as she watched the horizon. Joan spotted them both as she rode up the hill alongside Judith on the two horses they'd managed to find. Shakespeare hurried down to meet them, fury and relief battling on his face.

Joan tried to relax her tight grip on the saddle's horn but felt herself start to pitch to the side. She held fast and straightened her spine. She could do nothing about her injuries but she hoped neither adult would notice her exhaustion.

"You two will be my death, I swear." Shakespeare snatched up the reins of each horse. He glared at Judith. "I sent you to keep her from doing something foolish, not join her."

Judith leaned forward in the saddle as he led them back to the house. "What? Not know me yet?"

"Don't quote my words back at me," he said, pinching his lips together around a smile.

Joan stuffed her fist in her mouth to keep from laughing too loudly. They reached the yard and dismounted. Joan's knees buckled as her feet touched solid ground. Her mother grabbed her shoulders, eyes raking over Joan's injuries.

"Your father should look at you," her mother said, her grip on Joan's arm almost too tight. "You too, Judith."

Joan nodded and let herself be pulled into the warmth of New Place alongside Judith. Shakespeare watched them go before waving over a servant as the door closed behind them.

Inside, New Place bustled with activity. The house never felt overfull except in the morning; it seemed to swell with the movement of the fifty extra people who now resided there. They crowded in every room, pausing to whisper to each other as Joan and the rest passed by before Joan's mother hurried them into the candlelit drawing room and closed the door.

"Where is the doctor?" The king lay sprawled across the sofa, a fluffy pillow placed under his head and a thick wool blanket tucked around him. "Send for him immediately."

Joan's father kneeled next to him, dabbing a speck of blood from the small cut on the king's head. When he finished, he grabbed the pot of ointment with the yellow label from the top of his kit—a moisturizer meant to soothe the nerves—and began to apply it as the king winced and whined. Philip sat nearby, patiently waiting his turn, although his condition was far more grave. The cloth he held to his temple was dyed crimson with blood, though he made no move to complain.

"Doctor Hall will be here presently," Iya Mary said with a careful firmness. "Thomas will see to your wounds until he arrives."

She stood off to the side, her eyes shifting between the king and the drawing room door so she saw when Joan and the others entered. She whispered so to Joan's father. His head whipped around, his body seeming to relax before he turned back to his work. Iya Mary moved away from him and gestured for Joan, her mother, and Judith to join her.

"Is this why your father so desperately wanted to speak to me this morning?" She said as she looked Judith over. "So I wouldn't see through your disguise?"

Judith smiled at her grandmother. "Susanna and I thought it best if I go support Joan, and father agreed."

Iya Mary narrowed her eyes and hummed before looking to Joan's mother. Judith winked at Joan, the expression and Judith's show of support sending warmth through her.

"The king's wounds are superficial, and the young man will survive as well," Iya Mary said quietly. "We've called John to come take over his majesty's care. Roger and Martin . . ." She sighed as a weight seemed to settle over her shoulders.

A chill raced down Joan's spine. "Are they . . ." She couldn't bring herself to say the words for fear that speaking them would make them truth.

"They're alive," Iya Mary said. "Thomas was able to apply cursory aid before he was called here." She glanced back at the king, her brow furrowing. "He'll be able to do more as soon as His Majesty releases him."

Joan could hear the disdain in Iya Mary's voice as she spoke of the king and felt a matching anger rise within her. While her father tended to the king's tiny cuts, Roger might be close to death. They'd nearly been killed following King James, and he couldn't even allow others the care they needed. Even in exile, they had no choice but to obey the whims of the king.

"How badly are you hurt?" Iya Mary asked Joan suddenly.

Joan blinked, too surprised at her open concern to speak. Iya Mary hadn't offered her a single kind word in the week they'd been in New Place. Feeling her compassion now felt jarring, to say the least.

"It's always a fight to keep you from speaking, but you choose this time to be silent." She turned away. "Why must everything be so difficult with you?"

And there it was, Iya Mary's kindness gone just as quickly as it had come. Joan felt her mother's hand on her back as Judith touched her arm and knew her face showed too much. She tried to school her expression as Iya Mary returned to the king's side.

"Send that witch-child away," King James said, sniffing. He narrowed his eyes at Joan. "I'll not have it near me in this vulnerable state."

Her father tensed. He turned around as if to look through his kit of ointments, open fury crossing his face. Fear swept through Joan. King James wielded his position like the fiercest weapon, expertly bludgeoning whoever displeased him. Her father might want to defend her in this moment, but Joan knew the dire consequences he'd face should he displease the king.

She'd experienced first-hand how easily King James would end a life. Joan caught her father's attention and forced a smile to let him think she was unhurt by the king's words. Mr. Sands looked her over quickly, then—with a steadying breath that allowed him to shift back to pleasant blankness—turned back to the king.

Joan sighed and noticed Philip watching her. His eyes cut quickly to the king before turning back to her.

"I'm sorry," he mouthed.

She nodded, then, with a whispered "Pardon" to her mother, she slipped out the door. Even with all their magic, everyone knew who held the most power within this house. The king was wrong and reckless, but none of them could risk telling him so.

In secret moments like this, Joan wondered if she actually wanted to restore this man to the throne. She was certain that she couldn't let Titanea do as she pleased, but was King James much better? He'd been ready to have Joan executed before Titanea had unleashed her Fae on them all, and his disdain for the "witch-child" hadn't waned even though Joan had saved his life more than once now. What might he do should he discover all her community's secrets?

When the Pact was back in place, when everything returned to normal, would King James reward them for their protection or punish them for their magic? If he threatened to destroy those she loved as Auberon had, as Robert Cecil had, would Joan allow it because he was king?

She knew her answer and prayed she never met the moment where she'd have to prove it in blood.

Susanna burst into the house, her future husband, John Hall—and the only doctor in Stratford-upon-Avon—just behind her. He paused, hand pressed to his chest as he caught his breath while Susanna strode over to Joan.

"You're hurt," Susanna said. "Let John look at you."

Joan shook her head and stepped aside. "The king is waiting for him."

Susanna scowled at the closed door. The curse she wanted to give seemed to pass over her face in a thunderous shift of expressions. She huffed and waved John over. He straightened his spine before he disappeared into the sitting room with one last apologetic glance at Joan. Susanna touched her arm gently, then followed, leaving Joan alone with her traitorous thoughts.

CHAPTER SEVENTEEN
Point Against Point

ack in her room, Joan found a gown with matching sleeves laid out on her bed, the dark blue fabric embroidered all over with moss green swirls and waves. A quick glance showed James had stuffed the unlucky blue and orange set back in the wardrobe. She sent a silent thanks to her brother before switching out of his clothes and into her own. The thick skirt was a welcome change from her borrowed trousers. Her legs felt blessedly free and warm beneath the heavy fabric as she moved.

She threw herself face down on the bed, letting the silence of the room wash over her. It's how her father found her when he came to patch up her wounds, his eyes tired and hands fumbling. She didn't dare ask him about Roger or Philip, both not wanting to push and fearing the answer. He hugged her tightly as he whispered his love, then left.

Joan sat in her room for a while longer before venturing out into the rest of the house. It was approaching lunch by the time she made her way to the kitchen. The wide-open room was warmer than the rest of the house thanks to the fire burning in the large hearth that took up most of one whitewashed wall. Nan stood near it, turning several roasting chickens on an iron spit. She occasionally brushed them with oil from a nearby bowl that Joan knew to be the woman's signature seasoning mix.

Nan had preceded them to Stratford and had since integrated herself so well into the Shakespeare household that she'd practically become Iya Anne's second, taking on ale-brewing duties and coordinating the day servants who arrived to work every morning. Joan wondered if Nan would want to return to London with them when the time came. She'd been far happier this week than Joan had ever seen her since the incident with Auberon.

Now, she smiled up at Joan before turning back to her task. Iya Anne flitted about the room, her skirt tucked into her apron so she wouldn't trip and her hair gathered beneath a pretty forest green cap. She paced between the large, T-shaped table closest to the hearth and the sideboards that ran along the huge windows looking out onto the courtyard. Iya Anne handed off mugs of ale to a group who lingered after breakfast, clustered on the benches tucked into an alcove. She turned back, laughing with Nan as she passed and snatched up a basket of carrots and parsnips to give another servant. She spotted Joan in the middle of her next circuit and rushed over to her.

"You look a fright," Iya Anne said, guiding Joan over to the empty bench on the longer side of the large table. "Are you hurt? Has your father looked at you? Let me get you something to eat."

Joan tried to focus as people bustled past and around her. "He did. I'm fine."

Iya Anne patted her hand before heading over to get Joan a plate. Joan sighed and swung her legs around so she faced the table. Two older women stared at her from the other end of the table. Caught, one of them turned away. The other felt no such shame. She leaned close to her fellow, whispering something to her. Joan managed to catch "men's clothing" and "Mary said" but nothing more. She clenched her hands in her lap. Joan had seen both of them in passing, usually speaking with Iya Mary, but couldn't recall their names. Well, now she knew where she stood with these two, even if she couldn't name them.

Nan gave Iya Anne a plate loaded with warm sweetbread and a cup of small ale, which she brought over to Joan. Iya Anne looked up at the two women.

"Olivia, Alice," she said, laying a comforting hand on Joan's shoulder. "You can take that gossip out of my kitchen."

They flinched, the bolder woman snorting in outrage, but Iya Anne glared until they stood and left the room.

She patted Joan's back. "Now eat your food, dear." She smiled at her again before continuing to coordinate lunch preparations with Nan as if nothing had happened.

Joan nodded. Her mind spun with how quickly Iya Anne had dismissed the troublesome duo. She took a distracted sip of her ale. James suddenly slid into the empty spot next to Joan on the bench, grabbing a roll from her plate and slathering it with honey.

"I love these," he mumbled around a full mouth. "Are you all right?"

She sighed and picked up her own roll, exhaustion settling over her. It was barely noon, but the day already felt impossibly long. She pulled out the bread's soft center and rubbed it along the honey glazing the crust. Satisfied, she stuffed it into her mouth, humming in pleasure as the comforting taste exploded on her tongue. She reached for a second as James frowned at her. "What?"

"You really hate bread crusts, don't you?"

She scowled, the expression difficult with her cheeks puffed up around another mouthful of fluffy roll insides. She swallowed, then stared into her brother's eyes as she bit into the crust she'd been about to discard. She couldn't help but grimace at the rough texture. James laughed in her face before snatching the rest of the crust out of her hand. He tore away the part she'd bitten and tossed it back onto her plate. He popped the rest into his mouth.

"It wasn't a complaint," he said as he chewed. "Leaves more for me."

Joan rolled her eyes at her brother and took another sip of ale. She wondered how to ease into what she wanted to say next, but came up short. "I met a ghost," she blurted

"You what?" The previous cheer melted from his face. "What do you mean you met a ghost? Whose ghost?"

Joan pulled another roll apart, dropping the pieces back onto her plate. Bia felt strangely heavy at her wrist. "It was her, I'm sure of it."

"Wait, you mean *the* ghost?" James slammed his hands down on the table. "The one who knows how to seal the Pact?"

Joan nodded. "Yes, but something was strange. She attacked me."

"That doesn't make sense."

"I think she's under Titanea's control. If I describe her, would you be able to contact her?"

"I could try, but it'd be better if we had her name." James's face lit up suddenly. "Iya Anne," he called, "I have a question."

She looked up from stoking the fire in the hearth and approached them, wiping her hands on her apron. "What do you need?"

"If I wanted to contact a specific ancestor but I didn't have their name," James said, "how else might I do it?"

Joan sat up, listening intently. Iya Anne was a child of Oya just like James and held a similar affinity with the dead. She'd know how they might get the answers they desperately needed from that spirit.

Iya Anne frowned, pressing her fingertips to her mouth as she thought. "The simplest method is using something they felt strongly about for the ceremony—a treasured item or a favorite food or scent."

"I think we have that," Joan said. She touched the sword at her wrist. Bia was connected to that spirit and had likely belonged to her in the past.

James noticed the gesture and smiled at Iya Anne. "Thank you, that helps immensely."

"I won't ask more questions," she said as she pushed away from the table. "Be cautious. It's always possible to call the wrong spirits, ones that wish you ill."

Joan felt a chill race through her, James grabbed her hand and squeezed.

"Of course," he said, a grin crossing his face. "We'll heed your advice."

Iya Anne gave them one last suspicious glance before she headed back over to the hearth. Joan leaned close to James.

"We can't do this," she hissed. "That spirit—"

James shushed her. "We can and we must." He smiled at her. "I said I'll help you, so please trust me. I can do the ri—"

"Ah, here you are."

They both turned to see Sir Pearce looming over them, arms folded over his broad chest and his dark wool cloak tossed over one shoulder. He stared pointedly at Joan, a single bushy white eyebrow raised.

Joan glanced at her brother, then blinked up at man. "I am." She wondered what he wanted with her.

"There's swordsmanship practice happening out in the yard." Pearce jerked his head toward the garden door leading out from the kitchen. "Come along."

James frowned. "Joan doesn't—"

"It wasn't a request," Pearce said flatly.

James shook his head and muttered something unflattering under his breath. Joan pinched him before following Pearce out of the kitchen. Joan knew he'd been training some of their number in swordsmanship. She'd offered to help but had been rebuffed by both he and Iya Mary. His behavior now showed Joan that he didn't trust her skill. If her morning had been different, she might've been more inclined to play into his assumption and avoid potential conflict.

"Go change and don't dawdle," Pearce said as he stood in the doorway.

"There's no need for that." She snatched a cloak from the hook nearest the door and swung it around her shoulders, slipping past him and out into chilly air. She was too tired to be diplomatic or to change back into trousers.

New Place was built in a large rectangle so that the house surrounded a central courtyard and garden. The lawn was circled by an earthen walking path covered by a long arbor looped through with the bare vines of rose bushes. It branched off into five separate seating areas made up of stone benches tucked beneath flowered archways and trees. In spring, the whole courtyard would bloom and buzz with bees, but winter left its beauty in hibernation. Today, though, it was full of activity despite the cold January weather.

Pearce muttered something under his breath that Joan felt it best not to try to decipher and headed to where a group of twelve people were gathered on the lawn to stumble their way through what Joan assumed were practice fights.

Two boys—barely older than Joan herself—swung their blunted swords at each other with haphazard glee. Another duo stood several paces apart, tapping their blades together and flinching with each clang. The rest engaged somewhere between those two extremes. An overwhelming number of corrections raced through Joan's head as she watched. The weapons might be dulled—she'd managed that task herself—but Joan knew better than anyone the damage that even a blunted blade could do.

She hurried over to the boys first, feeling out some pattern in their movements as she closed the distance. She slipped between them on an upswing and snatched one sword easily. She parried the other's downswing on the dull blade, twisting it around and knocking it out of the boy's hand.

"A sword isn't a toy," she said. She pointed both swords at the ground. "Even if it's been dulled."

"You'd be their teacher?" Pearce frowned over at her.

The rest of the combatants had stopped their practice and watched her with rapt attention. Joan passed the swords back to the two boys before turning to look at the old knight..

"It's what I do with the King's Men," she said simply.

Pearce snorted. "As if teaching actors to play fight is comparable to *real* swordplay."

"Are you testing me, Sir Pearce?" Joan clenched her jaw as the man raised an eyebrow. "I assure you my skills are more than adequate."

He sighed and shook his head. "'Adequate' will get a blade buried in your gut, but if you need proof, I'll show you well enough." He unclasped his cloak and shrugged it from his shoulders. "I'll temper myself to account for your . . . unconventional attire."

Joan felt her anger rising at his dismissive words. She'd seen the man's form. He was a talented swordsman, far better than any of the people he instructed, but his skills came nowhere near her own.

She took a calming breath as she flicked Bia from her wrist, the sword growing to its full size. She snatched it from the air. Someone gasped. Pearce tensed, the shift near imperceptible but Joan marked it. She'd made him nervous.

Good. Let him eat his words.

"I'll not have you treating this as some frivolous sport like those two." He jerked his head toward the boys who even now tapped each other with their blades.

"Of course not," Joan said, now unable to keep her grin contained. "I doubt any have more respect for the art."

Pearce cleared his throat and gestured for everyone to give them space. They stepped back, forming a wide circle so they could all witness the day's spectacle. Joan slipped into a defensive stance as he flipped his blade up from where he'd dug its point into the ground and stood casually, sword held at his side. He watched her expectantly. It was a show of dominance, a posturing that said he felt confident enough to let Joan attack first. He'd soon be fighting her seriously.

The weight of crowd's eyes and Pearce's dismissal made her bold. She charged him, sword poised to disarm Pearce in an instant. He twisted and knocked her blade away with his own. Joan followed the energy of the hit, spinning with the momentum to attack him again on his other side. He stumbled back but blocked her at the last second. She swung at his other leg. He slammed his sword against hers. The heavy clang rattled both blades, vibrations running up her arm. He drove his elbow into her gut. She slipped to the side so his hit barely brushed the front of her dress and danced out of his reach. She tapped the flat of her blade against his back. He growled as she grinned at him. He sliced at her arm, the movement quickened by anger. She swung Bia up to knock his blow away, but he pulled back at the last moment drove his sword forward, straight toward her abdomen.

Joan didn't bother dodging. He noticed a moment too late that she wasn't going to dodge or parry. He couldn't stop himself. Someone screamed.

He cried out in horror as he rammed the sword into her gut. "You foolish girl!" His voice trembled as it echoed through the courtyard. "I didn't—Don't move."

"But we're not yet done," Joan said easily. Her palm pressed against the blade, curling it harmlessly around her waist.

Pearce's eyes widened as she pushed the bent sword away from her body. She grabbed his wrist and jerked his arm up, twisting until she pinned it against his back. He dropped to one knee with a shout. His sword dropped into the grass. Joan pressed Bia's flat side against his shoulder. She blunted the blade's edge just in case.

He tapped her arm twice, yielding. He dropped to his hands as Joan released him. She placed a steadying hand at his elbow to help him stand. He ignored her and awkwardly pushed himself to his feet.

Joan clenched her fist at the slight. "I don't know what you've discussed with Iya Mary"—she let Bia curl back around her wrist and picked up the fallen sword—"but I can assure you that I'm well prepared to fight." She ran her hand along Pearce's blade again. It straightened effortlessly at her touch. "Meferefun, Ogun."

"Meferefun, Ogun," he repeated, the words sounding more reflexive than reverent. "The rest of you, back to your drills."

She passed the sword to him with a smile. "Should I stay to help teach? I'm sure both of us—"

"Enough cheek." He snatched the weapon from her hands. "Go."

Joan scowled at him before walking away from the group. She hadn't been the one to suggest dueling. If anyone had the right to be angry in this moment, it was her. She'd only embarrassed Pearce, but she knew there was no greater injury for some men.

"Why's she leaving?" One of the two boys spoke loudly enough for Joan to hear. "Can she teach us that sword-bending trick?"

"No," Pearce said flatly. "Back to your pairs. Now."

Joan headed for the kitchen. If she hurried, she might still catch James and continue their conversation. They had some hope of getting the method of sealing a new Pact and, after the events of yesterday and this morning, Joan knew their safety could disappear at any moment.

The sooner the Pact was restored, the better.

James could perform the ritual tonight, and she'd have the answers she needed. A chill swept through her as she recalled Iya Anne's warning and her last encounter with that ancestor's spirit. The look she'd given Joan when she'd mentioned the Pact had been full of such venom. Now that her foes in life had somehow ensnared her soul in death, what might she do in their ritual?

No. Joan couldn't let fear overwhelm her. James was a powerful child of Oya. His understanding and connection with the dead were as impressive as her mastery of the sword. He'd know how to handle a volatile spirit, and she'd be right beside him to help should he need it.

Shaking her head, she swung open the kitchen door and walked straight into Tobias. Joan steadied him before he could fall.

"My apologies, Tobias," she said quickly. "My mind was elsewhere."

He cleared his throat, his cheeks going pink beneath his freckles. "It's fine. Thank you. For earlier, I mean."

"Of course." She smiled at him. "I'm glad we could help each other."

He nodded at her, then slipped past to head out into the garden. His palm brushed hers, and Joan felt him press a folded piece of paper into her hand.

She turned after him, but he gave no indication that he'd done anything unusual—hadn't even broken his stride in the handoff.

What could he possibly have to share with her that he would resort to such secrecy? Joan clutched the paper tightly, using her thumb to tuck it into her sleeve. She'd read it once she was alone.

CHAPTER EIGHTEEN
Things Small as Nothing

oan stepped back into the house, her curiosity about Tobias's message growing with every step. She looked for James in the warmth of the kitchen but saw only the day servants carrying platters of food, plates, and the like off to the dining hall for lunch.

Joan started that way, but changed course and headed upstairs in search of some privacy. She'd read Tobias's note first, then track down James. She couldn't focus on anything besides the edges of the paper scratching against her wrist.

She reached the top landing just as Nick's mother slipped out into the hallway. A smile spread over her face as she spotted Joan.

"Just who I wanted to see," she said. "May we speak?"

Joan nodded. Mrs. Tooley moved back into her room and beckoned Joan to follow. Joan shoved the note more securely into her sleeve, then stepped inside. A few toys lay strewn across the floor, obviously left behind by Margery and Matthew. She smiled fondly at the slight mess. Mrs. Tooley gestured for Joan to sit on the bench at the foot of the bed as she closed the door behind them. Joan obeyed, pressing her suddenly sweaty palms against her skirt.

She hadn't thought Mrs. Tooley would make her so nervous. Joan had no issues with either of Nick's parents, but she hadn't spoken to them since Nick had fled London with her a week ago. She'd not even made time to check in on them in the hours they'd been safely at New Place or to explain the sudden strangeness they'd been caught up in because of their son's involvement with her. Guilt surged through her.

"Joan—"

"I'm sorry Nick's been pulled into this," Joan blurted. She didn't want anything to stand between her and Nick's mother. "I never intended for him, for any of you, to be in danger. I've done everything I can to protect him but I—" She paused, struggling to find the simplest way to explain. "I don't want any harm to come to you. You're Nick's family, and he loves you."

"Just as you love him," Mrs. Tooley said plainly.

Joan's heart jumped in her chest. "Yes." She wouldn't deny it.

The woman stared at Joan for a moment, then grinned. Joan could see glimpses of Nick's beauty in his mother's rich brown skin, the curve of her brows and curl of her lush lips, and the way she tilted her head.

"I felt a"—Mrs. Tooley frowned, seeming to search for the words—"disturbance and noticed the change in London, but I couldn't put a name to the danger. Nick told me it's the Fae?" She frowned when Joan nodded. "I'd heard stories as a child of their dangers, but I'd never thought to experience such a threat myself."

Joan clutched her skirts. "It's because the Pact that kept the balance between their realm and ours was broken. But we'll restore it. *I'll* restore it. The task is on my shoulders alone."

"Alone?" Mrs. Tooley said, her expression gentle. She moved forward, crouching down to clasp Joan's hand in hers. "We both know that's not true."

The calluses along her palm, their positioning and hardness, felt familiar to Joan. She shook her head. The Tooleys were weavers; Joan had to be mistaken.

There's no way the woman had wielded a sword before . . .

"Thank you for taking care of my son," she said.

Joan jerked to attention at the sudden shift in their conversation. "Of course, but Nick—"

"Joan . . ." Mrs. Tooley held up a hand to shush her. "Nick is quite determined, but even I know he's not an expert fighter."

Joan felt the need to defend him, even to his own mother. "He has skill enough to serve him well. He does his best," she said emphatically.

"Yes, you would say such things." Nick's mother nodded, a sly smile spreading across her face. "But I think I can help him stand beside you. I thought there was no need to pass such knowledge on to my children, but now I see the folly of my ways. I wasn't protecting them at all." Her eyes suddenly looked sad, though she still smiled.

Joan wondered what the woman meant but didn't feel she could ask. "Thank you," she said instead.

"No, thank *you*." Mrs. Tooley stood, smoothing the fabric of her skirts. "I see why you've captured my son's heart so ardently."

Heat blazed through Joan's whole body at her blunt words. The older woman laughed heartily, the sound echoing in the room around them.

Joan let Mrs. Tooley head down to the dining hall without her and listened for the presence of anyone else upstairs. Satisfied with the silence, she pulled the note from her sleeve, unfolding it with quick fingers.

Dearest Joan,

If you are reading this, it means Tobias has delivered my message to you. I cannot describe by what miracle I find myself still alive, nor could I expect you to believe me should the words present themselves. News of your exploits at Whitehall reached me too late for me to join you in hiding.

I write to you now from the safety of the Globe. I found sanctuary here along with a few others you'll know. I am loathe to ask you to return to London, but I feel our haven will soon be discovered. Our time is short, but I know you'll be our salvation.

With all my love,

B

The sight of Baba Ben's familiar handwriting scrawled hastily in black ink buckled her knees. She stumbled into the wall, throwing out a hand to steady herself. She pressed the letter to her chest. When did he write this? If he knew about Titanea's coup at Whitehall, then Cecil's murderers hadn't killed him.

He was alive. Or someone was using her godfather's memory to lure her back to London.

She frowned down at the note, heat rushing through her body. How had Tobias gotten hold of it?

She pushed off the wall and bounded down the stairs. She spotted Tobias tentatively opening the door to the sitting room. He caught Joan's eye, then ducked inside.

"Stop," Joan hissed. She leapt forward, catching the back of his jerkin.

He yelped and grabbed hold of the doorframe as she dragged him backward.

"Enough roughhousing," Iya Mary said. She sat in her favored chair closest to the hearth, glaring at Joan. "You've seen the letter."

Joan released Tobias and stepped fully into the room. "Have you?"

Iya Mary shook her head. She held her hand out, expression daring Joan to refuse. Joan passed the paper to her. She heard Tobias close the door behind them but kept her eyes on Iya Mary's face as she read Baba's letter.

She finished and looked up past Joan. "You said you got this from Benjamin himself?"

"No," Tobias said. He flinched as Joan whipped around to stare him down. "But the person who passed it to me is someone I trust completely."

Joan burst out laughing, only feeling the slightest twinge of guilt when Tobias flinched. What was she meant to do with this? She pressed a hand against her chest as if that touch alone could calm her racing heart. Her eyes burned.

How could she do as the letter asked?

How could she not?

"This is mad." Joan swiped at the tears streaming down her cheeks. She felt hysterical. She needed to calm herself. She took a deep breath and pressed the heels of her hands against her eyes.

Iya Mary hummed. "It might be a trap, so Susanna and Judith can investigate along with you, Tobias."

"I'm going too," Joan blurted. She didn't have to weigh the options; the answer was clear. She blinked her tears away and turned to Iya Mary. "With or without your permission."

If Baba Ben was alive, Joan was going to save him.

She raised her chin as Iya Mary frowned at her. In this she would not budge.

"Petulant. Irresponsible. Ornery," Iya Mary grumbled. She pointed one long finger at Joan. "You'll go tonight and tell no one. Follow Susanna's direction and return immediately."

Joan nodded, clamping her mouth shut around the giddy hope that threatened to burst out of her. She hated keeping the secret of another London trip but didn't dare complain. That Iya Mary had allowed even this was a miracle.

She held out the letter again. "Don't disappoint me."

"I won't," Joan said firmly. She folded it quickly and slipped it back into her sleeve.

Her godfather was alive and at the Globe, but he wouldn't be safe so long as he remained in the city.

Hang on, Baba. I won't leave you behind this time.

CHAPTER NINETEEN
INTERLUDE: Finley & the Grindylow

inley avoided most errands after dark these days. Too many people had disappeared into the night, and the screams of the unlucky few who were caught out after the sun's descent haunted the city so that even the hours close to dusk felt dangerous.

Still, the market had to be visited, and his employer was never sympathetic to the needs of anyone beyond his precious self, so Finley found himself hurrying through the streets of east London, his bag of food clutched to his chest, as he raced the sunset. All around him, people slipped into their own homes, shuttered shop windows, and closed down for the evening. It was strange to see London quiet itself so early, long before the law necessitated. He missed the usual sounds and smells of evening: the aroma of family meals wafting from open windows, craftsmen burning the midnight oil in their workshops, celebrants straining the law for that last taste of good wine in the alehouse, working women selling their wares to eager customers.

But now, the threat of night sent them all into hiding, like mice when a cat prowled nearby. The buildings on either side loomed over him, their whitewashed walls and dark beams seeming sinister in the fading light. The shadows they cast felt out of sorts, although Finley couldn't articulate what made them so strange. He'd always been cautious of strange things, of what lurked just beyond his sight. Some sense told him they lurked closer now than they ever had before.

He felt the sudden chill of being watched and glanced up to see a dark shape on all fours slink around a corner. It seemed too large to be a dog, but it could be no other creature.

He prayed it was no other creature.

Finley turned down the next street along the canal, putting a lane of houses between himself and whatever he'd seen. It was different from his usual homeward route, but he didn't want to risk meeting that... thing again. His ears strained to hear any unusual noise. Nothing but the soft sounds of birds foraging in the late light echoed around him. Satisfied, he pulled his cloak more tightly around himself, set his head down, and quickened his pace toward home.

A cold wind buffeted him, bouncing off the row of houses he walked past. Up ahead, the sun kissed the horizon, its light so dim you could look directly into it without being blinded. Finley prayed his detour wouldn't keep him out past its setting.

He heard the splash of something large diving into the canal and froze.

He should turn and look. He listened for the sound of swimming or the cries of a shocked animal that had fallen into the canal. There was likely nothing sinister about it. He need only turn and look to be sure.

The water gurgled as if something swam through the water nearest him.

His heart raced. A window shutter slammed closed somewhere above and shot him back into action. He ran. His feet pounded the road as he raced away from the canal.

There was another splash and then the sound of claws on stone. Finley didn't need to look to know that whatever beast he'd heard had leapt out of the canal to chase after him. The horrible scraping echoed in a quick staccato, faster than any creature Finley could've hoped it to be.

This was nothing natural.

Desperate, he dropped his bag, freeing his arms to help him run faster. He heard it thud to the ground before the creature stopped following him to snorfle through its contents.

Finley turned back. His first mistake.

A child crouched in the road, rail thin and soaking wet. Their long, blond hair hung down over their shoulders, dripping with rivulets of water. They looked to be a boy, clothed as they were in a pair of dark trousers and equally dark shirt, but they didn't seem bothered by the cold January air as they crouched barefoot on the stones and dug through Finley's fallen bag. They pulled out an apple, then bit into it with a loud crunch.

Relief flooded through him. He'd heard of people swimming in the canal but only ever in the heat of summer. He wouldn't be surprised by a child doing the unthinkable and braving the chill waters in the middle of winter, particularly in these wild times. The sound of claws must've been his imagination. Whatever it was, he felt more than a little foolish for running from a child who clearly needed help.

As if sensing Finley's gaze, the child looked up. Their large blue eyes seemed to glow in the fading light of the sun, set in a perfectly pale, angelic face with too-sallow cheeks.

Yes, this was just a hungry child who needed help.

Finley took a hesitant step toward it. "Hullo, do you have somewhere warm to go before dark?"

"Yes," the child said, their voice soft and rasping but still pleasant to the ear. "I'm hungry."

Finley chuckled even as alarm raised in him. He pushed the feeling aside in the name of helping someone in need. "You can have some more of that." He gestured toward the bag on the ground and slowly crept closer. No need to scare the poor thing by being hasty.

"I'm hungry," the child said again, this time more insistent. They took another bite out of the apple, sending juice running down their chin.

Finley was nearly close enough to touch them now. He crouched down to their level, unfastening his cloak to wrap it around them. "How far do you live from here?"

The child pointed back down the road, never taking those vivid blue eyes off Finley.

"Is it far?"

They shook their head, still staring. Finley felt that sense of alarm blaring within him again and looked around for the four-legged thing he'd spotted in the alleyway earlier, as if it could creep around the corner at any moment and devour both him and the child.

"Why don't the both of us get home," he said. He stood and reached out his hand to the child. He needed to hurry them along. Some instinct screamed for him to run. He'd forget about the bag; he could get more groceries tomorrow. And damn his boss, he'd leave early enough to not be forced to outrun the daylight. He glanced behind himself to see the sun more than half tucked beneath the horizon.

It would be dark very, very soon.

Small fingers wrapped around his hand, the skin clammy and ice-cold.

"I'm hungry."

Finley turned back to the child, ready to tell them to take the whole damned bag of food if they wanted but they both needed to get off the streets now. The tiny hand squeezed around his, the grip far tighter than someone so small should be capable of.

"I'm hungry." A smile spread across their face. They were still far shorter than Finley, but something in their presence seemed to engulf the entire road. They looked up at him with those too-blue eyes and tossed the entire rest of the apple into their mouth, core and all.

Finley felt as if his stomach dropped out of his body. Panic surged through him. He tried to rip his hand away from the child's, but they held fast. They watched him struggle with growing pleasure before tugging him toward the canal, grabbing his forgotten bag as they dragged him along. Finley screamed. The sound echoed around them. He searched the nearby windows, praying for someone to see and help. He noticed a face peeking out of the top floor of a house. Eyes met his before the shutter swung closed with a heartbreaking bang.

The child looked back at Finley. "They've heard, but no one will come."

A chill raced down his spine as the truth of their words struck him.

This was his end.

He'd only wanted groceries. He'd only wanted to help. He felt tears spring to his eyes and let out a hopeless sob.

The child—no, a demon and not a child at all—climbed up onto the wall overlooking the canal, easily pulling him along. Finley shoved his hand and feet against the stones and tried to resist being dragged over it. The child frowned down at him,.

"Don't be difficult, food. I'm hungry." They jerked him forward, their strength immense.

Finley felt something snap in his arm as he was hauled over the wall. He wept harder as the demon dangled him above the water, holding his body aloft by one arm.

"Please . . ." he blubbered, tears and snot and terror making it difficult to get the words out. "Please, just let me go home."

The demon watched him, still scowling. "Stop that." It shook him hard enough to rattle his bones. "Crying makes you taste worse."

"Please. Please, I beg you, just let me go home."

"Stop it."

"Just let me go home."

The demon bared its teeth as it swung Finley close to its face. "No."

The demon tossed him toward the canal. There was a moment of horrifying weightlessness before he hit the water with a splash, and the sudden rush of cold stole his breath. He burst to the surface, sputtering and coughing. A heavy weight dropped onto his back. Water surged over his head as a hand tangled through his hair to force him back under. It held him down.

Finley fought with all his strength, kicking, punching, thrashing, anything to get himself back to the surface for a breath, but the demon's grip was relentless. Their face suddenly appeared before his. Those blue eyes seemed to glow and cast the only light in the darkening water. They smiled again. Finley clawed at their face.

He could feel his limbs getting heavier as his chest burned, craving just one more breath of air. The barest hint of sunlight reflected off the surface just out of his reach. His toes touched something hard below him—the bottom of the canal. Desperate, Finley shoved against it and kicked his feet, hoping to propel himself up through the water.

The demon yanked him again, hard enough to rip some hair from his scalp. Hard enough to make him scream. His mouth filled with water as his body tried to breathe and found no air. Panic like he'd never felt before raced through him. He needed to cough. He needed air. He needed the surface.

The demon swam around him, hand still gripping his hair, and settled their feet against his chest. They pushed. It felt as if an anchor crushed him to the floor of the canal. His vision went dark, a sudden calm sweeping through him.

He couldn't fight any more. He was so tired.

The demon's mouth opened, a massive maw full of sharp teeth. Finley welcomed the abyss.

CHAPTER TWENTY
Fast Find, Fast Bind

he bells of Holy Trinity Church tolled eight o'clock when Joan made her way into its grassy yard, a lantern clutched in her fist. Susanna told them not to travel as a group to avoid suspicion, so she'd navigated the dark streets of Stratford alone.

Up ahead, she could make out the distinct forms of Tobias, Susanna, and Judith standing around the entrance to the graveyard. They all looked up as Joan approached.

She had no idea why Susanna had named the churchyard as their meeting point. She worried it set an ill omen over the whole enterprise but not enough to challenge the decision.

"Are we all ready?" Joan looked to the other three, excitement and fear bubbling up within her at once.

Tobias shifted impatiently from foot to foot. His dark gray clothing blended seamlessly into the night, and when he drew the hood of his cloak over his head, Joan could imagine him disappearing completely in the streets of London. Susanna nodded to him. He laced his fingers together before stretching them outward. His knuckles popped loudly.

"Must you do that?" Susanna groaned.

Tobias didn't even turn to look at her. "Yes."

Tobias shook his hands out, then reached into the air before him as if he was grasping a doorknob. He raised the other and rapped his knuckles against nothing. Three sharp thuds echoed around them as if he'd tapped a wooden door instead of thin air. A sliver of light carved out the rectangular shape in the dark as he turned his invisible knob. A click sounded, then the creak of hinges revealed a dark alleyway and a rush of the distinct odor of London's streets. He presented the magical doorway with a flourish.

"Impressive," Susanna said, "but I would hope you can do that in silence as well."

Tobias shrugged. "I might."

Joan snorted at his sudden boldness. From their earlier encounters—and, zounds, had that been only this morning?—she'd thought him of a far more humble nature. Hopefully, this revelation wouldn't prove to be anything more than an annoyance.

She glanced over at Judith, who rolled her eyes.

"Ready." He turned to Joan, gesturing her through the door.

She'd agreed to be first as the most prepared to defend. Judith positioned herself so that she had the clearest line of sight through the doorway and around Joan's body. She swung her crossbow into her hands as she pulled a bolt from the full pouch at her hip. The arrow's iron tip sparkled in the light. She and Joan had worked to perfect the bolts in the hours before their excursion, making sure they'd inflict more damage without affecting Judith's aim.

Joan flicked her wrist, and Bia leapt into her hand at full size. She sent a rush of iron down the blade as she held it out before herself defensively. She glanced back over her shoulder one last time, taking in the group going with her to London. Judith with her crossbow poised to take out any approaching threat. Susanna, who had small iron-bladed axes at either of her hips. Tobias, armed with an iron dagger and his knowledge of the most secret ways through the city.

The desire to have James, Rose, and Nick with her hit suddenly. If not for Iya Mary's demand, she'd have all three of them by her side now. She hated keeping another secret from them but she'd had little choice.

She'd beg for their understanding after she brought Baba back to Stratford.

Joan took a deep breath, then she stepped through the doorway and found herself in London. Home. The shift in the air was enough to tell her she'd left the quiet countryside, even if the smell hadn't. The pungent odor of the Thames felt comforting and alarming in equal measure.

She moved further along the dark alleyway, making room for the rest to come through behind her. She held her lantern out ahead of herself, careful not to let its light creep out into the main road ahead of her. She heard the others moving slowly as their eyes adjusted to the dim light.

"Southwark," Tobias whispered, his low voice close to her ear. "I can get us to the theatre quickly, but we won't be able to avoid all the big streets."

Joan nodded. Bia vibrated strongly in her hand as Ogun's presence flared in her chest, burning as brightly as it had when she'd last ventured to London and reminding her that the city belonged to the Fae now.

They needed to hurry.

"Take us," she replied. She passed the lantern to Tobias and fell into step behind him. She could see the glow of their other one, held by Susanna, from the corner of her eye but kept her gaze ahead.

Tobias moved them along smoothly, leading the way through alleyways and hidden paths with easy confidence. He seemed far more comfortable here on the city streets than he did back in Stratford. Joan was glad for his help.

They came up along the backside of the Clink—the prison nearest the Globe—when a howl sounded from behind them, too close to ignore.

Joan spun, sword at the ready as she stepped around to shield Susanna and Tobias. She heard the sharp twang of Judith firing off an arrow and something yelped in pain in the darkness. The crossbow's string sang as she loaded another.

"Get to the theatre," Joan whispered, "Judith and I will hold them off, then catch up."

Susanna touched Joan's shoulder. "Flee if you're outnumbered." She placed her lantern on the ground and then was gone.

Joan heard their footsteps retreating. She nodded to Judith.

"Keep your eye—"

A snarling black dog leapt out of the dark, slamming into Joan. She hit the hard-packed dirt and shoved her arm against the creature's throat as it snapped at her. Its eyes glowed in the moonlight, mouth open to reveal sharp teeth dripping with saliva.

The dog pulled back and Joan covered her arm in iron just as the creature's jaw closed around it. It released her with a yelp, then growled and snapped at her again. Joan shoved her metal-coated forearm against its mouth, driving it backward as she surged to her feet. It took every bit of her strength to move the creature even though she'd surprised it. She swiped at it with Bia. The dog jumped away and Joan raised her sword between them.

She heard Judith firing rapidly from just off to the side and knew they were surrounded. The two of them would fight as many as they could, but there was no running now. She hoped that gave the others enough time to make it to the Globe.

The dog in front of her growled, the thick black fur along its back raising in anger as it braced itself to leap at her again. Joan extended her hand, feeling iron flow out of her palm to form another identical rapier except for the black dogs engraved along Bia's hilt.

Her chest burned suddenly, as her eyes quickly cut to the carvings. They seemed to move and shift under her gaze.

The idea that sped into her mind felt so ludicrous, she nearly laughed.

This creature was clearly Fae, but something about its current form felt true, as if this was its real shape beneath the magic. And black dogs belonged to Ogun.

Joan breathed deeply, reaching for the heat of Ogun's presence within her chest. She wasn't sure what she was doing or even if it would work, but she'd sure as hell try. Warmth rushed through her body. She reached out, calling to the creature the same way she called to the metal.

Heel.

The command felt so right, she half expected to feel the creature's essence sing back to her. It didn't, but there was the slightest shift in its posture. She pressed again, drawing more of Ogun's heat to her and exerting her will.

"Heel," she commanded, aloud this time. The word reverberated with power, Ogun's deeper voice overlaid with her own.

The creature yelped, ears flattening against its head. It didn't stand down, but its hackles lowered.

Encouraged, Joan tried again. "Heel," she said firmly, the echo of Ogun's voice coming through more strongly.

The dog suddenly dropped down, its belly pressed to the ground as it let out a high-pitched yip. Joan's eyes widened. She could still hear Judith firing off in the darkness. She extended her will again, this time reaching for any creature that might hear her.

"Heel."

She heard several soft thumps as five other shadows dropped to the ground and yowled softly. Joan flexed her hand, allowing the iron rapier to flow back into her palm as she approached the dog who'd first attacked her.

It looked up at her with wide, dark eyes, its ears lowered. As she got closer, its tail thudded heavily against the ground. Slowly, Joan reached out a hand. She'd snatch it back the moment it lunged at her, but her instincts told her such caution was unnecessary. The dog let out a cautious bark just before Joan laid her hand on its head and scratched behind its ears.

It leaned into her touch, wagging its tail happily and licking her palm. It barked again then scooted closer to get more attention. Joan glanced up at Judith, who eased toward her, her own eyes wide.

"I didn't think that would work," she said.

Judith choked out a laugh. "I shouldn't be surprised at this point, and yet . . ." She turned back to the darkness around them, crossbow still ready to fire. "What in God's name did you do?"

Joan blinked, trying to center herself as Ogun's energy still pulsed around and through her. "Black dogs belong to Ogun."

"Must wonders never cease?" Judith laughed. "How much strange magic must I bear witness to?"

Joan followed her gaze to where the other five doglike creatures lay on the ground. The one she'd been petting whined, alerting her of its displeasure that she'd dared stop scratching it. Joan rubbed its head.

"I wonder how much it understands." She glanced up at Judith, who only shrugged.

Well... in for a penny...

"Will you tell your"—she looked at the others—"fellows to leave us alone?"

The creature barked happily and jumped to its feet. Joan flinched back, sword flashing out at her side, ready to strike. It ignored her and bounced around to face the other five.

"Mother says go." It said the words as clearly as if they had been spoken with human lips. "Make Mother happy and go."

A chill raced up Joan's spine, and she heard Judith's whispered curse. She shouldn't have been startled that the Fae creature could speak, but it was still unnerving.

The other five barked normally before rising to their feet and trotting off into the night. Only the one nearest Joan remained. It turned to her, tail wagging hard enough to wiggle its entire bottom.

Joan stared back at it. "You speak?"

"Yes," it said. "All grim speak."

Ah, so this was a grim. How strange that Ogun's power managed to top Titanea's when it came to these creatures. Joan could investigate it further later, but for now, she and Judith needed to catch up to the others.

"Do you have a name?"

It tilted its head to the side and seemed to grin at her. "Names are powerful. Call me Arcas."

"Very well, Arcas." The name felt odd in her mouth, but she kept it. She filed away the grim's words on names and power for later before turning to Judith. "Let's go join the others. Farewell, Arcas."

Joan turned to head down the road where she'd sent Tobias and Susanna when Arcas stepped into her path. Now that they weren't trying to kill each other, she could see the grim's massive size clearly. Its body would tower over her if it stood on its hind legs. As it was, it came up to her waist standing on all fours.

"Me too, Mother," it said happily. "I'll come too."

Joan's mouth opened and closed in shock. She looked to Judith, who shrugged as she passed them.

"You invoked Ogun's power." She waved her hand at the dog, who'd sat directly in front of Joan. "These are the consequences."

Joan scowled and looked back to Arcas. The creature's ears flattened against its head as it watched her with large, dark eyes. Its posture slumped. "You don't want me, Mother?"

Joan sighed, then reached out to pat its head. "Come along." Black dogs belonged to Ogun, and by that blessed magic, this grim now belonged to her.

Arcas leapt up, placing its big paws on her shoulders easily as it tried to lick her face. Joan slipped her hand up to block its wet tongue.

"Not my face, please."

The grim dropped back to all fours, tail wagging furiously again. Joan sighed. Judith laughed up ahead.

"Meferefun, Ogun," Joan said the words confidently before following the older girl, Arcas loping happily beside her.

Judith snorted and shook her head. "Meferefun, Ogun."

CHAPTER TWENTY-ONE
This Great Sea of Joys

oan grew more and more uneasy as they approached the Globe with no sign of Tobias and Susanna. Judith seemed to feel the same. She'd gone from holding her crossbow casually at her side to gripping it in both hands. She stared out toward the building, her shoulders tense.

Up ahead, the rear entrance into the tiring house was shrouded in shadows save for the lantern hung beside the door like a beacon.

"What do you think?" Joan said, pausing far enough away from the door to draw her sword should anyone, or anything, charge from it.

Judith crouched down, touching the dirt gently. "No signs of a struggle or anything more than running." She stood, dusting off her hands and swinging her crossbow around to her back. "It looks as if they just went inside."

Somehow, that felt more foreboding.

Joan started forward, then turned sharply to the grim at her side. "Do you sense any danger?"

Arcus sniffed the air, then snorted as if something distasteful had assaulted its nose. "No."

"Ah." She paused for a moment, considering the reply. It wasn't a lie, but something about the grim's response felt incomplete. "Anything that would be a danger to Judith and me?"

Its head tilted to the side before it looked up at her. "Not nearby." Its ears flattened against its head. "Are you pleased, Mother?"

Joan felt guilt sweep through her. The creature might be Fae, but its utter devotion, sudden as it was, bonded her to it as quickly as if it had been a true dog.

"Yes, I am," she said, scratching the grim behind its large ears. It was uncanny to communicate with a creature that had the intelligence of a person but the manners of a dog. She glanced up at Judith and jerked her head toward the tiring house door. "Let's get inside."

Arcas barked happily, bounding ahead of them. When they reached it, Joan steadied herself and swung the door open.

Warm candlelight glowed from the top of the short staircase as footsteps hurried toward them. Joan gasped as a familiar pale face stepped out from the shadows on the landing.

"We've been waiting for you to arrive," Frances Cecil said. Relief swept over her face even as she clutched her skirts so tightly her knuckles had turned white. "Come along."

Judith started up the stairs, but Joan held her back with a hand against her chest.

"What are you doing here?" Joan struggled to keep the rage out of her voice. It bubbled up despite her efforts. She heard Arcas growl beside her as he sensed her anger.

Frances recoiled, her eyes wide. "Wait, I . . ." She looked helplessly off to the side, and Tobias stepped up beside her.

"It's all right." He laid a hand on the girl's shoulder, smiling in comfort before looking to Joan. "She's not a threat."

Joan frowned. She couldn't imagine how that could be true when she'd been the one to kill Frances's father, Robert Cecil. She doubted the girl had forgiven that in the week since his death.

"I said she's not a threat," Tobias repeated the words firmly, the force in his voice unlike anything Joan had heard him use before. His other hand moved to grip Frances's, and the girl smiled at him gratefully.

Judith pressed a hand gently against Joan's arm. "Let it lie, Joan." She made a show of heading up the stairs. "We can't waste time; we have work to do."

Joan clenched her jaw but let Judith move past her. She patted Arcas on the head, hoping to calm the grim's growls. It quieted and butted against her hand. Joan scratched behind its ear, then followed Judith. She let Bia slither back around her wrist as they moved into the candlelit backstage area.

"You've made it," Susanna said from where she stood near the open door to her father's dressing room. "I assume you handled—" She caught sight of Arcas and reached for her axes. Thunder rumbled in the distance as she called forth her magic. "One of those creatures followed you here!"

Joan threw up her hands. "Wait! It's with me." She stepped between Susanna and Arcas, just in case the older girl decided to attack. "Black dogs belong to Ogun, and it seems that applies to the Fae as well."

"Unbelievable . . ." Susanna said slowly, shaking her head.

Judith laid a hand on her sister's shoulder. "Our Joan is capable of many unbelievable things." She grinned at Joan as Susanna seemed to relax. "We'll speak more of that later. What's happened?"

"A small group has been hiding out for the last few days," Susanna said. She gestured for Frances to speak.

The girl flinched. "Ah, yes . . ." She glanced at Joan, then looked away again quickly. "Miss Lanier suggested we escape the palace and seek safety at the theatre. Ben and Roz were already here, so I passed his letter to you through Tobias." She smiled suddenly. "Ben said we need only wait for you to come, and you have."

"Where is he?" Joan felt like she'd been doused in icy water when she heard the casual mention of her godfather's name. She clenched her fists, nails biting into her palms. She had no idea what expression moved across her face, but it was enough to make Frances shrink back against Tobias's side.

Movement at the edge of her vision caught her attention, and she turned to see Aemilia Lanier step out of Shakespeare's dressing room, a boy only a few years younger than Joan pressed close to her side. She felt herself soften at the sight of the woman who'd helped her in the palace.

Aemilia's eyes widened as she saw the full group. "Joan, Susanna, Judith?" she whispered. She gently removed the boy's arms from around herself and rushed over to hug Susanna. "You've come. Thank you. Thank you."

"I'm glad you're safe." Susanna pulled away, her expression gentle. "My parents will be happy to see you."

Aemilia let out a watery laugh. "And I them. It's been far too long since I've laid my hands on your father"—her grin sharpened—"or your mother."

"Please," Judith said, pressing her hands over the young boy's ears, "not with children present." She said it in a way that made it clear she included herself as well.

Joan barely heard them. Roz, the lead tiringwoman for the King's Men, slowly guided Baba Ben out of the dressing room, his arm thrown over her shoulder. He looked far too thin, his cheekbones sharp on his face and his shirt hanging off him like it belonged to someone else. His curly hair had been braided back against his head, and bandages wrapped both of his hands. He glanced up, his exhausted gaze meeting Joan's. He smiled.

She couldn't breathe.

"Baba . . ." she said. Tears choked her.

He patted Roz's shoulder, pushing away to stand on his own. "I knew you'd come find me," he said, his voice raspy. "I knew it." He held his arms out toward her.

A sob burst from Joan's lips as she threw herself into his embrace. She pressed her face into his chest, soaking the front of his shirt with tears. He wrapped his arms around her back. His familiar scent of cloves with the slightest bite of metal surrounded her. It assured that part of her that could still hardly believe that what she saw, what she felt was real.

Her godfather was alive.

CHAPTER TWENTY-TWO
A Young Conception

nce Joan had calmed herself, the group settled in Shakespeare's dressing room. Baba Ben sat in the only chair, exhaustion pinching his features. Roz stood near him with Joan perched on the table on his other side. Frances stayed close to Tobias and as far away from Joan as the small room would allow. Susanna paced back and forth like a general, muttering to herself. Aemilia watched the tall girl and held her son, Henry, close to her once again. Judith half-leaned out the door, her attention divided between them and the rest of the tiring house.

Joan had asked Arcas to patrol the hallway. If she listened carefully, she could hear the soft thuds of its feet on the wooden floors.

"We should go back now," Joan said, resolutely. "It's too dangerous to remain here any longer." Her attention shifted to Bia, the sword cold against her skin. Every moment here risked alerting Titanea to her presence.

Susanna nodded. "Tobias, can you make us a doorway?"

"Wait," Baba said suddenly, looking directly at Joan. "There's something you should know." He gestured to Frances, who paled under his gaze. "Tell her what you told me."

Frances pursed her lips before speaking. "The queen . . . the false one—" She swallowed thickly. "She keeps a skeleton in her room, draped with flowers and ornaments. She speaks to it, taunts it. I think it's important."

Joan's heart jumped into her throat. Could it be?

"A name," she said, fingers tapping against Bia, "has she spoken a name?"

Frances frowned and seemed to search her memory for the detail. She shook her head. "I can't—"

"Rufina," Aemilia said. "I've heard that name whispered around the palace but like a curse." Joan felt Bia pulse at her wrist.

"What are you onto?" Susanna stopped her pacing, her total focus on Joan.

Joan leaned back against the table. She wouldn't usually discuss details of the Pact in such mixed company, but if Titanea was indeed holding their ancestor's—Rufina's—bones in Whitehall Palace, now wasn't the time to be coy.

"Rufina"—Ogun's heat pulsed in her chest as she said the name— "is the one who sealed the first Pact." She glanced at Baba Ben, and he nodded in confirmation.

As if he'd known all along . . .

Her voice died around her next words. She cleared her throat and tried again. "Baba, what is this?"

Confusion broke over his face. "What do you mean? Do you doubt me?" He looked from Joan to Judith then Susanna, and his thin shoulders slumped. "I see you all do. Joan, if I tell you something only your godfather would know, will you trust me then?"

"I . . ." She fought the sudden urge to tell him he needn't prove such a thing and leaned forward to take his hand. "Yes, if you can do that, I'll trust you."

He nodded. "I understand. I'm loathe to share this so openly but"—he slipped his hand from hers and leaned back in the chair—"the day Ogun chose you, whenever other Orisha were asked if they wanted to claim you, you cried and cried." Fondness swept over his face as he recalled the memory. "But as soon as Ogun was named, your face immediately cleared and you laughed, and even though you were yet a babe, you said his name as clearly as if you were grown. It was incredible."

"That's . . ." Joan's throat hitched, choking the word as she swiped at the tears clouding her vision. "Yes." She looked up at Susanna and Judith, who both understood the weight of the memory.

Only your godparent was present when an Orisha claimed you as their child. Not even her parents knew the details of this moment.

He'd told it exactly as he had every time she'd complained or cried to him over the years. The words stuck in her mind as clearly as if she remembered the event on her own. Without a doubt, this was truly Baba Ben.

"Why would your godfather lie?" He smiled at her, his eyes a little sad. "Still, I understand your caution. The Fae are quite sly."

Joan swiped at her eyes again and cleared her throat. "I need to get to the palace."

"No," Susanna said firmly. "We're going back to Stratford."

Joan shook her head. "I think Titanea is controlling Rufina's spirit through those bones. I've met her ghost twice now, and both times she used my sword to summon the Fae."

"Twice?" Susanna looked furious enough to make Joan flinch. "Why are you only sharing this news now?"

Joan wiped her sweaty hands on her skirt, the weight of Susanna's anger throwing her. "It was safer to have the situation in hand before I shared it."

"Safer for who?"

Joan frowned. That answer should've been obvious. "For everyone."

"When did she have time?" Judith said suddenly from the doorway.

Susanna sighed, her frustration seeming to leave her body all at once. She rubbed her temples. "You're not in this alone, Joan," she said. "I know it feels that way because you"—she paused and gestured to Baba—"you two are the only children of Ogun, but we are all in this with you."

Baba patted Joan's hand. She flinched and shifted Bia out of his reach. The pain that rushed through her the last time he'd held the sword was fresh in her mind. She didn't need that stealing her focus right now.

"You said the ghost has been summoning the Fae?" Susanna rubbed her chin. "Then I think you're right, Joan. My mother's always said bones are powerful ties for spirit work. Getting them back might break that control."

Joan looked to Tobias. "Can you get me to Whitehall?"

"I can make a doorway to the dock," he said. "Will that do?"

Joan nodded, jumping down from the table. "I think I can guide us from there." Grace's face suddenly sprang into her mind and she knew she needed to use this moment to rescue the young maid from the palace.

"You'll be caught as soon as you set foot in Whitehall," Susanna said.

Aemilia shook her head. "The palace is mostly empty at night. It's when they hunt."

A chill raced down Joan's spine. Aemilia's words weren't a guarantee of safety, but they couldn't let Rufina's bones remain in Titanea's control. It left them too vulnerable.

"You should take Baba and the others back to Stratford," Joan said. "Tobias and I will retrieve the bones and meet you there."

Susanna seemed ready to protest again when Baba held up his hand.

"I don't like this either," he said softly, "but those bones are a danger as long as they're in the hands of the Fae."

Joan turned to Susanna. "We won't tarry, I promise."

Susanna scowled but raised no more protest. Tobias took that as his cue and moved away from Frances to start making his doorway. The pale girl watched him carefully, wringing her hands and biting her lip. He gave her a small smile.

"You should take your dog with you." Judith stepped into the room fully. "I'll feel better if you do."

Arcas's shaggy black head peeked around Judith's skirts as it slipped past her. "Yes, I go with Mother."

"It speaks!" Roz shrieked suddenly. The woman looked ready to faint.

Baba placed a steadying hand on hers and shushed her. "I'm sure Judith can explain later."

Tobias swung open the doorway, revealing the soft grass at the center of New Place's courtyard. Judith guided Aemilia and Henry through. Tobias and Frances hugged quickly before she hopped over into Stratford-upon-Avon. Susanna and Roz took up Baba Ben's arms on either side, helping him walk.

He glanced at Joan. "Be careful."

"We will be," Joan said. "You too. I expect to see you once we get back."

He smiled as Tobias eased the doorway shut. He took a steadying breath before creating another. This one swung open to a dark wooden dock, Whitehall Palace rising up against the sky behind it.

Joan touched Arcas's head. "Let's go," she whispered, then stepped through to the grounds of the palace.

CHAPTER TWENTY-THREE
Rise by Sin

he sound of water lapping against the dock's wood supports filled Joan's ears as she came out on the other side of Tobias's doorway. She felt Arcas step up beside her, its large body brushing against her skirts. Tobias slipped through last and closed the doorway behind them.

Joan breathed deeply, trying to remember where the servant's entrance to the palace's riverside sat. For a moment, she was caught up in the memory of screams and gore and violence.

Goodfellow's hand burst through Phillips's chest, splattering hot blood across Joan's face.

Arcas butted against Joan's palm. The old man's horrified face disappeared from her mind as the grim pulled her from that terrible remembrance. She slipped her fingers into its thick fur and let it steady her. They were alone in the night. For now.

"How are we getting in?" Tobias whispered next to her.

Joan scanned the palace's exterior and finally found the plain wooden door. "There," she said. "That's where we get in."

Any other way they approached the palace would leave them extremely vulnerable, and she refused to have any more deaths on her conscience. They eased along the wooden walkway that would take them from the dock to the palace proper, boards creaking beneath their feet. The loud rush of the Thames thankfully swallowed up the noise. The full moon sat high overhead and lit their way. Arcas seemed to innately understand the situation, crouching beside Joan, slinking along with its head ducked down. Joan rubbed her hand along its shoulders, half to show her gratitude, half to hide her own nerves.

Finally, they neared the servant's entrance that would take them through a thin hall and into the palace kitchens. The door was so plain it was easily overlooked beside the more ornate ones used by the royals and their retinues. As was the intention; no one wanted to notice servants. Joan herself would've missed it in her short time at the palace had Grace not shown it to her. She prayed it hadn't been locked. Regret rushed through her at having left behind the maid who'd saved her life.

She'd remedy that tonight.

The door swung open silently on well-oiled hinges. Tobias looked into the dark hallway with trepidation. Arcas snorted at him and shook itself before loping through the door. He scowled at the grim, then slipped inside after it. With one last glance out at the moonlit night, Joan followed the others, swinging the wood door closed behind her.

She eased past Arcas and Tobias, one hand pressed to the wall to orient herself. The heat of Ogun's presence warmed her chest, and Bia vibrated at her wrist. Neither signaled immediate danger even though she stood within Titanea's palace.

Joan doubted that would be the case for long. They needed to hurry. She led the way. Unlike the main halls through Whitehall, the throughways intended for servants were poorly lit. But she had some idea of where to find Grace, and she navigated them there. It would take them away from the queen's rooms, but Joan had to try. They turned a corner and came upon a hallway lined with doors.

"Who's there?" a shaking voice whispered from the far end. Fire sparked and a candle flame flickered to life, revealing Grace's familiar face. Her hand flew to her mouth. "My lady . . ."

Joan rushed toward her. "Grace, you're alive!" She grasped her hand, discreetly letting Bia brush the girl's skin. Relief rushed through her as Grace didn't react.

"Why have you returned here?" She glanced around them and squeezed Joan's hand. "There's nothing but danger if you're discovered."

"I know, but there's something we must retrieve from the queen's rooms. Once we have that, we can all leave this place."

Grace blinked, her eyes welling with tears. "We? Do you mean . . ."

"You're my friend," Joan said fiercely. "And you saved my life. I never should have left you to face this alone."

Grace hiccupped a little sob and rubbed her tears away roughly. "It hasn't been as different as you'd think."

Joan clenched her jaw, but she understood. Hadn't she kept Titanea's secret because, unlike the mortal queen she'd impersonated, the Fae queen had treated Joan like a human instead of some exotic animal? She could imagine the same held true for Grace, who was only a servant in the palace and a Black woman as well. That the Fae might treat her better than her fellow mortals had was a frustrating reality that often gave Joan pause.

Yes, Titanea and the rest of the Fae wreaking havoc on the people of London needed to be stopped, but would that truly make their world better for people like her? If Joan restored the Pact and returned King James to the throne, would she come to regret it?

Enough.

She'd consider such thoughts later. For now, she had a task to complete and the more they lingered, the more they risked discovery.

"You need to get to the queen's rooms?" Grace wiped the tears from her face and straightened her spine, steeling herself. "I can get you there quickly. Come."

She opened one of the doors nearby to reveal a well-lit hallway. She gestured for Joan to follow. Joan glanced back at Tobias but couldn't make out his expression in the dark. Arcas nudged him forward, and the four of them slipped out into the main hall.

They moved more quickly now that Grace led the way. The palace around them lay eerily silent, though Joan found the quiet comforting after the carnage Titanea and her Fae had wrought upon the royal court. Arcas suddenly dropped into a crouch, its ears flattening against its head. Bia thrummed hard at Joan's wrist and her chest blazed with heat. She lunged forward to grab Grace by the back of her dress. Farther down the hall, the sound of booted feet thudded along the floors.

So much for the palace being empty . . .

Grace blew out her candle and motioned them all into a deep alcove that held a large statue. Joan tucked herself into the shadows, her fingers on Bia in case she needed to fight. The boots strode closer with a heavy, unhurried gait. It seemed an eternity before the sound was upon them. Joan held her breath as the person's shadow passed over their hiding place.

Candlelight caught on blond hair and a crimson uniform. Joan's heart seemed to stop before kicking back into motion at double speed as Lord Fentoun walked before her.

Confusion surged through her mind. It couldn't be the man, he was dead. She'd held his hand as he bled out on the floor of the Banqueting Hall and watched the light leave his eyes. Bia shook at her wrist and Ogun burned in her chest. Arcas pressed against her side, its body tense. It's touch somehow calmed her rising panic. No, Joan was confident that this was merely one of the Fae who wore the dead man's form. She sent up a quick prayer of peace for Lord Fentoun's spirit.

The creature strode out of sight, continuing down the hall away from them with heavy steps. Joan waited until it was silent again before she dared step out of the alcove. Grace and Arcas followed with Tobias coming last. Grace steadied herself again and led them further down the hallway. When they reached the end, she rushed forward, running her hands over the wall opposite them until she found a hidden trigger. She pressed it and a door slid open. She waved the others inside. They moved through to another dark servant's passage. Grace lit her candle again from the lonely taper that hung by the hidden entrance.

They walked several more paces down the dark corridor before Grace opened another hidden entry. The overwhelming scent of flowers immediately swept out into the narrow hallway. Arcas snorted.

They'd reached the queen's rooms.

Joan stepped in first, her eyes searching for Rufina's remains and finding a room changed almost beyond recognition. The plants and flowers that had decorated it when Titanea masqueraded as Queen Anne had become an infestation. They draped over every surface, greedily scaled the walls, and covered the ceiling. Vines hung low enough to force them to crouch and duck. It took three passes before Joan recognized the posts of the queen's bed beneath the persistent coiling of plants.

She gestured for Tobias to join her as she approached. They moved around to the side of the bed and found the skeleton laid out as if peacefully asleep. A blanket of colorful wildflowers, too vibrant to have bloomed in January's cold, was draped over its shape. More flowers fanned around its head like a halo, and a single white lily grew from each empty eye socket.

Joan tried to compose herself even as she felt Tobias shudder beside her. She gestured toward the skeleton and stepped back as he moved to draw a doorway around the body. He had to reach over awkwardly to swing it open and let the bones fall into the soft grass of the New Place courtyard. Joan snatched at the flower blanket before it could drop out of sight. Once Tobias closed the doorway again, she spread it back out across the bed. She nodded to him, and they turned back toward where Grace and Arcas waited.

Bia thrummed hard against Joan's wrist as the room's main door swung open, light flickering across the receiving area just beyond where they stood.

They'd be discovered in moments if they didn't move.

Joan grabbed Tobias's arm and half-dragged him back to their secret entrance as someone crept closer. Grace had already slipped into the passageway, but Arcas stood guard, waiting for Joan to go in first. She shoved Tobias inside, then scrambled in after, making room for Arcas. Grace pressed the trigger again just as the light swung into the sleeping area. The secret door slid closed but not before Joan caught a glimpse of Robert Cecil in the dim light.

"We need to get back to Stratford," she whispered, a shudder running through her at the sight of another dead man—one she'd killed with her own hands.

Apprehension crossed Tobias's face before he nodded. They moved far enough down the corridor that the sound of his magic wouldn't alert the Fae in Titanea's rooms. He swung the doorway open and gestured Joan through.

She stepped out the other side but not into the crisp air of Stratford-upon-Avon. This was single large room lit with low, flickering candles and lined with long wooden benches.

The palace chapel.

CHAPTER TWENTY-FOUR
Strange Bedfellows

hy had Tobias brought them to Whitehall's chapel and not New Place?

How had Tobias brought them to Whitehall's chapel? Children of Elegua could only travel between places they'd been before . . .

Joan spun just as Tobias swiped the doorway from existence behind Grace and Arcas. He wouldn't meet her eyes, his gaze shifting to something behind her.

"Joan Sands," a familiar voice half crooned, half spat her name. "To think I'd lay my eyes on your face again so soon."

Rage burst in Joan's chest as she turned to face William Cecil. He stood on the bottom step of the pulpit, his pale skin seeming to glow in the dim light save for the dark circles she could see beneath his eyes. He looked as haggard as his father had, even though he was years younger, and the satisfied sneer on his face boded ill for all of them.

"You have my payment?" Tobias said, his voice shaking slightly. "And you'll keep your promise?"

Had this been his plan the entire time? Had he brought her the news of her godfather's survival only so he could lure her to William Cecil?

Joan felt like she was on fire, the heat of her fury offering none of the comfort of Ogun's presence. She wanted to drive her sword through Tobias's chest to repay him for his treachery.

"Your payment and my promise?" William nodded slowly. "Yes, you can marry my sister. If you survive." He snapped his fingers and three Fae appeared on either side of him, two of the same six-limbed creatures they'd fought in the forest and the other still wearing Robert Cecil's face.

William flinched at the false version of his father. His eyes went shiny in the candlelight as his face contorted with rage. The Fae grinned at him before turning to Joan and the others.

"Kill them all," William sneered.

Joan flung Bia into her grip and called an iron machete into her other hand as the creatures sprang toward them. She heard Arcas growl beside her as it tackled one to the ground and ripped out its throat. She caught the claws of the other on her crossed blades. It hissed as it touched the iron, springing away quickly.

Someone cried out behind her, but the sound cut off abruptly. She swatted the creature away, then turned to see the one wearing Cecil's face had driven its hand through Tobias's gut. Arcas ran up behind it, trying to close its jaws around either side of its head. The creature dodged the grim and slapped it out of the air. Arcas yelped, skidding hard across the floor. On the pulpit, William laughed.

Enough.

Joan tossed her machete into the air, splitting it into two blades as she called forth the gold ornaments she could see in the space behind William. They flew toward her, a heavy gold basin striking the boy in the back of the head. He tumbled down the short set of stairs and sprawled across the floor.

The metal reached Joan and she formed it into a long pike with an iron blade at each end. She shrunk Bia and slapped it around her wrist, then snatched her new weapon out of the air. She spun it around her arm, slicing the creature coming at her across the face. It hissed in pain as blood poured from the wound and blinded it. Joan swung again and beheaded it with the rear blade.

Joan let the momentum carry her metal staff around her arm once more before spinning it in the opposite direction as she ran toward the false Cecil standing over Arcas. She changed the blade at one end of her staff into a heavy orb and slammed it into the Fae's jaw. It sailed across the chapel and lay still. Arcas leapt to its feet and they both ran to where Grace kneeled over Tobias, her hands covered in blood as she pressed them against his wound.

Joan dropped to the floor near the boy's head. His eyes fluttered as he panted with pained sobs.

"Stay with us, Tobias," Joan said as she laid a hand against his face. "We need you to get us home." Yes, he'd betrayed them, but she didn't want him to die like this. She could beat the hell out of him once they all got back to Stratford.

"You won't leave this place alive," William grunted, and Joan turned to see him struggling to stand, a gash on his forehead bleeding sluggishly. "You hear me?"

Joan ignored him and shook Tobias's shoulder. "Tobias, please."

The boy groaned again, tears streaming from his eyes. "I'm sorry . . . I . . . he wasn't supposed to kill . . ."

"Later, Tobias," Joan hissed. "Just make us a doorway."

Something screeched from up on the pulpit, and Joan pushed herself to her feet again. She glanced at Grace, who nodded and took up trying to get Tobias to use his magic.

Joan shifted her staff to both her hands just as two more creatures crawled out from behind William. The one Arcas had taken down stood slowly, the skin around its throat stitching itself back together. The grim growled.

"You're dead, Joan Sands!" William screamed. "I promise you!"

Joan spun her staff on her palm, rage surging and her making her bold. "I'll send you to meet your father first."

"Kill her!" William roared. "Kill her now!"

The creatures seemed to regard him dispassionately before they leapt from the pulpit and skittered toward Joan on their six limbs. She braced her feet, sharpening the end of her staff. If Tobias was still alive, he needed only enough time to open a doorway. If he wasn't, she'd hold the Fae off until Grace could escape.

Either way, she'd fight.

There was a sudden rush of cold air, and then she was falling, a terrible weightlessness overwhelming her as the chapel floor flew up past her eyes. She slammed into solid wood with a thud that jarred the staff from her hands. Above her, a rectangular opening showed the chapel's vaulted ceiling. Two grotesque faces peered through before it seemed to fold in on itself, leaving nothing but the sparkling stars in the clear night sky and a ceiling painted with gods and angels triumphant.

Tobias had done it. He'd gotten them out—but not to Stratford.

He'd brought them back to the Globe.

CHAPTER TWENTY-FIVE
By Virtue Fall

here have we gone?" Grace asked. She'd somehow kept her hands pressed to Tobias's wound even as they'd crashed into the stage.

Joan scrambled over to them. "We're at the Globe. Tobias," she said gently, turning his face to hers.

"Frances..." His eyes fluttered open and focused on her face after a long moment. "Frances... I..."

Joan gritted her teeth. She hoped her anger and panic didn't show on her face. "You got us to safety; well done."

His head started to roll away from her, his eyes drifting closed.

"Tobias? Tobias!" She grabbed his face again, patting his cheeks until he looked her in the eye. "Tobias, listen, I need you to make another door to take us to New Place. Can you do that?" She could feel the shiver of fear creeping through her.

If Tobias died here, so would they all.

He blinked at her slowly. "'s cold... Frances?"

"I know, I know, Tobias." Joan clasped both hands around his face, hoping to share some warmth and keep him focused. "I know it's cold.

We'll get you warm once we're back at New Place, yes?" She jerked her head up and down, trying to get him to nod with her. He gave the tiniest bob of his head and Joan felt relief surge through her. "Yes, just get us to New Place."

"You want to leave so soon? You've just arrived, dear Joan."

The voice sent a deeper chill through Joan than any rush of icy wind. She turned to see Titanea, queen of the Fae, floating in the air above them.

"You should stay," she said, a vicious smile sliding over her face. "You and that new pet of yours." Her gaze shifted over Joan's shoulder to Arcas. "Although it seems less than trustworthy."

Joan pushed herself to her feet, calling the staff to her hand and closing her fingers around the cold metal as it slammed into her palm. "Grace," Joan said as she squared off with Titanea, "if Tobias makes a doorway, go without me."

She didn't expect to encounter Titanea here, but she'd give the Fae queen a hell of a fight.

"What's happening?" Grace shouted. "Wait, not—" Her voice went abruptly silent.

Joan spun to see Arcas standing alone before an empty spot on the floor stained with blood, the magic of a doorway fading around it. Tobias had taken himself and Grace somewhere, and she only prayed it was New Place.

"A lovely trick," Titanea said. "Something like your mother's?" She disappeared from sight and reappeared directly in front of Joan's face. "We have some injuries to pay back to her as soon as we've finished with you."

Her hand shot out, wrapping around Joan's throat. Joan swung her staff at Titanea's head, but the Fae queen caught it in her other hand, fingers locked around the center where there was no iron. She tossed it aside. Arcas leapt up, biting the arm that held Joan. Titanea hissed at it before blasting it away with a burst of magic. Arcas yelped as it slammed into the stage below them. It rolled across the wood and lay still.

"No!" Joan gasped. She clawed at Titanea's arm, hoping to weaken her hold.

Titanea laughed and shook her sharply. "Foolish child. This is the end for you."

Joan let her body go limp as if she'd run out of air. She shifted her hand so her palm hung close to Titanea's belly, then called forth an iron spike. She drove it into the Fae queen's gut.

Titanea cried out, tossing Joan toward the stage. Joan tucked her arms around her head as she rolled across the floor, then scrambled to her feet, gasping for air. She hurried over to Arcas. The grim whined and huffed out a pained breath, the singed fur along its side already healing. Joan flexed her wrist, calling Bia to her hand at full size. The sword sang as it slipped into her grip, and she sent a sheen of iron coursing down its blade.

Titanea tried to pull the iron spike free, hissing as it scorched her skin. It glinted in the moonlight where it protruded from her belly.

Suddenly, a rush of water crested over the roof of the theatre, slamming into Titanea with a roar. Joan spun to see Shakespeare standing at the back of the stage, his arms outstretched and face set in deep concentration. Behind him, her mother held a magical doorway open, the white and timber walls of New Place shining on the other side like a moonlit beacon. Judith ran out, her crossbow aimed at Titanea. Susanna appeared after her, axes drawn as thunder rumbled in the sky.

Joan had never seen more welcome faces.

"Hurry," Shakespeare grunted, "this won't hold her long."

Joan nodded and urged Arcas to its feet. It snuffled, limping after her. Judith kept her crossbow aimed at the wall of water engulfing the Fae queen as Susanna's hand at her back guided her toward the door.

Joan suddenly heard the flapping of large wings over the thundering rush of water. Arcas snarled, its attention turning to the sky. The dark shape of the wyvern cut across the bright light of the moon, huge and familiar. Joan's whole body went cold.

"Get through the door," she shouted, "now!"

Shakespeare twisted his hands to turn the swift-moving current on itself. It locked Titanea in a swirling ball of dark river water. Sweat beaded across his face as he fought to hold it steady.

The wyvern's deep roar rumbled through the theatre as Titanea burst free of Shakespeare's magic, sending the water gushing across the stage. Joan shouted as it swept her feet out from under her. She hit the wood hard and tasted blood in her mouth. Susanna ran forward, hurling both axes at Titanea, who dodged easily.

"Enough, playwright." Titanea raised her hands and a hundred motes of flickering blue flame sprang into the air.

They danced around her outstretched arms, moving with an intention that showed these were living Fae beings. She caressed one, and it released a tinkling laugh like the crackling of wood in a hearth on a winter's night. Joan felt a wave of comfort wash over her at the sound. Her whole body relaxed as if she were back in the warmth of her father's workshop. She lay across the stage, swatting Arcas away when it nudged her side. She hummed.

Titanea smiled directly at Shakespeare. "Go," she whispered to the flames.

Bia jerked hard enough to lift Joan's arm. Ogun burned hot and sudden in her chest, shocking her out of her reverie. She shook her head to clear it.

The tiny blue beings shot out across the theatre. A few danced along the thatched roof and in the dark stalls. Everywhere they touched, the wood and straw ignited. Heat surged over them as the Globe burst into bright orange flames.

Shakespeare released an anguished shout. He raised his hands to call forth more water from the Thames. He grunted, his power already spent, and dropped to one knee. He tried again. The wyvern roared again, this time much closer.

Panic surged through Joan. She shoved herself to her feet as water swirled weakly around them. She scrambled across the stage to where Shakespeare struggled to douse the fire threatening to devour their beloved playhouse. A sudden gust of unnatural wind buffeted her, but she didn't dare look up. She shoved Shakespeare to one side as she dove to the other. Titanea crashed through the stage where they'd just been, the force of her landing shattering the wooden floor.

Joan called to her metal staff. She burst it into pieces that spread across the hole like bars, blocking Titanea in. Shakespeare stumbled to his feet nearby. He raised his hands again, trying to extinguish the flames that had grown out of control. Black smoke surged around them.

The theatre was lost, and if they stayed, they would be too.

Joan ran to him and used all her supernatural strength to heave the tall man over her shoulder. She grunted as he twisted in her grip, but she held fast. Susanna and Judith came up on either side of her as Arcas stood near the magical doorway, refusing to go through without her. The ground rumbled as the wyvern landed in the center of the yard.

Shakespeare suddenly stopped struggling. "God above," he whispered.

The fear in his voice sent a chill down Joan's spine. She knew exactly what lurked behind them and the destruction it wrought. They were still too far to make it to Stratford before the wyvern attacked. She caught her mother's eye. The wyvern roared again.

Determination overtook her mother's face as she took a deep breath and shoved the doorway across the stage toward them. It sped across the floor, swallowing them up. Joan felt the magic shiver over her skin as they tumbled through into the interior courtyard at New Place. Her mother slammed the doorway closed behind them, and the roaring of fire went silent. The bells at Holy Trinity Church tolled midnight.

They'd made it back, chased by the acrid smell of smoke as the Globe burned.

· 22 JANUARY ·

CHAPTER TWENTY-SIX
Break Not Hours

houts echoed around the courtyard, bouncing off the house's walls until they seemed to multiply into a hundred voices. Joan coughed and rolled onto her side. The smoke made every breath itch and prickle in her chest. Arcas dropped down beside her, whining as it nuzzled her face. She pressed a hand against the grim's back to leverage herself up, careful to keep Bia away from its still-healing wounds. Shakespeare lay still on the ground nearby, and a bolt of panic raced through her before she saw the steady rise and fall of his breaths. Judith crouched beside him, her hands hovering over his arm. Susanna groaned and flopped over, her eyes screwed shut.

Iya Anne burst out of the kitchen door, bandages clutched in one arm and a familiar medicine case in the other. She raced to where Joan's father knelt over Tobias. Frances stood close, wringing her hands as Aemilia steadied her with an arm around her shoulders. Grace still held pressure over Tobias's wound, her face severe.

James and Nick had found Roz and helped the woman sit on one of the garden's stone benches. Her wide eyes seemed to barely take in her surroundings as Nick spoke softly to her. Rose lingered near them. Her gaze shifted rapidly between Joan and Arcas.

"London?" Her mother shouted, her furious face filling Joan's vision. "What were you thinking going back to London?"

Joan blinked at her. "I—"

"I don't want an answer." Her mother held up a hand, her eyes shining too brightly in the lantern light. "What madness made you attempt this again?"

"Give me the blame," Baba said from behind them. "I asked her to come." Joan turned to see him approaching slowly, hand pressed to his side. Something deep in Joan's chest unclenched at the sight of him. She rushed over, and placed his arm around her shoulders to steady him. Arcas sat silently where she'd left it, watching them with its tail wrapped around its feet like a cat.

"Benjamin..." Mrs. Sands's gaze locked on Baba, tears fully sparkling in her eyes. "You... how did you..." She paused, taking in his gaunt face and sunken eyes, the clothes that hung a little too big on his slim frame, and the set of his shoulders that spoke to a great exhaustion. She came up on his other side to hold him upright. She looked to Joan, warm understanding replacing her fury. "I see." She laid her hand over Joan's where it rested on Baba's back and squeezed gently.

"Make use of yourself"—Iya Mary gestured to Joan as she strode over to them, Tobias's blood covering her white sleeves—"and let him hold your sword." She glanced over at Baba. "We must be sure of no tricks."

Joan clutched Bia, her heart racing in her chest. "Bia won't allow any other child of Ogun to hold—"

"Enough," Iya Mary snapped. "We haven't time for your possessiveness—"

"It's not possessiv—"

"You return with a clutch of strangers and Tobias near dead—"

"Tobias—"

"—and now you want to behave like a spoiled *child* with a toy they refuse to share."

"He knows about my initiation!" Joan shouted. "Is that proof enough? Will that satisfy you?" She clenched her hands, trying to keep her own anger in check. Yelling at Iya Mary was improper, but she refused to listen.

Iya Mary pursed her lips, the expression on her face saying Joan had only proven her immaturity. "It suffices." Then she turned back to the house and gestured for Baba to follow her.

Behind her, the group caring for Tobias had already moved the boy inside. Joan glanced over at her mother, who smiled back.

"I've got Ben," she said and adjusted her hold to help Baba along the path.

Shakespeare was finally pushing himself to his feet, his movements jerky and slow as he ignored Judith's helping hand.

Joan moved toward them. "Master Shakespeare—"

"Don't," he grunted, not bothering to look at her. "Do not speak to me."

She flinched at the rage in his voice. He'd never addressed her so harshly. She blinked back the sudden burn in her eyes.

"Father . . ." Judith placed a hand on his arm to steady him.

He pulled away from her, ignoring her flinch. "I expected better of you, Judith." Then he disappeared into New Place.

Judith swiped at her eyes and cleared her throat. Susanna hurried to her sister, slipping an arm around her shoulders and whispering intently as she led her deeper into the courtyard.

Joan shivered. She felt numb, as if the cold night air had swept over her, stealing any warmth. She let Bia slither around her wrist again and sighed. Arcas butted its head against her hip.

"This isn't your fault, Mother," it said gently.

She fisted a hand in its fur but didn't speak. She heard footsteps approaching and looked up to see Rose standing before her, her expression pained. Joan felt guilt surge through her.

"Why—" Rose took a steadying breath before continuing. "Why did you leave me behind again?"

Joan stared at her, unsure of what to say. She'd done it because Iya Mary had demanded it, but the admission stuck in her throat.

She looked away. "I'm sorry."

"You should be." Rose suddenly grabbed Joan's hand. "I know you might not trust me"—she glared when Joan shook her head and pressed on—"but if you'd spoken to me first, you'd've known that, no matter what, my loyalty is to you. I made the wrong choice before by siding with Titanea instead of following my heart. Instead of staying with you." She brought Joan's hand up to her face, pressing her palm against her cheek. "I swear to you, I won't make that mistake again."

Joan's chest went tight as she looked into Rose's eyes. How could Rose think she didn't trust her?

"Joan," James blurted as he and Nick hurried over. "Why in the hell did you go without me?"

"Without us," Nick added.

James waved a dismissive hand at him. "Yes, yes, but she's just started up with you. She and I have been together from the moment we were created. Hold this." He shoved the lantern into Nick's hands and glared at her, waving a finger in her face. "We shared the water of the womb, Joan. How dare you leave me out!"

Joan looked between her brother and her two loves, unsure of what to say to the three of them. "Iya Mary told me not to—"

"So, you're agreeing with her now?" James said.

She clamped her mouth shut. He was right; she'd challenged Iya Mary's words so often but had simply agreed this time. She hadn't asked herself why she'd left them behind so easily until this moment. The answer came to her in an instant.

"I only wanted you safe," she said, her tight throat making the words difficult. "I couldn't . . ." She swallowed. "I needed you safe."

It was the truth and, despite her good intentions, she'd only managed to hurt them more. She should've expected their disappointment; the four of them expressed their love in that same stubborn way.

Rose squeezed Joan's fingers again. "I know you worry for us, but you have to let yourself lean on us too."

Joan nodded, her chin trembling as she struggled to hold herself together and then realized she didn't need to, not in front of these three.

"It was a trap," she said. "Tobias betrayed me to William Cecil and . . ." The words hitched in her throat. "Titanea burned down our Globe."

She looked up at Nick and James's horrified expressions and burst into tears. Rose pulled her into an embrace. Joan felt the two boys wrap their arms around them both and sobbed harder. She let herself be held by the most important people in her world as all the night's stress washed over her, until her cries turned to sniffling and her tears dried. She had no idea how much time passed while they stood there.

"Why have you brought back a dog?" James said suddenly.

Nick and Rose pulled away and all three stared down at Arcas, who'd lain on the ground beside Joan's feet.

"Bark," the grim said in a perfectly human voice that made the others jump and Joan roll her eyes.

She tried to calm Nick with a look as she grabbed James and Rose, the only two she could reach. "It's fine. I promise. Arcas belongs to me now."

"Mother is my mother now." It wagged its tail happily.

Rose stared from the grim to Joan then back again, a laugh bubbling up in her throat. "Of course, you've tamed a grim."

"Is this because black dogs belong to Ogun?" Nick flushed when all eyes turned to him. "I've been doing my best to learn."

James kneeled in front of Arcas. "Make sure you don't talk in front of Iya Mary or she'll see you booted from the whole village."

Arcas nodded and let James scratch behind its ears.

Joan felt warmth rush through her. How cruel of her to leave them behind when they sought so fervently to support her?

She wouldn't make such a mistake again.

CHAPTER TWENTY-SEVEN
Too Hard a Knot

unlight poured through the window of Joan's room, marking the start of the day. She groaned and threw her arm over her face. Hadn't she closed the curtains when she'd fallen into bed the night before? Had Judith opened them when she came in? She turned her head but found the other girl's side of the bed empty.

Her stomach clenched.

"How much longer should we let her sleep?"

She flopped onto her back, taking a deep breath before pushing herself upright to scowl at her brother. He sat at the foot of her bed and watched her with one eyebrow raised as he scratched Arcas behind the ears. Rose stood over by the window, her traitorous hands still on the curtains that she'd just opened.

"You might have given me a while longer," Joan groaned and fell back against the pillows. She screwed her eyes closed, wishing she could stay here and not face the consequences for last night's events. She felt the bed dip on one side and opened her eyes again.

Nick glanced over at the others, then smiled down at her. "I argued that we should wait for you to wake on your own, but I was overruled by the impatient." He leaned close, pressing a gentle kiss against her forehead.

Joan felt a flush run through her as he pulled away. The place where he kissed her burned with searing heat.

"Don't lie." James swatted at the tall boy.

Nick dodged and James went sprawling across Joan's legs. She grunted as Arcas snorted and flopped out of the way.

Joan shoved her brother off. "Enough. I'm awake." She swung her legs out of the bed. "Are you all satisfied?"

"Quite," Rose said. "Now you can tell us everything that happened yesterday."

Joan stilled as she reached for her robe before continuing to pull it over her arms. "It's a long story." She wrapped it around herself, then turned to James as she tied the sash. "How is Tobias?"

"That traitor's alive," James snorted.

Joan and Arcas had recounted their confrontation with William Cecil and the other boy's role in it. They'd had to physically restrain James from racing into the house to pay back Tobias's perfidy.

"They patched him up well"—a sly grin slid over James's face—"but you should've seen Father's face when I told him what Tobias had done."

Joan stilled, staring at her brother with wide eyes. "What do you mean when you told him?"

"Oh please, do you think I would've kept quiet about Tobias betraying you to William Cecil when you were getting raked across the coals for letting him get hurt?" He scowled, arms crossed. "I'm glad you didn't leave him to die, but I'd have passed no judgment if you had."

Joan's mind raced. "I need to find out what else he revealed to William," she said. She turned back to the wardrobe in her room, searching for a gown before James gently shouldered her out of the way.

"No need," Rose said. She hadn't moved from near the window and her expression was dark with anger. "We've already spoken to him." She looked to Nick.

Joan followed her gaze and swallowed again. If Rose's eyes had been a storm, Nick's were a tempest. She'd never seen him look so enraged.

James grinned at Joan as he laid a cheery blue gown across her bed. "I thought we'd need to use violence, but then Nick..."

"I spoke to him alone," he said quietly, his voice betraying none of the anger written all over his face. "He was quite verbose, with encouragement."

Rose leaned close to Joan. "He was absolutely terrifying. I'm glad I haven't crossed him." Something in her voice made Joan glance at the other girl. Contrary to her words, excitement spread across her face as she gazed at Nick.

Joan felt her pulse quicken as she felt that same emotion reflected in herself. Joan's stomach flipped. She wanted to dig into it, discover what that feeling meant to Rose, what it meant for them and this trio they'd formed. She had hope for what it signified and worried she'd be mistaken.

But now wasn't the time to pull at such personal threads. She shook her head to clear her thoughts.

"Nick refused tell us what he found out until you woke up," James said, the words further grounding her in the present moment. "She's awake now, Nicholas."

Nick sighed. "Yes, yes." He gestured toward the bed and the four of them clambered back onto it, Arcas getting up only to lean against Joan's back. "Besides bringing you to where William Cecil could ambush you"—a dark look crossed his face as he mentioned Cecil, and Joan laid a hand over his. He took a steadying breath, turning his palm up to clutch her fingers—"Tobias told him about New Place and revealed that this is where we're hiding the king."

Joan and James groaned in unison.

"Damn you, Tobias," James cursed. "You really should have left that rat to die, Joan."

She almost agreed, but something held her back. The part of Tobias's betrayal that angered her the most was how it had caught her completely off guard. Even Judith and Susanna had missed it, and they were two of the most observant people Joan had ever met. The why of it was obvious. William had promised him money and, perhaps more important to Tobias, marriage to his sister.

Joan tried to imagine Rose or Nick doing such a thing in order to be with her and couldn't fathom it. Whatever the complications in their relationship, neither would act on their love with such duplicity.

"I'm sorry you had to deal with Cecil," Nick said. "It won't happen again."

William's selfish machinations had nearly gotten Joan killed while she was at court, even though he'd never raised a hand to her himself. The last she'd seen him, he had been a helpless, frightened boy surrounded by monsters and death, clutching his dying father's hand as she left him behind in the Banqueting Hall. She should've known he'd become a future difficulty.

This time, she'd fight him in earnest and send him to meet his father.

The thought felt cold, but she wouldn't take it back.

"Why were you in the palace at all?" Rose said. "If your godfather was at the theatre, you had no reason to risk Whitehall."

Joan sat up suddenly, staring directly at James. "The ghost, do you remember? Titanea had her bones." A sudden chill raced through her. "Tobias sent them here before..."

"You mean the skeleton that's growing flowers in the middle of the courtyard?"

Joan flopped back against the bed in relief. At least he'd been honest in that.

"They belong to the ancestor who sealed the first Pact?" A grin slipped over James's face at her nod. "Then we can use them for the ritual. We'll do it tonight."

Joan agreed, but something within her hissed caution. Susanna had mentioned that bones had strong ties to spirits, so using them in this way made sense, but what did it mean when the spirit itself was one Joan was loathe to trust? Besides, James had never done the ritual without their parents or at least another elder. Joan had never attempted it at all. They'd be working from her brother's written notes and whatever else he'd gleaned from Iya Anne.

"We can meet in my room after dark," James said as he pushed himself off the bed.

Nick stood as well. "All of us?"

James seemed to consider it for a moment before he nodded. "Yes, all of us." He grabbed Rose's shoulder, urging the girl to stand, before he started maneuvering her and Nick out of Joan's room.

"What are you doing?" Rose said, swatting his hands away.

James frowned, putting himself between them and Joan's bed. "Joan needs to get dressed, so you two need to get out."

"I know why you're sending him away"—Rose gestured toward Nick—"but I'm a girl."

James shook his head. "A girl who constantly has her hands all over my sister." He shooed them toward the door. "You're both distractions. Out!"

Rose snorted and Nick burst out laughing. He took hold of Rose's arm and dragged her from of the room, closing the door behind them. Arcas glanced at James before it leapt down and settled its large form directly in front of the door so it couldn't be opened again.

James nodded at the grim and strode over to start unlacing the gown on the bed.

"She could've stayed," Joan said as she swung her legs down to the floor.

James snorted at her. "As if she'd help me get you dressed and not attempt the opposite. No thank you." He held the gown out for her to step into. "I know how you three are. You're worse than Shakespeare and Burbage."

Joan laughed until her nose ran.

CHAPTER TWENTY-EIGHT
The Breath of Kings

oan finished pinning up the ends of her two long braids, both woven through with thick blue ribbon that matched her dress, and turned to her brother. "Why do you suppose Titanea kept that skeleton in her bedroom?"

"It was a trophy." His voice was muffled by the crush of clothes in the wardrobe until he pulled himself free. "She's beaten the Pact and, if what you said is true, this was her revenge on the person who sealed it."

Joan nodded. What her brother said made sense, but something made her feel like it wasn't the complete story. Rufina's body had been handled with great care. If Titanea held the bones purely out of revenge, why had they been cleaned of the marks of more than fifteen hundred years of burial? Why had she been laid out like a saint and dressed with a garden's worth of flowers?

Revenge wasn't cause enough for that, and Joan hoped to discover the truth when they spoke with Rufina's spirit. It might reveal some weakness of Titanea's that she could exploit.

"The queen made a very bad deal," Arcas grumbled from near the door. "Very, very bad."

James sent Joan a look, and she felt like smacking herself. Arcas was pure Fae—of course it knew of the Pact.

She crossed over to crouch beside the grim, her skirts pooling around her legs. "What did the Pact do?"

"Blocked our path." It huffed out a frustrated breath. "Those with great power and those who eat mortal flesh could no longer cross into this plane."

James made a noise, his face paling. "Do *you* eat mortal flesh?"

"As do bears," Arcas said as it regarded James. "And wolves and other beasts of this realm. As you too eat meat." The grim turned to her. "Is it not the same, Mother?"

Joan opened her mouth to say it was but found she couldn't. What would the fox or the hind or the stag say of the humans who hunted them? What would the lamb or the chicken of those who eat them?

"Were you starving," she said instead, "all this time?"

Arcas tilted its head to the side. "No, not starving, but never full. Life was lived but not enjoyed. We are of both realms, but suddenly we were trapped within a single one."

"Why did Titanea agree to such a bad deal?" James frowned. "How was she overpowered?"

"I do not know, but Auberon sought to overthrow her because of it."

Joan caught James's eye as the same thought seemed to cross his mind. Titanea had maneuvered Joan to eliminate Auberon when she could not put down the threat herself. It protected the Fae queen's position and likely the truth of the Pact she'd made with Rufina. This was another answer they'd seek tonight.

"It was miserable, being trapped in one world when we are meant for both." Arcas laid its chin in Joan's lap. "Please, do not send me back, Mother." It nuzzled her hand. "Please."

She raked her fingers through the grim's thick fur but didn't speak. She had no choice but to reseal the Pact if she wanted things to return to what they had been.

But is returning the right path?

For once, Joan couldn't be sure if the voice she heard within her was her own or Ogun's.

Joan had let Arcas slip out the high bedroom window to roam Stratford—with the promise that it wouldn't eat any people—before she headed down toward the kitchen with James. They'd reached the main staircase when Master Burbage slipped out of the room Shakespeare and Iya Anne had been using after King James laid claim to their original one.

He pulled the door closed behind him and released a deep sigh, then wiped his hand over his face as his shoulders slumped. He had to know of the fate that had befallen their beloved theatre by now. Joan felt a chill rush through her as she remembered Shakespeare's reaction to her last night and wanted nothing more than to flee before Burbage caught sight of her. She couldn't bear the betrayal in his eyes too.

She must've made some noise in her retreat because he looked directly at her then. Her heart raced in her chest as he approached. She felt James slip his hand into hers and squeeze.

When she'd told her brother and Nick about Titanea's Fae setting fire to the Globe, they'd mourned but hadn't blamed her.

Might she hope Burbage would do the same?

"Master Burbage," she said once he was close enough, "I—"

He pulled her into a tight hug. "I'm glad you're safe." He stepped back, a sad smile on his face. "The theatre we can rebuild. You're much harder to replace"—he shared a look with James—"as we've all seen."

Joan snorted out a watery laugh and swiped her hands across her eyes. Burbage patted her arm.

"Will's hurt is aimed at you, but you're not its cause," he said. "Give him time; he'll come round."

She nodded, grateful for the man's words. He pulled her close again, tucking her under his arm and continuing down the hall with her and James.

"Master Burbage, might we speak?"

The three of them turned to see Philip standing just at the bend in the hallway. His expression was pleasant as he approached them, though Joan noticed the strain in his eyes. The injury he sustained at the hunt yesterday morning had healed completely, thanks to her father's treatment. Joan was glad to see that.

"His Majesty wants to see *Twelfth Night* performed," Philip said abruptly.

Burbage laughed. "Not going to ease us into it, my boy?" He ran his fingers through his beard. "I'm sure we can arrange that in a few days' time."

"Tomorrow." Philip somehow infused the single word with both authority and resignation.

It was how they all existed under the king's command, and Joan found herself hating it more and more with each passing moment.

Is returning the right path?

Joan shook her head to clear the treasonous thought and tried to put her attention on what Master Burbage was saying.

"... not well." He glanced back at the Shakespeare's door. "I'm afraid tomorrow is far too soon."

Philip sighed. "You know this isn't an actual request. You can't say no."

Burbage's whole body tensed as he clenched and unclenched his fists. Philip took a cautious step back.

"I'll speak to the king?" Joan said, positioning herself between the two men, hoping to soothe the situation. "Come along, Philip." She headed toward the king's rooms without waiting for Philip to lead the way.

Master Shakespeare was in no condition to perform, nor could they lower their guard for such sport. They couldn't bend to the king's whims again, not after everything that had happened yesterday. She'd twice saved his life, which had to count in her favor somehow. It was a risk, but she had to try to change his mind.

If she needed to burn what little leverage she held with King James to give Master Shakespeare and the company the time they needed to grieve, she'd offer it up happily.

"What are you doing?" Philip said as he caught up to her.

Joan shook her head. "Now isn't the time to hear a play, believe me." For a moment, she thought to tell him everything. That Titanea knew King James hid within this house, that she'd burned down the Globe.

That it was only a matter of time before the Fae arrived to finish what they'd started in the Banqueting House.

"I must try to change his mind," she said instead. "Will you announce me?"

Philip sighed and slipped into the room, closing the door behind him. He was gone for only a moment before it swung open again and he beckoned her inside. Joan took a deep breath and entered.

The king stood by the window, his hands clasped behind his back. Sunlight poured around him like a halo, exaggerating his already impressive height. Joan faltered for a moment as the sight suddenly made her feel too small for the task before her.

She grabbed her skirts with shaking hands and dropped to one knee. "Greetings, Your Majesty."

"What do you want, witch?"

Joan kept her head low as she forced the grimace from her face. "Regarding the King's Men, Your Majesty, they are in need of your grace and a few days' time to fulfill your command."

"No."

Joan flinched at the brusque response. "I beg your pardon, Your Majesty, but one or two days more is not—"

"No," he said again. He looked over his shoulder to regard Joan, his expression obscured by the window's light. "What of 'no' do you not understand, witch? They are the King's Men, and as *my* players, they shall perform when I desire it." He turned fully, seeming to tower over Joan even with most of the room separating them. "Do not think your magic gives you power, girl. It is only because of your usefulness to me that you have not yet burned."

Joan cast her gaze at the ground and fought every urge that told her to run. She refused to let him know how much he frightened her.

"Learn your place or you'll live out the rest of your days in the Tower," he said coldly. "I will hear the play tomorrow. Now, get out of my sight."

He turned back to the window, and Joan let Philip bustle her out of the room. Once safely in the hall, he grabbed her arms, face intense as he leaned close.

"Do not anger him, Joan," he pleaded. "He is not patient. He is not understanding. He is vengeful and petty, and he will have you killed if it pleases him. Do you understand?"

Joan nodded, though she didn't need Philip's words to see the king's nature. He'd shown her time and again all on his own.

She struggled to calm herself as thoughts of her *usefulness* raced through her mind. This was the life she had to look forward to now that the king knew of her magic, and once she sealed away Titanea and the Fae, she'd spend the rest of her days as a tool in the king's arsenal until he tired of her.

Philip pulled her into a sudden, tight hug. "I'm sorry he has this over you," he whispered, "but compliance makes it easier. Believe me." He squeezed her one last time, then let her go and ducked back into the king's room.

Is this the right path?

Joan unclenched her hands, her knuckles aching with the release, and went back to find her company.

CHAPTER TWENTY-NINE
Make the Body Follow

nce Joan had informed Burbage of the king's command, he'd gone back to confer with Shakespeare. She hadn't waited to see whether the man's anger had cooled overnight. Instead, she'd headed to her parents' room. After her unsettling encounter with the king, the desire to be with them overwhelmed her, hurrying her steps until she knocked on their door.

It swung open immediately. Her mother stood there dressed but with her hair hanging down around her shoulders in thick twists. She gestured Joan inside without a word before closing the door behind them. Joan's father sat in the chair by the window, mixing some powders together with great focus.

He looked up from his work, his eyes catching Joan's. "I'm making another poultice for the traitor." His gaze turned sharp. "It'll heal him, just not as quickly as my best would."

"Serves him right, the rat," Mrs. Sands spat, crossing her arms. "I could've killed the boy myself."

Joan burst into tears, dropping down into a crouch on the floor of her parents' room. She heard her father's chair scape loudly before he came over. Both her parents wrapped their arms around her as she cried.

"Oh, Joan," her mother said softly, "you didn't think we were angry with you, did you?"

Her father passed her a handkerchief as he squeezed her shoulder. "We know Tobias's injuries are his own fault." He glanced up, his gaze meeting her mother's over Joan's head. "We are upset that you didn't see fit to tell us what you were doing, but we also understand."

"Iya Mary allowed me to go, and I couldn't . . ." Joan sniffled, unable to articulate that she wasn't struggling against any single pressure but the combined weight of everything together.

"Things have been . . . difficult here." Her mother hugged her again, somehow understanding Joan's silence. "Iya Mary means well even if she doesn't show it." She pulled away, looking into Joan's eyes. "She has the pressure of leading our entire community on her shoulders. Not everyone handles that with grace in all things."

Joan opened her mouth to say something against the old woman but clamped it shut again. Her mother was right; both she and Iya Mary were responsible for the safety of not only their Orisha community but also the entire country. Joan's reaction had been to drive forward as fiercely as she could, ready to face down Titanea with all she could muster. Was it so wrong that Iya Mary proceeded with more caution? Had her age and experience taught her to move in such a tentative way?

The old woman had never been in a war nor had to spill another's blood. Joan knew those experiences had changed her and the people around her, but hadn't she hesitated in the beginning as well?

Some of the anger that had surrounded her while in Stratford dissipated. She sagged in her mother's arms, breathing through her emotions.

"And now that Ben is back," her mother continued, "neither of you should feel the need to carry that weight alone."

Joan nodded, snuggling deeper into her mother's embrace.

Her father touched her cheek tenderly. "I'm sorry you've felt so alone, my love," he whispered, and Joan felt her eyes get watery again. "Know we are immensely proud of everything you've done and we stand behind you."

Joan smiled at her father. "Thank you."

Judith still hadn't returned when Joan entered their room, so she sprawled across the bed without hesitation. She pulled the thick wool blanket over her head and stayed there, shielded from light, from fear, and from the doubts that raced through her mind.

Holy Trinity's bells tolling twelve woke her from her doze. She sat up to find Judith in the chair by the window, sharpening crossbow bolts with a knife.

She held one up, squinting at it. "Would you tip these with iron once I'm done?" She placed it in a pile of others on the table and reached for the next unfinished bolt.

"Of course," Joan said. Her hands clenched and unclenched the sheets. "I'm sorry."

Judith shook her head. "I'm not angry with you." She finally looked at Joan, her expression gentle. "You were right to go to the palace yesterday, so there's no need for you to apologize."

Joan felt herself relax as relief coursed through her.

"Besides," Judith continued, going back to her bolts, "we've all heard of Tobias's treachery by now, so expect more apologies to come your way today."

Joan shoved herself out of the bed. "You heard?"

"The whole house has. You know how gossip travels here." Judith sent her a hunter's grin. "I'll speak to him when he's healed enough to run."

Joan laughed. She hugged Judith until she shook her off and sent her to get lunch.

The hall had mostly cleared out by the time Joan sat down with her plate. On her second bite of roasted chicken, Nick and Rob hopped onto the bench on either side of her. Both boys looked thrilled, Rob bouncing in his seat, clearly struggling to keep some news to himself. As soon as Joan turned to him, the words burst from him.

"We're to perform *Twelfth Night*!" He clapped, laughing and grinning at Joan. "And you right along with us."

Joan blinked at him. "I what?"

"You're to perform *Twelfth Night* with us," Nick smiled down at her. "How do you feel about playing Sebastian?"

Joan snorted and shook her head. "Absolutely not . . ."

"Ah, there she is." Burbage's voice echoed through the courtyard from behind them. "I've found her, Will."

She looked up to see both men striding toward her, their eyes set on her.

"No," she said, as they reached her.

Shakespeare frowned. "But you did so well playing Hermia . . ."

"And His Majesty has allowed it," Burbage said proudly. "You've made quite the impression on him."

Joan clamped her mouth shut. She knew the "impression" she'd made on the king. She was a spectacle to use as he saw fit. She hated it even as a part of her rejoiced at the prospect of performing with the King's Men again.

"Sebastian is Rob's part," she said before turning to the other boy. "Are you not to perform?"

He shook his head, his eyes sad. "I'll be taking the part of Maria."

Joan's heart lurched. That had been Samuel's part, rest his soul. Had the company not played *Twelfth Night* since before his murder? A quick glance at the others' suddenly somber faces told her they hadn't.

"We thought you'd enjoy playing Sebastian..." Rob raised an eyebrow at her before looking pointedly at Nick.

Nick's role was Olivia, the lady destined to love Sebastian at the end of the play.

Joan glared at Rob's unsubtle urging and sighed. "Very well..." She held up a hand as they started to cheer. "But we must drill the fights first thing."

"Of course," Shakespeare said, an apology in his gaze. "I, for one, have grown quite sloppy in your absence."

Burbage cleared his throat and elbowed Shakespeare. "Will..."

"Ah, yes." Shakespeare flushed before looking to Joan. "I apologize for my words and behavior last night. You did nothing to deserve that. I'm truly sorry."

Joan received it gratefully, sending him a radiant smile in response. Relief settled in his shoulders.

"Well done," Burbage laughed. "Tomorrow, we'll rehearse most obscenely."

Joan shook her head at the bastardized quote from *Midsummer* but couldn't stop the joy that crept into her heart.

She hadn't dared hope to speak Shakespeare's words again, but tomorrow she'd set foot onstage for the second time in her life as a player with the King's Men.

Word of the impending performance spread through New Place, then out into Stratford until the whole town simmered with excitement. The King's Men would hold their usual morning rehearsal, taking time to ensure Joan, as well as the old farmer they'd employed to speak the part of Malvolio, knew all their marks. That role—Olivia's puritanical servant—had always been played by Master Phillips. The ache of missing two of their company and the knowledge that their beloved theatre likely lay in ashes covered everything with an air of melancholy. They'd push through their sadness because of their king's demands, but Joan wished they'd all been given more time to grieve. The losses felt like too many, and the looming performance scratched at open wounds.

Joan left the elder players at the town hall as they rearranged the space to suit tomorrow's performance and returned to New Place. She slipped into the main part of the house, hearing raised voices echo from the sitting room.

"Benjamin, I remember what was said that day even if you don't."

Her mother's voice, thick with frustration, carried to Joan's ears. Baba was obviously there with her, and Joan could assume so were her father and Iya Mary. She didn't know what the conversation was about, but something within her told her to barge in even if it was improper.

Iya Mary disliked her for no reason; why hesitate to give her one now?

Joan swung the door open, and all eyes turned to her as she stepped into the room. She'd been right. Iya Mary sat in her chair before the hearth with Joan's parents standing together on one side and Baba Ben on the other. Her mother's face was red, her expression showing she'd been arguing. Baba glanced at Joan before he turned back to Iya Mary.

"It's too heavy a burden." He leaned toward the old woman. "How can we justify the risk after last night?"

Her mother hissed out a breath. "Benjamin—"

"This isn't for your ears, child," Iya Mary said to Joan. "See yourself out."

Joan took a deep breath. "But it seems as if you're talking about me . . ."

"Enough. Enough." The old woman rubbed her fingers against her forehead. "The Pact is no longer your concern."

Joan frowned, glancing at her mother, who bore a matching scowl on her face. "What do you mean? Ogun said—"

"I know what you believe you heard Ogun say in the tower." Iya Mary shook her head and gestured toward Baba Ben. "But Benjamin thinks we should find another option."

Joan's mother glared at Baba Ben. "Benjamin is mistaken."

"I agree with him, Bess." Iya Mary stared down Joan's mother until she looked away, eyes on the floor. "I thought you'd be happy to know your daughter doesn't have to shoulder the burden any longer. She is only a child."

Joan felt her whole body go cold as she listened to the old woman's words. What did she mean, Joan wasn't responsible for the Pact? She looked up at Baba, who was watching her with a calm expression.

"Leave off this Pact business, Joan," he said gently. "It's safer for you that way." He placed a hand on Iya Mary's shoulder. "You are only a child, and this shouldn't be your fight."

Joan opened her mouth to speak, but the words wouldn't come. She glanced over at her mother, who wouldn't meet her eyes.

"What changed?" she blurted, unable to keep the hurt from her voice. "What changed—"

He mother grabbed her arm. "Joan, that's enough . . ."

"No!" Joan pulled away, advancing on her godfather. "What changed to make you leave me out?"

Baba Ben sighed, a sudden weight seeming to droop his entire body. "Don't do this, Joan. It's unnecessary and unbecoming." His gaze drifted to her wrist and the sword that rested there before he straightened himself, staring directly into her eyes. "I only want you safe."

Joan flinched as he threw her own words back at her. Regret crossed his face before it hardened again. She felt her mother take up her arm and lead her from the room. Soon she stood alone in the hallway again as the door swung closed behind her mother.

Bia vibrated strongly at her wrist, but Joan ignored the blade. She couldn't focus through the buzzing in her ears. Her heart thudded in her chest.

She'd spent so long preparing herself for this battle, for the role she needed to play. She'd bled and killed defending this realm with Ogun's blessing. She'd stomped down her grief and fear and pushed forward through everything, and now . . .

Now nothing.

If she wasn't meant to restore the Pact in Ogun's name, what purpose did those sacrifices serve?

She felt all her energy leave her in a sudden rush. She barely made it around the corner and to the stairs before her legs gave out. She slid down the wall, arms wrapping around herself as she dropped to the bottom step.

She buried her face in the fabric of her skirts and used the mass of fabric to muffle her sudden raw scream.

It had happened, the very thing she'd feared Iya Mary would do. They'd cast her out, determined her useless because she was still a child.

She should be relieved. She no longer had to risk her life to restore the balance between mortals and the Fae.

Bia thrummed, the gentle pulse steady at her wrist. She touched the sword and felt it sing beneath her fingers. Warmth bloomed in her chest as Ogun made his presence known. Joan breathed deeply and let the feelings bolster her.

No.

She knew her purpose, even if Iya Mary and Baba Ben wouldn't see it. Once she discovered the method of sealing, she'd have everything she needed to set the world right again, even if she was only a child.

CHAPTER THIRTY
Many a Watchful Night

Nightfall found Joan in her brother's room. She watched him bustle around, gathering candles before hurrying back to drizzle another few drops of scented oil into a basin of fragrant water.

"James . . ." She caught his arm as he passed her again on one of his circuits. "We don't have to do this."

He stared at her. "I've had all day to ponder this and now that I'm actually excited by the prospect, you want to talk me out of it?"

"This is excitement?" She raised an eyebrow.

"Yes," he said, resolve setting his shoulders before they slumped again. "No. I only . . ." His hand squeezed Joan's. "I've never done this on my own. What if I can't come back?"

Ah, this Joan understood intimately.

James held a special connection with the dead. The skill was impressive but required its user to open themselves up to possession, not only by Oya and the other Orisha but by any spirit. And, if he wasn't careful, those spirits could decide to remain within him.

Joan remembered how she'd felt when Ogun would overtake her body, how the more she fought, the less control she had. But that was an Orisha. She'd never felt the spirit of another person slip into her skin.

James's fingers had gone cold in her grip. She kept hold of his hand, hoping some of her confidence and warmth would pass along to him. He couldn't go into this wavering as he did. His fear might open him up to things they'd rather not deal with, might clear a path for some malevolent spirit.

"It will be frightening," she said gently, "but I'll be right beside you." She squeezed his hand again. "I won't let you disappear. I swear it."

She'd support him however she could. Even if that meant facing down an unwelcome ghost.

He nodded as a smile slid across his face. "Let me finish these final preparations and we can leave."

Joan nodded and watched him go back to gathering items, his movements calm and steady.

Yes, she thought to herself. *We can do this.*

We can't do this.

Rufina's skeleton lay in a patch of grass in the courtyard, exactly where Tobias's doorway had dropped it the night before. That Joan had anticipated. That she had prepared herself for.

But she hadn't expected to see the area around the bones fully bloomed with wildflowers as if it were spring instead of deep winter. She swallowed thickly and glanced over to see James, Nick, and Rose equally disturbed.

Arcas sniffed near the bones. The grim sneezed and backed away. "This is nasty magic."

Joan shook her head. She clutched the basin of scented water, her hands suddenly slick with sweat. She turned to James. "We don't have to—"

He snatched the bowl from her hands and gestured for the rest of them to settle on the ground around the skeleton and its garden. Joan obliged, finding a spot where the flowers didn't quite reach. The cool grass pressed against her shins as she moved her skirts out of the way for Arcas to flop down beside her. Nick settled on her right and Rose on her left. Each of them had brought a lantern, which they placed in the grass. The skeleton seemed to twitch in the shifting light. Rose glanced at Joan with wide eyes, her hands fisted in her lap.

"Don't. Don't do that," James snapped. "You'll only make me nervous."

Rose nodded and tried to school her expression. James finally kneeled across from Joan, placing the basin and the single white candle beside him.

"Ready?" His voice shook a little but his expression warned Joan not to mention it.

She nodded.

"You can do this, James," Nick said fervently. "And we're all here with you."

James smiled at him and it took every bit of Joan's will to keep from leaping over to hug them both. Nick knew nothing of the ritual, but his faith in James's abilities was absolute. Hers was too.

James bowed his head and whispered his prayer too quietly for them to make out. Joan didn't try to decipher his words. Some secrets were kept by only the children of a specific Orisha, and the way to open the path to the world beyond was closely guarded by the children of Oya. He finished and took a deep breath. Then he laid his hands on Rufina's skull.

A breeze kicked up around them. The candle and lanterns wavered, flames dancing. Suddenly, they flared high and bright as the wind strengthened to a gust. It whipped around them, tugging at their clothes though their lights stayed steady. Joan could feel her hair threatening to unravel as the wind blew hard enough to have to brace against. The skull's teeth clattered together. The flowers leaned away, some stems snapping completely.

Arcas growled. The sound vibrated against Joan's side as Bia gave a mighty shake at her wrist. Heat bloomed in her chest.

Caution, child, Ogun whispered within her.

Joan placed one hand on Arcas's back and pressed the other against the ground, ready to pull James out of the ritual if things seemed wrong. His eyes stared straight ahead. He stiffened then relaxed, his posture shifting into something unfamiliar. The wind died down, the air suddenly still. The skull rattled twice more before settling down beneath James's hand. He frowned and traced his fingers over it with a kind of reverence. He blinked, his jaw setting into a slight scowl before his gaze shifted to Joan.

She gasped as their eyes met. It was as if she looked at a stranger.

Because this wasn't James any longer.

"Rufina?" Joan spoke the woman's name softly, half afraid to be wrong.

The spirit possessing James appraised her with his face. "I am." She raised an eyebrow and hummed softly. "You are the one my sword chose?"

It was unsettling to speak to someone this way. Yes, it was James's voice and body, but something in his tone and his expressions was wrong. This was and wasn't James just as it was and wasn't Rufina.

"I am," Joan said but didn't offer up the sword. "Meferefun, Ogun."

Rage spread over Rufina's face. "Don't." She bared her teeth. "If you were smart, you'd leave that sword to rust and your Orisha along with it."

Joan flinched, the words and the fury on Rufina's face alarming. Arcas leapt to its feet, black fur on edge as it growled again.

Rufina looked suddenly to the grim. "You . . ." Her gaze shifted to Rose and her eyes narrowed. "And you . . ."

"Speak to me," Joan said. The disgust in the spirit's voice made Joan want to keep her attention locked on her. "How did you seal the first Pact?"

"With blood and betrayal and lies from a honeyed tongue." She watched Joan again, unblinking. "The price Ogun asked was high. Will you pay it?"

Joan frowned.

Rufina's head jerked to Rose, addressing her. "You love her, and she'll see you locked away forever." She turned to Arcas. "You too. Will you allow it? Will you forgive her?" Her voice raised with each word. She turned back to Joan again. "Or I can end it now."

She leapt at Joan, clearing the skeleton between them in a single move. Joan shouted and dove to the side. Arcas jumped on Rufina, using its body to pin her to the ground as she reached for Joan. Rufina stilled, then went limp. She twitched and when she looked up again, Joan saw her brother clearly.

"James," she said.

He nodded, then his back bowed, knocking Arcas to the side. His mouth opened wide with a soundless scream before Rufina's dark rage overtook his face again.

This wasn't right. The spirit should've been released once James came back through.

"I won't let her be betrayed again," Rufina growled. She shoved herself up and snatched Joan's arm. "I owe her that."

Joan shoved an elbow against Rufina's chest as she tried to grab hold of Bia. If the spirit touched the sword again, the Fae would immediately converge on the house. That they hadn't yet was good fortune that Joan wouldn't see lost this night. From the corner of her eye, she could see Rufina's hand gripping the skeleton's foot—the only bones she could reach as she struggled with Joan.

"Make her let go!" Joan shouted, but Nick was already snatching her hand away from them.

Rufina gasped, her eyes going wide before her face went slack. She collapsed forward, and somehow Joan knew it was James who caught himself on his hands. His elbows shook as he released a shuddering breath.

"James?" Joan watched him, not even daring to breathe as she awaited his response.

He nodded and coughed a bit. "The basin . . ." he said, voice hoarse. He looked up at her, panting as he tried to collect himself.

Rose brought it over. He scooped out a palmful of the fragrant water and ran it along the back of his neck. He flicked it away, hands trembling.

"Well"—he cleared his throat as his voice shook—"I think we can say the bones were effective." He took another deep breath, steadying himself.

Joan grabbed his hand and pulled him farther away from Rufina's bones. "That's enough for tonight."

James looked relieved, though he didn't say anything. He moved opposite Joan again, giving the skeleton a wide berth before whispering the prayer to end the ritual and close the path—so the spirit couldn't come through again.

Joan had plenty to think about with the little Rufina had revealed. It wasn't near enough to forge the Pact anew, but it still felt monumental.

She glanced over at Rose, who was clenching her hands so tightly her knuckles had gone white. Arcas lay on the ground, its chin on its paws as it watched Joan. They'd both been disturbed by what Rufina had said to them.

What had she meant about the original being sealed with lies and betrayal? What had been Ogun's price? Joan hadn't known her Orisha to deal in such a mercenary manner, but she doubted Rufina had lied.

Tonight's words and the way Titanea had treated Rufina's bones...

There was far more to the story of the Pact than any of them realized. But without the cooperation of Rufina's spirit, Joan feared she'd never have the answers they so desperately needed.

· 23 JANUARY ·

CHAPTER THIRTY-ONE
Things Small & Undistinguishable

oan stayed in her brother's room all night. They'd fallen asleep holding hands just like they'd done when they were small children afraid of the dark. She shook him awake just after dawn, knowing him well enough to dodge the swing he took at her in retaliation.

"Come on," she said as she made her way to the door. "We have to rehearse."

Joan was happy for the distraction of the play. It would give her relief from the fear and frustration of last night's failure.

Rufina's skeleton still lay in the courtyard, Joan knew. An uncanny awareness of those cursed bones tugged at Joan's senses, and not even the full distance of the house separating them could dull it.

Perhaps that was why they remained there, because of that strange energy warning everyone away. Iya Mary and their parents would know not to touch them. If Joan and James had been more experienced, they likely would have too. But what was done was done.

She shivered as the sensation washed over her again and shook her head.

James groaned and rolled over. "I feel like death."

"Don't joke," Joan said. She turned to him and frowned.

His face looked far too pale, and dark bruises marred the skin beneath his eyes. She placed a hand against his forehead. It was burning hot and slick with sweat.

"You can't perform like this."

He grinned at her. "I can." He swung his feet out of the bed, stood, and immediately pitched forward into Joan's arms.

"You cannot," she said firmly, settling him back beneath the covers. "We'll figure out how to proceed while you rest." She tucked the blanket around his neck. "And you *must* rest."

James sighed but nodded. Joan waited until he'd closed his eyes before she slipped out of the room. She pressed her back against the door, trying to calm herself.

The strain of last night might've been enough to leave her brother vulnerable to a normal, wintertime sickness. Their father could handle something like that easily. She held on to that thought tightly as she went to find him and refused to consider any other possibility even as those thrice-damned bones tugged at her senses.

She left James in their father's care and headed off to meet the rest of the King's Men at the town hall for rehearsal. She had no idea how they'd manage *Twelfth Night* without Viola, their heroine, but she knew Master Shakespeare would devise some solution.

She rounded the corner leading to the stairs and noticed Baba Ben returning to his room.

He still had that exhausted air about him, his eyes seeming to droop as he turned and spotted her. She had no desire to speak with him after what he'd done yesterday, but guilt ran the thought away nearly as soon as it had been born.

This was her godfather back from the presumed dead. He was the only other child of Ogun besides her, a gift that had felt so lonely only days before. She couldn't turn her back on him now, no matter how angry she felt. She sighed and walked over to him.

"Joan," he said, smiling warmly. "Good morning. I thought you were with the players."

"I'm on my way—" She paused, wondering if her next words were too bold, but continued anyway. "Why have you cut me out of everything?"

Baba Ben looked shocked for a moment before sighing. "Joan . . ." He waved her into his room and closed the door behind them. "I know you're angry, but surely you understand why I want to keep you safe?"

"I . . ." Guilt rushed through Joan again, stilling her words.

Of course, she understood that need. She'd spoken those same words to James, Nick, and Rose just yesterday. All her mistakes in the palace had been because of her struggle to ensure the safety of everyone she loved. Despite how betrayed she felt now, how could she fault Baba for doing the same?

He seemed to read all of this in her expression as he pulled her into a tight hug. "I'm sorry I've hurt you, but I won't apologize for wanting you far from this fight." He released her, pressing his hand against her cheek. "I love you as if you were my own child." He stared into her eyes. "No matter what happens, remember that."

Joan nodded, her eyes burning as memories of that night in the Tower—the night she thought he'd died—rushed through her.

"Baba—" She breathed deeply and prepared to ask the question that had weighed on her mind since she'd received his letter. "How did you come out of the Tower alive?"

Baba Ben stepped back, his hand rubbing the stubble at his chin. It was strange seeing him with facial hair, as he usually preferred to keep his face clean shaven. It had been an odd sight in the Tower as well, though she'd brushed it off in favor of more pressing matters.

"It was quite strange," he said finally. "But Goodfellow . . ." A small smile crossed his face. "One moment the murderers burst into the cell, and the next Goodfellow stood over their bodies, both of them dead. There was a shift of some kind of magic, then one of the men transformed so those who came later would find the body of Benjamin Wick on the floor. Then we disappeared to some hidden realm."

Joan nodded, feeling relieved and sad all at once. "Then you made your way to the Globe." She thought of telling him about Goodfellow's final betrayal but couldn't bear to break this moment. Instead, she surged forward to hug him, just because she could.

"I know it's been hard," he said. He patted her shoulder again and guided her to the door. "But it's best to leave those thoughts behind. Believe me."

CHAPTER THIRTY-TWO
How Many Fathoms Deep

Joan held the long hair of her black wig out of the way as Roz helped lace her into her gown.

"I won't tie it too tightly," Roz said. "You only wear this for a single scene."

Joan nodded. "I remember, thank you." And she did. *Twelfth Night* was her favorite of Master Shakespeare's plays. She could recite nearly every line in the entire thing herself. A blessing, because today she'd play both Viola—the girl who survives a shipwreck and dons boy's clothes to secure employment from the local duke—and her twin brother, Sebastian.

She'd seen many performances where James would rush backstage to change from Viola's dress into the hose and jerkin that disguised her as Cesario. Rob would wear an identical costume when he played Sebastian as the siblings in the play were meant to look enough alike to each be mistaken for each other.

The way the roles imitated life wasn't lost on Joan.

"Will they give you a beard to make you a more convincing boy?" Rose said sweetly. She sat on the table watching Roz finish dressing Joan.

"They tried," Roz said, "but she wouldn't stop sneezing."

Joan rolled her eyes as the two of them laughed at her misfortune.

"I hate to disturb your fun, but I think I'll need help as well," Nick said as he slipped past the curtain separating out Joan's dressing area. His held his black gown to his chest, his shoulders bare as the black chemise he wore hugged them just low enough to expose the smooth line of his neck.

Joan tried not to stare and only noticed Roz had finished tying her laces when she cleared her throat. The woman raised an eyebrow, a sly smile sliding over her face.

"I'm afraid I must go assist the rest of the company," she said. "But I think there are enough hands here to help you." She winked at Joan, then slipped out of the dressing area.

Joan shook her head and glanced over at Rose, who watched Nick openly. She licked her lips, eyes traveling over his form. A mischievous idea slid into Joan's mind.

"Can you help him, Rose?" she said. "I'm not yet ready."

Rose cleared her throat. "Yes, I can . . . yes." She pushed herself off the table and walked over to Nick. "Turn around, please."

Nick did as she asked, glancing over his shoulder as she grabbed the laces that ran along the bodice of his black gown. Joan watched as a shiver passed through him, her own pulse racing. Rose pulled the laces tightly and drew the bodice close around his waist. Nick gasped, Joan breathing along with him as their eyes met. They stayed locked as Rose worked. When she finished, she slipped her hands around Nick's waist.

"You're ready," she said softly.

Nick slid his hands over hers and glanced back over his shoulder. "Thank you."

Joan could almost feel the moment the two's eyes met, and she wanted nothing more than to slide herself between them again. Not to interfere but . . .

"Joan, are you ready?" Shakespeare said from just beyond the dressing area, breaking the tension in the room.

Rose and Nick jumped away from each other as Joan's head whipped to the curtain.

"I'll be but a moment," she said.

She listened until his footsteps retreated fully before looking back at Nick and Rose. A smile slipped across Nick's face as he moved toward the curtain. He leaned over to press a quick kiss to Joan's lips. She leaned into him, only pulling away when Rose snorted out a laugh. Grinning, she leaned back and touched Nick's cheek with one hand. He turned away from the curtain, catching hold of Rose's hand.

"Thank you again," he said. He pressed a soft kiss to her knuckles, eyes locked on hers as she blushed bright red.

Joan giggled, not used to seeing Rose so embarrassed. Her eyes cut to Joan before she jerked her hand backward, tugging Nick toward her, and pressed a firm kiss against his lips.

He blinked rapidly as she pulled away, his face half-dazed. Rose smiled again and shoved him through the curtain.

"Have a good show, Nick," she said, before pulling the fabric closed behind him.

Joan watched Rose, whose eyes were locked on the still swinging curtain. She turned to look at Joan, her cheeks red. Joan felt the smile on her own face widening as confidence bloomed in her chest.

Nick and Rose felt something for each other. Joan couldn't be sure how strong the attraction between her two loves was, but the fact that it existed at all made her feel hopeful.

They'd need to speak about it, to be sure that all things stayed equal between the three of them, but this unusual arrangement of theirs would work. She was sure of it now.

They still had some time before the start of the play, but Joan couldn't wander far—she had the opening scene. She wished she could speak to her brother. Just as when she'd gone on as Hermia in *A Midsummer Night's Dream*, she felt that clawing fear creeping into her belly. His calm reassurance had guided her through it then.

She took a deep breath and sat on one of the chairs that had been placed backstage so the actors could rest between their scenes.

"Joan . . ." Nick approached her, wringing his hands as he stared down at her.

She smiled and patted the seat next to her. He dropped into the chair, his lips turning up the barest bit at the corners. He looked like he didn't know what to do with his hands, and fidgeted before finally setting them on his knees.

Joan watched him struggle and decided to have pity on his poor nervous self. She had a good idea what weighed on his mind anyway.

"You want to talk about Rose?" She said the words softly, watching his face and hoping her frankness didn't scare him off.

He flinched. "Yes . . ." His gaze skittered along the floor before focusing on something over her shoulder. "I think I . . . I believe that . . ." He shook his head, clearly trying to gather his thoughts.

"Are you attracted to her?" Joan waited until he finally met her gaze before she clasped his hands within hers. "It's fine if you are." She felt her own cheeks heat up with what she was about to reveal. "It's better than fine, actually."

The tension in Nick's body disappeared as he sagged with relief. "It was ... unexpected ..."

"I'm sure," she laughed. "She's quite dynamic."

"She is. And so are you."

Joan blushed harder and squeezed his hand. "Thank you." She watched his face, noticing the slight furrow in his brow. "Were you afraid I'd be jealous?" She touched his cheek softly before running her fingers across his brow. "I'm not. I'm thrilled to hear that you feel something for her too." Nick raised an eyebrow and Joan continued. "I haven't been sure of how to navigate this thing between the three of us, and being the sole point of connection was intimidating." She took a deep breath, moving through her insecurities to speak plainly to the boy she loved. They all deserved honesty here; it was the only way any of this would work. "I was afraid at first too, but not so much that I wasn't determined to figure it out. You're both worth the effort to me."

Nick smiled and kissed her knuckles. "You're worth it to me as well." He caressed her fingers, as much for her comfort as his. "I don't feel as strongly for her as I do for you but ..." He frowned, not upset but considering. "But I think I could grow to love her too, quite easily."

Joan felt as if her grin might split her face, but she only nodded. Nick shook his head but couldn't hide his answering smile. He tugged Joan in for a hug, tucking his face against her neck.

"If this is a fraction of what you feel for us, how can you stand it?"

Joan laughed and pulled away. "'Tis the sweetest agony, loving you both." She leaned in and pressed her lips against his. She felt him pull her closer and fought the urge to climb into his lap, to be as near to him as she possibly could.

Even if none of them knew the path such a relationship would take, they could figure it out together. That's all the three of them needed.

CHAPTER THIRTY-THREE
INTERLUDE: Frances Cecil's Folly

rances slipped out of the back of the meetinghouse as the audience guffawed at the antics of William Shakespeare and Richard Burbage. The two actors, as Sir Andrew Aguecheek and Sir Toby Belch, respectively, held the crowd rapt with every chaotic interaction. She'd always enjoyed hearing *Twelfth Night*, but today, the play only weighed down her heart.

If Tobias was to be believed, her own brother used her to try to kill both the boy she loved and Joan. Her heart broke with the truth of it, that her brother was all the family she had left in the world, and he had betrayed her.

But hadn't she done the same to him by seeking out the very person who'd murdered their father?

She searched within herself for some feeling toward the man who'd barely been in her life beyond presenting her at court like some prize mare, but she could find none. Her father had ensured she was raised properly, sending her off to her aunt, guaranteeing she received the best education and had a wardrobe befitting her station. But while he'd exceeded at providing material things, she'd never felt the glow of his affection. Not like William, his only son, had.

She wondered if things would've been different had their mother lived. Perhaps she might've curbed some of their father's harsher instincts and saved him from his tragic end.

Frances glanced back at the meeting hall, the sounds of the audience's reactions muted from within. She should return to the play, but her head ached with all these terrible thoughts.

"Frances?" Ben Wick, the man she'd come to know over the days they'd hidden together at the Globe, strode up to her. "Why aren't you inside?"

She looked away, wringing her hands. "I . . . It was . . ."

"Ah." Sympathy crossed his face. "I doubt this play brings up happy memories for you." He patted her shoulder gently. "Why don't you take a walk near the river and clear your head?"

The thought of a riverside stroll appealed. She and William had often enjoyed quiet time along the Thames. Better to find herself stuck in those happy memories than the ones that dogged her now.

"Thank you," she said sincerely. He stepped back and she noticed the item he carried, a strange skull with pure white lilies growing from the eye sockets. A chill raced down her spine. "Why do you have that?"

Ben followed her gaze. "I—" He doubled over suddenly as pain racked his body.

Frances reached out to steady him, rubbing his back until his breathing calmed again.

"I'm fine. Thank you," he gasped. He straightened slowly and smiled at her. "And don't mind this. I must give it to someone." He looked sad for a moment before he nodded to her and turned back toward New Place. "Please try to enjoy your walk, Frances."

She waved, watching him until he disappeared into the house. His advice was sound. She'd indulge in a small walk about the town. The sun still hung in the sky, slowly making its descent. It wouldn't set for another few hours yet.

Sighing again, she strolled along the road toward the River Avon. She could hear the noises of waterfowl growing louder as she approached and welcomed that over the sounds of merriment back at the meeting hall.

She wished she didn't begrudge them their enjoyment or Joan's deep, loving bond with her own brother, but she couldn't deny what she felt. She doubted James would ever betray his sister. She also knew Joan would be brave enough to stand up to him if he had done half the things William had.

She wondered if Joan would be strong enough to strike James down if that became an absolute necessity.

Frances felt like Joan would do it. She was that kind of person.

Sometimes, Frances could understand what William saw in Joan, why he'd been so determined to have her as his wife.

It didn't make what he'd done right. Not then and definitely not now.

She reached the river and sat in the browned grass on its bank, wrapping her arms around herself. The air was cooler here by the water; she could already feel the tip of her nose aching with the bite of cold, but she refused to go back yet. She'd sit here with her thoughts a while longer, and hopefully, when she returned, the audience would be applauding the end of the play and she could go back to pretending she didn't care what her brother had done.

"Frances? Is that you?"

Her head jerked up at the familiar voice calling from across the river, her eyes wide. There, on the opposite bank stood her brother, William.

He looked exhausted and beaten, his clothes stained with rust-colored splotches that had to be dried blood. His face lit up when their eyes met and he dropped to his knees.

"It is you," he said, tears making his words waver. "Thank the Lord I've found you."

Frances scrambled to her feet. Her heart raced in her chest. "What are you doing here?" She hugged herself again. "How dare you come here after what you've done?"

"I'm sorry, Frances, but I wasn't myself." He dropped his face into his hands. "I know words aren't enough to make you forgive what I did, but you must know how those ... beings, the Fae"—he half-whispered the word, eyes glancing around as if he was afraid they'd overhear—"can control your mind."

She shivered, the horrors she'd seen in Whitehall Palace fresh in her mind. She couldn't leave him on the other side of the river where those creatures might snatch him up again before she'd be able to help him.

"Thinking of you is what helped me break free." He pressed his hands against his chest, clutching his heart. "I love you, sister. You're all I have left. Do you believe I would truly leave you alone if I was in my right mind?"

Frances bit her lip, eyes boring into her brother's as if she could pull the truth from his gaze. Nothing in him seemed insincere, and she wanted to believe him with every beat of her aching heart. He was right—they were all they each had left.

William wasn't a strong fighter; he'd always relied on their father's power to bolster his bad behavior, and in absence of that he had used the Fae. But now that he had neither, he couldn't truly be a threat to any in this town.

Decision made, she stood, dusting the grass and dirt from her gown.

"Meet me at the bridge," she said, pointing farther down the river. "You'll be safer here, and we can speak to His Majesty."

A smile bloomed across his face. "The king is here? Thank you, Frances."

She smiled back and picked up her skirts to hurry to him. Once he was safely inside the town, they could seek the king's protection and force Joan to leave him in peace. Then Frances would confront him about what he'd done to Tobias.

She'd keep them apart until she could broach the idea of her love forgiving her wayward brother just as she had. She felt confident it would happen.

As she approached the bridge, she could see William coming up on the other side. Before long, she held William's hand clasped in hers. They grinned at each other, and she dragged him forward into a hug.

"You still have much to answer for, William Cecil," she said as she pulled away. She brushed the tears from her eyes and sniffled.

William nodded, glancing around them in wonder. "In due time."

CHAPTER THIRTY-FOUR
Private Pleasure, Public Plague

oan took a deep breath before she entered the stage, Armin following behind her as Feste the fool.

Moving about in trousers still felt so odd to her, but it seemed that wearing men's clothes made her natural fighter's swagger more distinct. She hadn't done much to change how she moved and had only lowered the pitch of her voice slightly, but she'd seen at least two girls her age in the audience giggling whenever she stepped into a scene.

Joan found an opportune moment to wink at them, fighting her broad grin when they squealed in delight. Moments like this made her wish she could make the stage her home as her brother did, as if her wish of becoming a goldsmith wasn't lofty enough.

"*Will you make me believe that I am not sent for you?*" Armin said as he dogged her steps.

He played the fool employed by Olivia. She'd fallen in love with the disguised Viola and sent Feste to find the "boy." Instead, the fool now found himself face-to-face with Viola's identical brother, Sebastian, who, of course, knew nothing of this lady.

Joan waved him away in frustration. "*Go to, go to, thou art a foolish fellow. Let me be clear of thee.*"

Undeterred, Armin followed her around the stage, trading lines and half-concealed humor.

King James sat in the center of the very first row, guffawing at everything Armin spoke. Philip enjoyed the play in a more subdued manner to the king's right and Iya Mary, on the king's left, laughed not once. Joan had only bothered to make eye contact with Philip. The one time she'd caught the king's gaze, she hadn't liked the considering look that crossed his face.

She preferred he despise her as a witch than admire her.

Burbage and Shakespeare burst onto the stage in a cacophony of noise as the drunken Sir Toby and the disappointing knight Sir Andrew. The local man they'd hired to play the part of Fabian followed behind them, script pages clutched in his hand. Fabian and Sir Toby had convinced Sir Andrew to challenge Viola for Olivia's love. They followed now to see the fruits of their urging play out, not knowing he faced Sebastian and not the "boy" Olivia loved.

Shakespeare jabbed his finger at Joan. "*Now, sir, have I met you again?*" His voice quaked with false nervousness as he strode toward her. "*There's for you.*"

His fist flashed out, and she reacted as if he'd hit her. He smacked a hand against his chest to mimic the noise of a slap. The audience gasped and murmured as she seemed to shake off the blow, clenching and unclenching her fist.

"*Why, there's for thee,*" Joan said in her lowered voice, then pretended to backhand Shakespeare. He cried out and let the fake hit send him stumbling. She rushed after him to deliver two more false punches. "*—and there, and there. Are the people mad?*"

Shakespeare fell to the ground, cowering as she drew her sword—Bia dulled like one of their stage blades—and pointed it at his chest.

"*Hold, sir*"—Burbage stumbled over to them, stepping between the two—"*or I'll throw your dagger o'er the house.*"

Something tugged at Joan's awareness. She tried to focus on the lines that the others were speaking, but she couldn't pay them any attention. The quality of light changed, as if a storm cloud had drifted over the sun.

She glanced toward the door and noticed the windows darken suddenly. She turned back to see Burbage watching her. As soon as their eyes met, he gave the cue for the quick sequence of blows they were about to exchange. Joan shifted to her left, allowing him to punch past her head. She followed the sequence with half of her mind on the encroaching darkness outside.

She could hear more hushed whispers from the audience. Her parents leaned together before her mother seemed to pull the iron cane Joan had fashioned for her from thin air. She laid the weapon across her lap as Joan's father began to make his way to the front. Iya Mary slid to the edge of her seat.

The king noticed nothing.

Shakespeare had long ago scrambled to his feet and now he stared openly at the windows, forgetting he was in the middle of a play.

That was proof enough. Joan caught Burbage's next blow and stopped their fight. He opened his mouth to speak but she shook her head.

"Something's wrong," she said.

The door to the meeting hall blew off its hinges with a bang. It landed heavily on a few of the people in the seats farthest back, sending those around them screaming and scrambling away. Iya Mary leapt to her feet as

Joan's father and Pearce rushed to her from either side. The three of them surrounded the king and bustled him up and across the stage.

"This way!" Joan shouted, waving the crowd after the king. She let them flow past her, then raced toward the danger.

A hooded figure rode through the broken door astride a horse so black it seemed to absorb all of the light that dared come near.

Joan remembered both the horse and its rider from that day in November after *Midsummer* and again from the attack on Whitehall.

Herne, leader of the Wild Hunt, surveyed the chaos as people rushed out of the meeting hall, shrieking and threatening to crush any who moved too slowly.

Joan flicked out her hand. Iron cascaded down her arm and shot out of her palm toward Burbage. It slid over his fists as he shouted his thanks and followed Shakespeare back across the empty stage. She pressed her palm against Bia's blade. The sword sharpened and glinted in the light as iron flowed down it.

Through the commotion, Joan could see Susanna and Judith struggling to move the panicked crowd out and away from Herne. The Fae remained still as her horse's hooves thundered against the ground. As if to answer, howling shadows streamed out of the meeting hall, their true shapes obscured within the writhing gray cloud.

"Iron Blade," Herne finally spoke, her raspy voice echoing around them. "Did you think you'd be safe here?"

Joan scowled as Ogun's presence flared in her chest. "Who says we aren't?"

"I do." Herne suddenly appeared in Joan's space, her hood thrown back to reveal a too-beautiful face framed by a set of long, curling horns and spiraling black hair. She backhanded Joan, sending her crashing into the stage.

Joan shook her head and jumped to her feet. She knocked Herne's next swing away with Bia. The Fae grinned and kicked Joan through the first row of empty chairs. Joan coughed as she struggled to stand again. Bia had slipped from her grip and lay just out of her reach. She raised a hand to call the sword to her when she saw the shadow of Herne's approach. Joan brought both her arms up in front of her face, blocking the kick meant to take her down. She grabbed Herne's ankle with both hands and heaved her across the massive room. Chairs clattered across the floor as Herne skidded through them.

She'd be up again soon. Joan turned to scramble over to Bia and stopped. Baba Ben stood over the sword, his expression blank.

"Baba, what—"

He picked Bia up and Joan braced herself for the mind-piercing screams that had overwhelmed her the last time her godfather held the sword. But as he turned the blade over in his bandaged hands, it remained silent.

Joan sighed in relief and dropped back on her heels. "Hurry, throw me the sword." She held out her hand.

"I'm sorry, Iron Blade." Her godfather looked up at her, eyes sad. "For all of it."

Joan felt her blood turn to ice as that name fell from Baba's lips. His shape shivered in the air. His arms and torso filled out with muscle, his brown skin flushing with health. His dark braids unraveled and the color seemed to drip from the strands like water until his hair turned stark white. His face melted away, then solidified into the familiar features of Goodfellow.

Joan's hands shook as the Fae regarded the blade they held, the bandages protecting their skin from its iron.

"No..." Joan leapt at them. She grabbed for Bia.

Goodfellow stepped out of her reach, watching as she slammed back into the floor. "I'm sorry, Iron Blade." They sighed heavily. "There may still be time to save your brother." Then they vanished before her eyes, Bia along with them.

CHAPTER THIRTY-FIVE
Thy Disturbed Sport

oan couldn't breathe. Baba Ben hadn't come back to them after all. It had been Goodfellow the whole time. They'd infiltrated Stratford and now they likely returned to Titanea with the very blade needed to restore the Pact.

She heard laughter behind her and turned to see Herne push herself to her feet, the two of them alone in the hall. Outside, the shrieks of the Wild Hunt blended with the cries of the people of Stratford and the shouts of the children of the Orisha. She couldn't focus on what might be happening beyond these walls, not while Herne stood before her, not with Bia gone. She needed to fight.

But her sword . . .

"I remember you." Herne's gaze shifted beyond Joan, a slow smile sliding over her lips. "Both of you."

"Know me as I was, Hunter, not as I appear."

Joan went cold as the voice behind her drowned out the sounds of battle beyond the walls of the meeting hall. She knew she shouldn't take her eyes off Herne but . . .

She turned to look.

James strode across the empty stage, clutching Rufina's skull to his chest. Blood dripped from the dagger he held, the crimson liquid staining his hands and the sleeves of his untucked white shirt, though none of it appeared to be his own. His face still hadn't regained its healthy color though he moved like a seasoned warrior, like Rufina.

The spirit using James's body brandished the dagger, her gaze on Herne. Joan felt locked in place as her fingers went numb.

James was supposed to be resting safely in New Place. How had he gotten hold of Rufina's skull? After their disastrous ritual, he'd never have touched them again on his own.

"There may still be time to save your brother."

Goodfellow's words echoed in her mind, and she felt bile rise in her throat. They'd taken Phillips, her sword, and now her brother. How many more betrayals would Goodfellow heap upon her? How many more could she bear? Her chest ached and her stomach roiled as she pressed her hands against the ground to steady herself.

It didn't work. The world spun.

"Tell the queen that the king is dead by my hand," Rufina said with James's mouth. "I gift her this realm that I might earn forgiveness."

"What?" Joan whispered, horror cracking her voice as she realized just whose blood the spirit wore.

Herne sneered. "Tell her yourself, traitor. You'll get no absolution from me."

"I'll give her more," Rufina said before her eyes alighted on Joan. "I'll kill the Iron Blade."

She leapt onto Joan from the stage, tackling her to the ground. Joan grabbed Rufina's wrist and stopped the dagger before Rufina could drive it into her chest. Joan focused on the blade, curving it away from herself.

"No," Rufina growled, "you don't get to do that."

The dagger straightened again, and Joan felt as if she'd been doused in icy water. Rufina grinned. She tucked the skull into the crook of her elbow, then brought her other hand atop the dagger's hilt and pushed. It dropped lower, digging into the skin of Joan's throat.

"Draw your sword, Iron Blade," she hissed. "Or are you too afraid to fight me in this body?" She pressed harder. "Draw your sword!"

Joan's hands shook as she struggled to keep the dagger at bay. Her nails dug into Rufina's arms and blood bloomed from the crescent-shaped wounds. Joan's hands slipped

A dark shape slammed into Rufina's side, knocking her away from Joan. The spirit hit the stage but managed to keep hold of the skull. Arcas growled as it stood over her, its sharp teeth bared. It leapt at Rufina again, and Joan felt her heart stop.

"Don't hurt him!" she screamed as the grim reared back to bite.

It snapped its jaws shut and instead shoved its paws into Rufina's chest. She shrieked, swiping at Arcas with her dagger. The grim dodged the first blow, but the second caught it across the face. It yelped and retreated, paws shielding it from another attack. Rufina surged to her feet as the dagger sparkled suddenly in the light. As iron covered its blade, Joan realized.

Rufina threw it at Arcas, the grim still distracted by its wound.

No!

Joan reached for the dagger and pulled. It spun to a halt in the air before flying into her hand. She snatched it by the blade, not caring if it cut her palm as relief rushed through her. Arcas shook its head and bounded out of Rufina's reach.

"Leave my brother's body," Joan growled.

Rufina laughed. "Come take it from me."

"Is that despair I smell on you, Iron Blade?" Herne laughed from the back of the meeting hall. Her horse cantered over to her, knocking chairs aside in its wake. She swung herself into the saddle, a wide grin on her face. "It seems you have this in hand, traitor. I'll leave the rest to you."

The horse reared up as a cloud of black smoke swirled around its legs and burst toward the ceiling. When it cleared, Herne was gone.

"Draw Bia," Rufina said. She narrowed her eyes, then grinned suddenly, the expression ugly on James's face. "Oh, have you lost your sword? Shame. What will you do now?"

Rufina dove at Joan again, her fist raised. Rose appeared suddenly between them, blocking Rufina's fist with her crossed arms. "She's going to fight," she grunted and shoved the spirit back across the stage. Rose looked at Joan over her shoulder. "Are you hurt?"

"I . . ." Joan couldn't form the words. She'd never felt so lost, so stuck before. How could she attack James even if he wasn't in control of himself? How could she do anything?

Rose wrapped an arm around Joan's waist and suddenly they were outside, crouched in the space between two buildings as the sounds of fighting echoed around them. A dark shape swooped past them followed by strikes of lightning. A woman screamed, then went abruptly silent.

Had the lightning been Susanna? Had the scream? Was she lost? James was. The sword was . . .

Joan's hands shook. She felt unmoored without Bia.

Rose gripped Joan's shoulders and forced her to look into her eyes.

"That spirit is trying to kill you," she said. "I know it's hard, but you need to fight back."

Joan blinked at her, her mind still feeling far away. "Did you know?"

"Know what?"

She scowled and pulled away from Rose. "Did you know that Goodfellow was pretending to be my godfather this whole time? They stole my sword and gave James that thrice-damned skull! Did you know?"

"Zaza?" Rose's eyes widened in shock. "Zaza was here this whole time? I didn't . . ." Rose frowned before staring directly at Joan. "I never met your godfather."

Joan opened her mouth to refute what Rose said when the words actually hit her. She racked her brain, trying to recall any moment when Rose and Baba Ben had been in the same space either before his imprisonment or after his false return. Her eyes widened. They hadn't ever met; even now, Baba had been conspicuously absent whenever Rose was around, instead sticking close to Iya Mary, who Rose never approached.

It hadn't seemed odd at the time, but now it was clear that Goodfellow had avoided Rose intentionally.

"I can't fight James," Joan said softly, her mind still reeling. "And my sword, I can't reseal the Pact without my sword."

"Then we'll get them back." Rose grabbed Joan's hand. "But we both know you're far from helpless without that sword." Joan's eyes met Rose's, the girl's fierce belief in her shining through. Joan breathed deeply. She missed the gentle vibrations of Bia at her wrist, but Ogun's presence burned as brightly as ever within her. She flexed her fingers, calling iron from around them and hearing it sing back. It flowed toward them, swirling around them both as it awaited Joan's command.

"Can you handle iron?" She shaped the metal into two heavy cudgels but paused when Rose shook her head. Joan ripped her sleeves away, wrapping the fabric around the base of each weapon. She handed them carefully over to Rose. "These won't bend under any force you use."

Rose smiled as she took the batons, standing and swinging them with ease. "Oh, these will do nicely."

"Excellent." Joan stood as well, flexing her hands again. Iron flowed down her arms, forming a sharp machete in each of her fists. She tightened her grip. "Let's go."

"Right behind you, Iron Blade."

CHAPTER THIRTY-SIX
Think & Die

s they stepped out into the main road, nothing but chaos reigned around them. The darting shadows of the Wild Hunt swooped and scurried after anyone within reach. Joan tried to tune out the panicked noises around her and focus.

"What should we do?" Rose said from beside her.

Joan scanned the crowd, looking for a specific figure. "Take me to James—to Rufina. We need to get my brother back." Even if she had to tear that damned ghost out of him with her bare hands. Rose nodded, wrapping her arm around Joan's waist and transporting them to just outside of New Place. A cacophony of screams echoed from within the house.

"Go help the others," Joan said. "I—"

Hooves thundered behind them and an arrow whistled past Joan's ear, striking Herne's horse in the eye as it raced toward her and Rose. Rose pulled her back as the creature collapsed at their feet. She looked up to where the arrow had come from and saw Judith standing on the pitched roof of someone's house, her feet braced and crossbow still aimed at Herne's mount. She nodded to Joan before firing at another creature.

"Help James," Rose said as she shoved Joan toward New Place. "Leave the rest to us." Then she disappeared.

Joan broke into a run and burst through the door into utter chaos. Joan could see her father dashing between people, directing all the other children of Yemoja around him as they cared for the wounded. Joan's eyes swept over the room, taking in all of the injured—both children of the Orisha and people of Stratford-upon-Avon. She caught the quickest glimpse of several women rushing out into the courtyard carrying stacks of white sheets. Joan turned away, unwilling to follow those them any further.

Another scream echoed from the sitting room, two discordant voices overlaid together. Her father's head whipped in that direction, hands stilling. He shook himself and caught sight of Joan, fear in his gaze.

Joan ran toward the noise.

Her mother and Pearce struggled to restrain Rufina as she bucked and tore against their hold. Iya Mary stood nearby, her arm lashed to her side and a black bruise forming on her cheek. The skull had rolled into a corner, both lilies snapped at the stems. Iya Anne shouldered past Joan as she raced into the room with candles and a basin of water sharp with the scent of herbs. The strong smell drove Joan into action.

She grabbed hold of Rufina, slipping her arms and legs around her brother's body to lock his limbs in place. Rufina shrieked again as she strained but couldn't break past Joan's superior strength.

"Go," Joan said at her mother's helpless look. "Help start the ritual. I can hold her."

Mrs. Sands and Pearce jumped to their feet, helping Iya Anne place and light the candles. Rufina bucked again. Joan tucked her fist into her elbow and tightened her hold. Rufina clawed at Joan's arms but couldn't scratch through the thick sleeves.

"How did you seal the first Pact?" Joan hissed.

Rufina growled back. "I'll never tell you."

Joan closed her eyes and tried to breathe through the sudden burst of rage. When she looked up again, Iya Mary stood over her, easing her way down onto the floor. Her mother, Iya Anne, and Pearce sat at the other points around her and James. Faintly, she could hear Iya Anne whispering her prayers.

Rufina jerked against Joan, breaking an arm free. Joan shouted and scrambled to restrain her again.

"Enough!" Iya Mary shouted.

She turned her palms out, and wet, tan clay seeped up through the floor. It oozed together, coalescing into a giant hand on either side of Joan and Rufina, the damp, earthy smell overwhelming. Iya Mary clenched her fists and the clay constructs clamped around Rufina's arms. They dried instantly, locking her in place. Rufina screamed. Joan tightened her grip.

"Leave the boy's body," Iya Anne said, her voice echoing with a slightly higher one, "and go in peace."

Rufina growled and tried to headbutt Joan. Joan dodged.

"Rufina," Joan said. "Her name is Rufina."

Iya Anne nodded. "Rufina, leave James now." Iya said the words with no hesitation or gentleness. "Leave him and we'll send you off with light."

"No." Rufina spat. "I'll see you dead first. All of you."

Wind gusted through the room as hard as if they sat in the midst of a hurricane. Nothing could be heard over its rushing. Joan could feel the vibrations in the floor as the furniture rocked in the buffeting gale.

Just when she thought they couldn't stand it much longer, the air went still. Rufina stiffened as the candles flared. She shook her head, relaxing in Joan's grip for a moment.

"You won't," James's voice whispered. "I won't let you hurt—" He jerked and choked as Rufina took claim of his body again. She screamed.

It wasn't working. Joan looked up to Iya Anne. The woman cast her eyes about helplessly. They'd never faced something like this before, but James would be lost to them if they didn't do *something*.

Please, Joan prayed, reaching out to Ogun, *please help us*.

She wasn't sure if the Orisha would answer or what he could do even if he did. Dealing with the dead fell outside his domain. Still, she cried out for help.

Please, I can't lose my brother.

Gusting wind suddenly buffeted Joan as the sharp smell of a storm swirled around her. Rufina shook violently in her hold before going still. Her head fell back against Joan's shoulder.

"You've overstayed your welcome," she said, but the voice had changed again. The lilting tone matched the one that had echoed beneath Iya Anne's, only this time stronger. "This child is mine. You won't have him."

Joan's chest felt light as hope rushed through her.

Oya had come.

"Get out," Oya said with James's mouth.

The wind stopped and something in James shifted to show Rufina's spirit had resurfaced. She shuddered. Joan held tight, fear rushing at her again. If this didn't work—

No. It would. Oya's power would prevail.

Rufina's head thrashed back and forth. She screamed loud and long before slumping forward in Joan's arms. For an agonizing moment, nothing happened, and Joan thought her heart had stopped. But then James groaned, his voice only his own. He twisted in Joan's arms to look up at her. A sob burst from her chest. She heard Iya Anne whispering prayers rapidly to close out the ritual, but she was only focused on her brother.

The supernatural stillness that had frozen everything in the room released. The flames of the candles dwindled, almost going out completely, before they flickered back to normal, dancing in the slight shifts of air in the room.

"Let's not do that again," James whispered. He shook his arms and the clay hands crumbled and fell off of him.

Joan choked out a laugh and hugged him as tightly as she could.

CHAPTER THIRTY-SEVEN
The Unkindest Cut

James lay back on the sofa, looking wrung out and tired. Joan clutched his hand in hers, half for his comfort and half for her own. She figured he knew and that's why he had yet to complain.

Their parents stood behind them, their father applying a salve to the cut across their mother's brow. Iya Anne had retreated to the yard to help settle the dead while Shakespeare came in, bandages wrapping both of his arms. Joan caught the barest glimpse of Susanna limping along helped by Rose before the door had swung closed again.

"The Hunt's departed," Shakespeare said abruptly. "Susanna and the others cleared out any stragglers."

Iya Mary nodded as she sat heavily in her high-backed chair. Pearce leaned against it with his head in his hands. Shakespeare lit a fire in the hearth, the sound of him stacking the logs and striking the flint loud in the silent room. The fighting had stopped outside as the Wild Hunt fled—a sign of good fortune, Joan hoped. Once the fire crackled to life, Shakespeare slipped into the chair across from Joan and James. He frowned in deep thought.

"What are our losses, Oscar?"

Pearce's head jerked up at the sound of Iya Mary's voice. "I . . ." He glanced at Joan, taking her in for a moment before he spoke again. "We've fifteen too injured to fight and another ten dead, including the king."

A heavy silence settled over them all. With King James gone, England's throne was truly empty with no one to take it even if they did defeat Titanea. Joan had no idea who of the royal court remained alive beyond Philip, and the man who'd placed King James on the throne in the first place was long dead by Joan's own hand.

She'd hoped to resolve her treasonous thoughts about the monarch, but not like this.

What path did they have forward now?

Iya Mary sighed, her shoulders slumping with the weight of every death. "How did it come to this?"

"It was Goodfellow," Joan said abruptly. They all turned to her, so she continued before anyone could speak. "It was never Baba—" Her voice broke. She took a breath and tried again. "Baba never returned to us. It was Goodfellow in disguise. They took the sword. I . . ."

Joan hadn't thought anything could hurt her more than the betrayal of Goodfellow murdering Master Phillips with their bare hands. She'd been wrong. The sight of that transformation, of Baba Ben's features melting away to be replaced by Goodfellow's as they'd taken her sword cut her as brutally as if they'd stabbed her. And then they'd offered up Rufina's skull to James, so she'd nearly lost her brother. She clutched her belly, the pain stark enough that she half expected her hand to come away covered in blood. She felt James's arms wrap around her, pulling her into a tight hug.

"We should've been more careful," Iya Mary said. "I shouldn't have taken your word."

Joan flinched. "I thought it was Baba. They knew things only he—"

"But you were wrong, and look where your folly has put us." The old woman shook her head. "Ten lost, fifteen injured, your sword gone, and the king murdered. We're as good as dead."

Joan gritted her teeth, fighting down the scream that threatened to burst from her throat. She felt a hand on her shoulder and looked up at her mother, who glared fiercely at Iya Mary.

"Stop putting this on Joan. She's a child," she said, anger bleeding into her voice. "Goodfellow deceived us all. Even you believed his words when he said we didn't need Joan to seal the new Pact. What of that?"

Iya Mary pursed her lips but didn't speak.

"With the forces we have left," Joan's mother said, "we should take the fight to the Fae queen."

Pearce snorted. "You've seen how poorly we stood against the Fae. You think we'd survive a direct run on their queen?"

"Some of us have fought her before, Pearce," Joan's mother said through gritted teeth. "We still have numbers on our side."

The man exploded forward, enraged. "What do numbers matter when that girl couldn't even keep hold of her sword?"

"Oscar is right," Iya Mary said, leaning against the chair's arm. "What does it matter when we have neither the method nor the means to seal a new Pact? When we haven't a king to put back on the throne?"

Joan felt her father press gently against her back as he leaned forward to speak into her ear. "Why don't you take your brother upstairs and let us speak alone?"

She knew it wasn't a suggestion, so she didn't bother protesting. She was grateful for the escape. She helped James to his feet and guided him out of the room, aware of Shakespeare's eyes on her back. They slipped out of the drawing room and closed the door. The shouting began as soon as the latch clicked into place.

"Iya Mary is wrong," James said firmly. "It's not your fault."

Joan nodded, only half believing him. She felt tears burn her eyes again. She clenched her jaw and sucked air in through her nose. She was so sick of crying. These tears were useless, doing nothing but make her head ache.

"Help, please, someone help us!"

William Cecil stumbled through the open door, Frances's bloody body clutched in his arms. His eyes widened as he saw Joan and he tried to move faster.

"Please," he said, his voice breaking over the word. "Please, she needs help." He took another step before his knees buckled, bringing him and Frances both to the ground.

The pleading in his voice cut straight to Joan's heart. Whatever she felt about him, she couldn't bring herself to match his cruelty. She glanced at James before hurrying back toward the Cecil siblings. She dropped to the floor and looked over Frances.

The girl's already pale complexion was stark white under the smears of blood. One of her legs was bent at a terrible angle, and the front of her black gown seemed dark and wet. Joan laid a hand there and felt no movement. When she pulled away, her palm was covered in crimson.

Something heavy settled in Joan's stomach before she faced William again. The boy kneeled on the other side of Frances, wringing his hands as he watched her expectantly.

"Aren't you going to help her?" He half hissed the words, his face twisting in anger.

Joan clenched her jaw. "She's dead." She watched shock overtake his face. "There's nothing we can do. I'm sorry."

"You're lying." He looked from her to the others behind her and clambered to his feet. "All that *magic* you people have, surely you can do something. You can save her."

"We can't raise the dead," James said as he came up to kneel beside Joan. "Your sister is gone."

"No, you're doing this to punish me."

Joan blinked at him. Why would he think she would be so petty? "If I had, you'd be the one lying here, not her."

He flinched as if she'd slapped him, his face going white. "What?"

"You never think about the consequences of your actions." Joan clenched her fists, struggling to find some gentleness for this spiteful, violent boy but finding none. "You wanted to punish me for rejecting you, for killing your father, because you thought it would satisfy the rage inside you." She sighed, suddenly feeling nothing but exhaustion. She was tired of dealing with the men of this family. "And now what do you have left?"

He stared at her, blinking silently before his face crumpled. Sobs wracked his body as he threw himself over his sister's corpse. Joan shook her head and stood. She lifted her hand, calling forth some metal. It gathered in the air before her and she twisted her fingers, forming it into a single cuff on a thick chain. She directed it to clamp around William's ankle as she secured the chain to the ground with a thick spike.

Even if she wanted to give him some peace to mourn where his choices had left him, she couldn't stomach the risk of him escaping. To Frances, she might've offered grace, but William had earned none. He looked up at her as the cuff clanked shut, his eyes filling with tears.

"Someone will come retrieve you soon," she said quietly. She stood and helped James up. They started away before she turned, speaking to William over her shoulder. "Nothing had to be this way. I wish you could've seen that."

He stared at her and his face crumpled again.

"Let's get you to your room," she said to James. "You need to rest."

She let James set their pace as she guided him up the stairs, refusing to turn back even as William's sobs echoed around them.

"So, I killed the king," he said as they reached the landing. "Will you visit me when I'm just a tarred head perched atop London Bridge?"

Joan flinched. "That wasn't you. If Goodfellow hadn't—If I hadn't . . ." This was yet another harm she'd caused with her desperate desire for Baba Ben to be alive, because of her weakness.

Fresh tears blurred her vision. She blinked heavily, pressing her fingers against the bridge of her nose to hold them back. The silence of Bia's absence hung like a weight around her neck. She tried to breathe, her chest feeling tight.

She jumped as James pinched her cheek hard.

"Don't do that!" he said, glaring at her. "Goodfellow can deceive even the Fae. How can you be expected to defend against that kind of power?"

Joan rubbed at her eyes as her brother's words soothed some of the hurt Iya Mary had inflicted.

"*You* defeated Auberon and Cecil, not Iya Mary. Who gives a shite if she doesn't believe in you?" James braced his feet and clutched her shoulders. A sheen of sweat covered his face but his expression was fierce. "The rest of us do. *Ogun* does. Hold that truth in your heart."

Have faith.

She heard Ogun's words as clearly in her head as if they'd been spoken out loud.

You will know how to move. That is why I chose you.

The Orisha's voice cut through her panic, the calming warmth starting in her chest and spreading out through the rest of her body.

She had been chosen, first by Ogun and then by the sword Bia. She'd risen to fight from the moment she'd been called. There was no need for doubt now, no matter how daunting the challenge ahead of them seemed.

Joan would have faith in herself, despite her mistakes. She had no choice if she wanted her loved ones to be safe. There was no other that she'd make.

"Thank you." She pulled her brother into a tight hug.

He groaned as she squeezed some injury, and she let him go quickly.

"Help me lie down," he said, gesturing down the hall. They started off toward his door slowly. "I swear, if I never have to wake up covered in blood again, I'll be grateful for all eternity."

CHAPTER THIRTY-EIGHT
Stern Tyrant War

Joan eased James's door closed, careful not to wake him as she slipped back out into the hallway. He needed his rest, and she'd prefer he remain ignorant of what she was going to do. She slipped down the stairs. The shouts of the adults arguing in the sitting room were muffled by the door although their intensity was apparent. They couldn't decide their next move, but Joan had a plan.

A desperate plan with only the slightest possibility of working, but what was there to lose?

She made her way to the kitchen. Tobias sat alone at the large table, his head in his hands. He looked up as she entered and Joan saw that a bruise discolored one whole side of his face.

"Joan," he said, his voice hoarse. He swiped his palms across his eyes. "I . . ." He leapt to his feet. "I'll leave."

She held up a hand and he froze. "I need a favor. You owe me."

He flinched but nodded. Satisfied, Joan walked out into the courtyard. Tobias followed. The two of them cut a wide circle around to the center of the lawn, avoiding the ten shrouded bodies that had been laid there until they could receive a proper burial. Joan heard Tobias's breath hitch behind her and tried to calm her own racing heart.

She needed to focus if she had any hope of this working.

They walked across the grass until they stood over Rufina's bones. Tobias frowned. "What are you—"

"This isn't the favor," Joan said. "Wait."

She stepped closer to the skeleton and crouched down. Someone had replaced the skull, and the broken lilies still drooped from the empty eye sockets. Joan took a deep breath, reaching out to Ogun. She felt the Orisha answer with a warm pulse in her chest. Then she grabbed Rufina's hand.

Magic ripped through her as soon as she touched the bones, and Joan felt herself drift away, her senses dulling. Her heart thudded with fear.

Open your eyes, Ogun said softly in her mind.

Joan took a steadying breath and did as the Orisha commanded. She opened her eyes to see New Place's courtyard all around her and Tobias standing wide-eyed to her left. Before her was Rufina's ghost, her form hazy.

Rufina glared. "You . . ."

"Tell me how to seal a new Pact," Joan said.

The spirit sneered and shook her head. Joan felt fury rise within her, her patience depleted.

"You will tell us." She channeled her rage into her words and felt Ogun's deeper voice overlaying her own. "Tell us how to seal the Pact."

Rufina's eyes locked on Joan's, fear spread across her face. She pressed her lips together, then blurted, "Why do you allow him to use you?"

"Ogun doesn't use me," Joan said. If Rufina had said those words months ago, when Joan had been confused and unsure in her relationship with her Orisha, she might have faltered. But now she knew. "We work together. That's how it's meant to be."

Heat flared from her chest as Joan felt Ogun come through into her body to confront Rufina.

"Tell her," the Orisha demanded, his voice ringing with the command. "You were my child once too. You understand justice."

Rufina looked stricken for a moment; her form flickered before it grew solid again. "Justice," she whispered and shook her head. "Justice?"

Rufina...

She flinched. "Yes, I'll tell her," she hissed. "Betrayal is how, lying is how." Tears sprang to her eyes. "She loved me and I used it to trap her, to trap all of them, because that's what Ogun asked of me."

Joan blinked at her, feeling the Orisha's confusion as clearly as her own.

No.

"You did!" The spirit screamed. "You made me betray her to protect this realm!"

I'd never demand such a thing.

Joan heard Ogun's words in her head and knew them to be true. He would never ask one of his children to lie, to betray someone. A sudden rush of memories invaded Joan's mind, as clearly as if she experienced them herself.

Rufina in her centurion armor, meeting Titanea in the forest. This version of the Fae queen radiated beauty and mystery and danger, and Joan felt Rufina's heart swell with love as if it were her own. Then the vision changed, and Rufina was surrounded by other soldiers, their clothing adorned with medals and sashes that marked them as her superiors.

"Cleanse this land," one of the men said. His face was obscured by a strange shift of shadows within the memory, but Joan got the sense that this was someone Rufina trusted implicitly.

My godfather, Rufina thought.

Suddenly the gold chains that draped the man's armor made sense. This was a child of Oshun.

"It's your responsibility," the man said, laying a hand on her shoulder. "Use *every* weapon you hold to your advantage." His tone left no mistake as to the meaning behind his words.

Rufina flinched, and Joan knew who'd set her on the path of betrayal.

"It wasn't Ogun at all." Joan spoke the words aloud, suddenly finding herself fully within her body again. "Your godfather told you to wield your love like a weapon, and you did as he commanded."

Rufina still stood before her in the courtyard. Realization shifted over her face before her expression shuttered again, unwilling to accept the truth. "He spoke with the Orisha's authority."

"He spoke with only his own." Joan shook her head.

Rufina clenched her jaw. "They demanded I lie to her." She swallowed thickly and continued. "People were dying, and when my commanders saw the power I had over the Fae, over her, they demanded I stop her. I couldn't disobey them, especially not my godfather." The words flowed quickly, as if they were torn from her chest and forced from her mouth. "And he was right; there was no other way. I needed to get her to make a vow to seal all her most dangerous subjects away, but no queen would allow herself and her people to be trapped like that. So, I made her believe we'd be going to the Fae realm together."

Her voice broke and steadied again. "She thought it was a ritual of marriage, but instead, I used the sword to mingle our blood. And when she repeated my false vows, she spoke the very words that would trap the Fae as long as the Pact remained.

"That is how you seal the Pact," Rufina spat. "Draw her blood with Bia and blend it with your own, then get her to speak the words you desire, a promise she must keep."

Cold flooded Joan as she realized the true depth of Rufina's betrayal. She thought about telling such a lie to Rose or Nick, one that would leave them separated and forever haunted by that betrayal, even in death. Bile rose in her throat.

"Did you not think to ask? If—" Joan blinked back tears, suddenly feeling nothing but pity for her ancestor. "If she loved you, you could've made her understand."

Rufina stilled, her eyes locking with Joan's. "I . . ."

"Your love might've birthed peace had things ended differently."

She thought of how willing Auberon and the other Fae were to die for their freedom. Of Arcas mourning being locked away from this realm. Of Rufina's actions now. The Pact had caused so much pain . . .

Joan refused to continue down that path. Conviction flowed through her, the thoughts she'd allowed to only half form in her mind blooming completely.

No, she wouldn't return the Pact to what it was. She would forge something new, something just. That was the only way she would wield Ogun's power.

The Orisha's presence burned warmly in her chest like a blessed confirmation. She looked down at Rufina's bones, clasping the hand in both of hers.

"I'm sorry you saw no other way," Joan whispered. She felt Ogun's warmth flow out of her palms, a deep green light washing over the skeleton before her. "Go with light and rest now."

Rufina gasped, the same glow emanating from her spirit. She closed her eyes as tears flowed down her cheeks.

Be at peace, Ogun whispered as the magic swept over both body and spirit.

Rufina sighed, her palms pressed against her chest, and then she was gone.

Joan took a steadying breath before releasing Rufina's hand. Her mind raced with everything she'd heard and seen and what she wanted to do to move forward. She shook her head and stood, freezing when she looked to Rufina's bones again.

The flowers surrounding the skeleton had overgrown it in an instant. They wrapped around the legs and burst up through the ribcage. The lilies in the eye sockets had multiplied into clusters of white blooms.

Ogun's magic had done this, somehow combining with Titanea's to enfold the body of this woman they'd both loved. Joan couldn't tell if it was meant as a prison or a shrine. Deep within, she felt it was both.

She finally turned to Tobias, who'd gone white while watching everything unfold. "Make me a doorway to Whitehall."

"What?" He blinked at her. "I—"

Joan glared. "I know you can do it. This is my favor."

Tobias clamped his mouth shut. He strode past Joan to trace his magic in the air. He knocked once before swinging the doorway open to reveal the wide-open courtyard of Whitehall Palace.

And Herne the Hunter stepped through. Tobias stumbled back, his face stricken.

"Seems the traitor can only break her word," Herne said as her feet alighted on the grass. "Typical."

Tobias turned to Joan. "I didn't—"

Joan dove at Herne, tackling the Fae through the doorway and back into London.

"Close it!" Joan shouted. She punched Herne across the face. "Close it now, Tobias!"

Herne growled, shoving Joan away. Joan stumbled back, afraid she'd fall through the door and bring the fight into Stratford again, but she met only the open air of the palace courtyard.

Tobias had done as she asked.

"I tire of you, Iron Blade," Herne growled as she pushed to her feet.

Joan flexed her hands, an iron machete flowing from each of her palms. "And I you."

"Enough."

Joan spun to see Goodfellow standing at the far side of the courtyard, watching her carefully.

She scowled at them. "Have you come to fight me too?"

"No," they said, expression carefully blank. "The queen wishes to see you." They glanced at Herne. "So, stand down, hunter."

Herne glared at Goodfellow but turned and strode away from Joan. Joan's heart thudded in her chest. She could face Titanea now and risk no other life but her own. She might be able to resolve this with no more fighting.

"Take me to her," she said, drawing her weapons back into her palms.

Goodfellow nodded and headed toward the palace. Joan took one last steadying breath, and, with a quick prayer to Ogun, followed.

CHAPTER THIRTY-NINE
The Storm Is Up

cross the courtyard, King James sat on his throne at the top of a dais, even though Joan knew the king's dead body was back in Stratford-upon-Avon, being prepared for a respectful, if discreet, burial. Robert Cecil, the man Joan had run through with her sword, stood beside him. Queen Anne—killed in the explosion at the House of Lords—perched on the stairs leading down to the ground, flanked by her three ladies, all murdered by Titanea. Lord Fentoun—who'd died in the Whitehall attack—stood at the base, clothed in his crimson uniform with his sword at his hip. All were Fae wearing the forms of the deceased.

Herne moved to stand alongside the others. She watched Joan silently. Goodfellow gave Joan one last look before striding away from her. Joan addressed the false king.

"Titanea," she said, watching as a smile slipped across King James's face, "I'm not here to fight you."

He leaned forward on his throne. "Wise, since you've come alone."

"I want to negotiate a new Pact."

The king's eyes widened as laughter bubbled up from deep within. The royal entourage joined in until a cacophony of cackling echoed through the courtyard. Only Goodfellow refrained, but Joan didn't allow her gaze to linger on them for too long.

Laughter she could handle, though it pricked at her pride. She could push down that budding anger for now if it meant she might end this without more bloodshed. The thought filled her with doubt, but still she had to try.

"I know how the first one was sealed," Joan called over the noise. The king quieted as his eyes locked on Joan and the others went silent around them. Joan cleared her throat and pressed on. "I know what Rufina—"

His hands gripped the throne, wood splintering in his grasp. "Don't speak that name."

"I know—" Joan reached for her wrist, for the reassuring presence of Bia, and found nothing. She let her hand drop back to her side. "I know that Rufina betrayed—"

"Don't speak that name!"

"—you. Betrayed your love. We can—"

"Do not speak!" Titanea thundered as the king's image exploded off her in a thick pulse of magic.

It surged out over the courtyard, rattling the palace walls with its power. The throne tumbled over, cracked perfectly in half. The other Fae dropped their glamours, cowering and clambering away from her. Only Herne and Goodfellow held their positions in the face of their queen's power.

"You know *nothing*, Iron Blade," Titanea spat.

Joan raised her chin. "I know it didn't have to be that way."

"Enough," Herne snorted. "You mortals get hold of some magic and think it's your duty to subdue us? Never again."

Joan glared. "I'm speaking to Titanea, not—"

"The queen has heard enough." Herne glanced up at Titanea, who gave a slight nod, magic still sparking around her. "You deal with me now, Iron Blade."

The Fae queen gestured, and one of her subjects returned to her side then dropped to their hands and knees before her. She sat on their back, raising her arms as Goodfellow and another Fae came up to clasp her hands and support her back. Herne stood, stretching her neck before she grinned at Joan.

"I don't want to fight," Joan said, shifting her gaze between Herne and Titanea. Ogun's warmth burned hot in her chest as she called iron machetes into each hand.

Herne laughed. "So you say with your blades drawn." She flexed her hands, nails extending into sharp claws. "I almost hate to kill you, Iron Blade."

"Don't worry, you won't," Joan said.

Herne surged toward her, clawing at Joan's face. Joan smacked the blow away with the flat of her machete. The Fae hissed and spun out of reach of Joan's next swing. Around them, Joan noticed other Fae creeping forward, slinking out from the palace gardens, crawling up from the banks of the Thames. She was beyond outnumbered, but she couldn't let her thoughts drift that way. She needed to keep her mind on the one in front of her, on Herne.

Joan shifted her stance, feet wide, blades outstretched. Her focus narrowed until it was only her and her opponent. She flipped one of her machetes in her grip, snatching it by the blade and throwing it at Herne.

Herne threw herself to the side, but the machete sliced across her arm as she slipped away. Her severed hand dropped to the ground, dark red blood oozing from the wound left behind. Herne hissed as she clutched it.

Joan rushed her, swinging for Herne's neck. The Fae caught her wrist before the blow could land. Joan swung her legs forward, kicking Herne in the chest with both feet. Herne released her as they both hit the dirt. Joan reached out toward the ruins of the royal Banqueting House and called forth a fount of liquid metal. It wrapped around Herne's waist, bolting her to the ground. She screamed in frustration.

Joan pushed herself to her feet and turned to Titanea. "I said I want to negotiate a new Pact." She released her machetes, letting them flow back into her palms. "Please."

"Foolish," Titanea growled, the Fae beside her cringing as she crushed their hand in her grip, "arrogant, impudent mortal child." Her expression cleared suddenly, a smile slipping across her face. "Oh, Joan, we won't even dirty our hands with your blood."

A distant roar sounded, signaling the wyvern's approach. Fear spiked through Joan's heart. She clenched her fists to hide her shaking hands and kept her eyes on the Fae queen.

She stepped forward. She needed to try again. "It doesn't have to be like this." She tried to ignore the roars growing closer and her mind screaming at her to draw her blades again. "We can negotiate a fair deal. One with no lies."

"Never." Titanea whispered the word, but it seemed to echo around them. Her gaze shifted over Joan's head, her eyes lighting up in pleasure. "You'll die alone here, Iron Blade."

The huge shadow sliced through the air above Joan as the wyvern crested the riverside buildings. She saw the creature in the full light of day for the first time and stumbled back.

Water sloughed off its serpentine body, nearly as long as two men were tall. The rising sun sparkled along thick, dark green skin. It flapped its massive wings, sending gusts of wind across the courtyard as it landed on the roof of the nearest building with a creaking thud. Broken tiles skittered down to the ground beneath its talons. It raised its slender neck and snorted out a breath before swinging its massive head around to stare at Joan.

Its gaze locked her in place. Its golden, catlike eyes sparkled with intelligence. Joan flinched as it shook its head, sending water in every direction like a sudden downpour. She turned back to where Titanea still sat on the dais, her smile unchanging.

"This is your end, Iron Blade," Titanea said, "and the rest of your gods' sycophants will fall after."

Another gust hit Joan, nearly knocking her from her feet as the wyvern thudded to the ground in front of her. She straightened, weaponless and terrified. The creature lowered its head toward her. Someone screamed her name. The wyvern snorted out a hot, foul breath. It reared back.

An arm wrapped around her waist, tugging her away as jaws snapped closed in the space where she'd just been. Joan blinked, suddenly on the opposite side of the courtyard. Her mother steadied her and closed the magical doorway.

"How many times do I have to tell you," her mother said, the panic still on her face, "we go together or we don't go at all."

Joan threw her arms around her mother as doorways opened all around them and the children of the Orisha converged on Whitehall.

CHAPTER FORTY
Disordered, Debauched, & Bold

oan stayed close as her mother drew her iron cane from the air beside her. Thunder echoed overhead, dark clouds rolling over the palace, the acrid smell of coming lightning filling the air. James and Susanna ran toward her. Both looked angry enough to fight her themselves.

"Berate me later." Joan held up her hands. "Are you two armed?"

James held up two iron daggers, and Susanna wielded her twin axes. Satisfied, Joan flexed her hands as twin machetes formed in each. The sky above them darkened, clouds blocking out the sun in grim, gray clusters. Around them, more shadowy forms of the Fae began to materialize. They shifted from between hedges and slithered out from beneath bushes. Seven jacks-in-irons converged on them from near the rubble of the destroyed Banqueting House.

Pearce raised a hand. "With me!" He ran off toward them, his group of five following closely behind.

The wind around them picked up, buffeting the wyvern and attempting to knock it over. The creature stood at the other end of the courtyard, completely unaffected by James's magic. "What is that?" he shouted to Joan. He strengthened the wind, sweat beading along his forehead.

Thunder rumbled as lightning struck nearby, and Susanna incinerated two goblins sneaking toward them.

"It's a wyvern," Joan said. She glanced up as Titanea disappeared from the dais, Goodfellow fading from view right behind her. "We need to take it out." Three six-armed Fae shot out from their shadows. One clashed with James, knocking him off his feet. Susanna shouted and shot it through with a bolt of lightning as Joan's mother caught the other across the face with her iron cane. It yowled as the blow split its head open and dropped to the ground dead. Joan pulled James back up to his feet.

The wyvern nosed the air as if to sniff her out. It leaned forward, supporting itself on its hind legs and the tips of its wings. There was no way she could take down this massive beast alone. Thankfully, she didn't have to.

She looked around, taking stock of the people in the courtyard as plans formed in her mind. This was her strength: She could find advantages in the midst of battle. She felt Ogun's heat in her chest push her to move.

She pointed toward her brother. "James, use your wind to keep the wyvern from flying. If it gets into the air, knock it off balance."

James nodded and spread his arms wide. Joan could see dust kick up around the creature as wind swirled around it, this time far stronger.

"Master Shakespeare," she yelled, catching the man's attention, "sweep the yard for any other threats." She spotted Avalee, one of her mother's godchildren, nearby. "Avalee—"

Quiet singing floated toward them from the river and Joan saw the older girl stiffen and pale. The memory of the girl appearing at their house, bruised and frightened and with a story of something attacking her on the bank of the Thames, struck Joan. If this was that same creature, her terror was understandable, but she couldn't let it immobilize her. That wouldn't help any of them survive.

"Avalee," Joan called her name again and waited for their eyes to meet. She tried to pass some encouragement to the girl. "Whatever that is, can you handle it?"

She stared back at Joan, blinking rapidly. "I—"

"We'll handle it, Joan." Susanna clasped Avalee on the shoulder. "Right?" Thunder echoed overhead, and when Susanna looked back at Joan, lighting seemed to spark in her brown eyes. "We'll go together."

Joan turned away as the pair moved toward the palace docks. She trusted Susanna to keep Avalee alive and fighting. If anyone could banish someone else's fear, it was her.

The wyvern seemed to finally catch Joan's scent. Its eyes locked on her and it attempted to rise into the air. James grunted as he strengthened his wind, knocking the creature back to the ground. Two arrows struck its body. Joan followed their arc to where Judith perched on another roof, already reloading her crossbow.

"Mother, can you get me close?" Joan asked.

Hesitation crossed the woman's face before she nodded. "How close?"

Joan flexed her wrists, machetes slipping back into her grip. "Near its heart."

Her mother sliced her hands through the air to form another doorway. It swung open and Joan saw the pale green skin of the wyvern's underbelly. She sprinted through, thrusting her blades up. They barely caught on the creature's skin before it twisted out of reach. Its spiked tail swung at Joan.

She flipped one machete around, spreading the metal into a shield. The wyvern's tail slammed into it. She tumbled back across the ground and put the shield up again just as it struck once more. The force drove her into the packed dirt.

The wyvern's large head swung overhead. It knocked her shield to the side and snapped at her. Joan sliced its nose with her other machete. It screeched and pulled back, giving her just enough time to scramble to her feet. Its wing slammed into her side.

She crashed through the garden hedges, branches and thorns slicing her face as her shield and machete clattered to the ground. Grunting, Joan forced herself up, then dove under another wing swipe. A dark shape bounded over Joan's head and charged the wyvern with a familiar howl.

The wyvern shrieked as Arcas grabbed hold of the fine skin between its wings, tearing viciously with its teeth. It threw the grim off and hissed as it rolled across the walkway. Arcas leapt up. It shook itself and growled as it positioned itself between Joan and the wyvern.

"Arcas?" Joan whispered, watching as the grim's bushy tail wagged enthusiastically.

It howled again; the sound ricocheted off the buildings around them before a cacophony of yowls answered. Satisfied, the grim turned back to Joan. "We protect you, Mother."

Relief rushed through Joan as ten grim bounded into the courtyard with seemingly no regard for walls or gates. She smiled, reaching her hands out to call back her shield and machete. They flew into her grip and she spun the blade in a quick arc.

"Let's go." She sprinted toward the wyvern, Arcas and the other grim falling into formation around her.

The wyvern attempted to take to the sky before a swirling wind knocked it off balance. It tilted back to the ground and two grim clamped sharp teeth around both of its legs. It snapped at them, curving its long neck around to reach the smaller creatures. The wyvern's teeth closed around one. The grim yelped as it was jerked into the air before another grim rammed the wyvern, forcing it to drop its prey. The wyvern swung its massive head back up and swept away another grim with its spiked tail. Arcas growled but stayed near Joan.

None of them could get close, the black dogs instead dancing around the beast's feet and tail. Joan couldn't see an opening that would get her to its heart. The wyvern was far too nimble, even on the ground. It swung its neck low again, ramming a grim with its head.

She took in the battlefield. Lightning bolts touched the earth over near the dock where Joan knew Susanna and at least three other children of Shango helped Avalee clear the river's shore. Martin and Roger had joined Judith on the rooftop, taking out enemies from a distance. Roger's lost arm forced him to shoot slowly but with no less accuracy.

They were managing, but Joan knew they couldn't keep up this level of fighting forever.

She looked over to where the wyvern was still being swarmed by grim, its belly close to the ground. It knocked one grim off its back with a swing of its long neck, and a plan formed in Joan's mind.

She might not be able to reach its heart, but she could take its head. Joan turned, catching her mother's eye and pointing toward the air above the wyvern. There was no time to explain, and she prayed her mother would understand without words. Awareness sparked in the woman's eyes before she sliced her hands through the air, making a new doorway. A matching one opened in the air above the wyvern's head.

"James," her mother shouted, "don't let your sister fall!"

Excellent.

"Distract it, Arcas," Joan said and ran toward her mother's doorway.

The grim sprinted ahead of her. It bounded around the doorway to tear into the wyvern's wing. She slapped her shield and machete together, merging the metal into one massive blade as she dove through.

Her mother's magic shivered over her skin before she barreled through the sky in a heart-stopping free fall. The wind rushed against her face. She raised the blade above her head, willing it to sharpen. The wyvern snapped at Arcas, and its head shifted just enough to take it out of Joan's range.

No!

"I've got you," Rose whispered in her ear suddenly. She wrapped her arms around Joan before they disappeared and reappeared directly above the wyvern's neck.

Joan held out the blade, feeling Rose's hands wrap over hers, before it struck true. Their combined weight drove the machete through muscle, flesh, and bone with ease. The head dropped away from them, the body collapsing into the packed dirt. A swirling wind swept under them and eased Joan and Rose to the ground.

Arcas and the other grim closed in on the creature, barking at the body as if daring it to move again. It didn't so much as twitch. It was well and truly dead.

Joan breathed out a sigh of relief as running feet approached her. Her brother slammed into her, his arms wrapping around her in a hug.

"That was madness," he shouted in her ear, half in rage and half in admiration.

She hugged him back. "Thank you for catching me." He pulled away and she flicked her wrists, forming her shield once again. "I need to get to Titanea."

A roar sounded behind them, followed by another, then another. Joan's heart dropped at the familiar sound and three more wyvern landed in the center of the courtyard.

Shite.

CHAPTER FORTY-ONE
Once More unto the Breech

"This can't be real," James whispered. He held out his hands, ready to command the wind, but a fine sheen of sweat dotted his forehead.

Joan could tell he was already approaching exhaustion and could feel the weight of it pulling her down as well. Despair clawed its way through her, but Joan shoved it down viciously. They couldn't bear much more, but they couldn't fall here.

She needed to find Titanea.

"We divide and conquer," Joan said. She flicked her hand out and shifted her shield back into a machete, and caught James's stricken look. "We can do this."

"You're dead, Iron Blade," Herne screamed from over near the dais. She shoved herself upright with her remaining hand, the exposed skin around her waist smoking where Joan's iron restraint had held her.

Joan rushed at Herne before James could stop her. The Fae shrieked, the piercing sound tearing though the air and rattling in Joan's ears until she feared they'd burst. Her machetes clattered to the ground as she tried to block out the noise.

All around them, Fae and children of the Orisha fell to the ground in pain. Joan winced as she felt wet blood on her palms. She straightened and Herne's foot slammed into her chest. Joan skidded across the dirt, crashing against one of the beams supporting the dais.

Joan coughed, her mouth filled with blood, and tried to stand. Herne shoved her heel into Joan's back, forcing her face-first into the dirt.

"You'll regret taking my hand," Herne growled, pressing Joan harder and harder into the ground.

Joan screamed. Her ribs strained under the pressure, on the verge of snapping. Suddenly, Herne shouted and the Fae's weight disappeared. Joan gasped, forcing herself up onto her hands and knees as Nick stepped between her and Herne.

They lunged for each other, Nick scoring wounds across Herne's face with a sword Joan didn't recognize. He danced under the Fae's swing and sliced off her other hand and flicked it across the courtyard. She screamed, scrambling after her lost limb. Nick rushed over to where Joan still knelt, gaping at him.

"What—" she gasped as he helped her up.

He smiled at her even as he checked her over. "Family heirloom." He held up his sword and Joan was struck by the memory of the familiar calluses on his mother's hands. The blade was wide as her machetes, with a hilt long enough to be wielded with two hands. "But it's not iron."

He glanced over at Herne and Joan followed his gaze to see the Fae letting her newly severed hand reattach itself. If all Nick needed was iron, Joan could provide that.

She touched her fingers to the blade and watched the shining liquid metal coat Nick's weapon.

"Excellent," he said, a dark smile crossing his face. He turned to swipe at Herne as she rushed them.

She dodged but not quickly enough to escape a deep slice across her cheek. She shouted as her skin smoked where the blade had struck and dove for Nick. He blocked her hands with his arms. Joan called her machetes to herself again, pivoting around Nick to slip behind Herne.

Nick grabbed Herne's upper arm and jerked her toward Joan, who slammed the butt of her machete into the Fae's face. Herne grunted as dark blood spurted from her nose.

That was all the opening Joan needed.

She flipped the machetes in her grip and drove them down into Herne's chest. The rough fabric of the Fae's black robes tickled Joan's hands as the blades drove through Herne's body and out the other side. Blood burst from Herne's lips. Her eyes glazed over and she collapsed into the dirt, dead.

Joan spun, forming another machete to behead the red cap attempting to gut her. She took a deep breath and stumbled. Nick caught her arm to steady her and looked up to see panic on his face.

"I'm all right," she said but still leaned into him for a moment.

He held her until he was sure she was steady. "Are you fine to fight?"

No. I need to rest.

"I am," she said instead.

She could see other children of the Orisha struggling to take the Fae down. For every creature they destroyed with water or lightning or wind, another took its place, and the three wyverns were still untouched.

They needed an advantage, and Joan could give it to them.

Joan reached out her senses, calling as she had that day in the forest. The ground trembled beneath her feet and the heat in her chest seemed to scorch her skin. She pressed a hand against the growing pain but held her focus.

The metal song started as a whisper beneath the screams, then grew louder and louder.

Focus...

Ogun's voice echoed through her mind, calming her.

Joan took a deep breath and pulled. Her whole body tingled, sending a familiar shiver along her awareness. The ground heaved beneath her, and only Nick's hold kept her on her feet. The song burst in her ears as fine bits of iron exploded out of the earth.

The motes of metal sparked in the air as they caught the sunlight and attached to any of the Fae still standing. Without knowing where they were, Joan commanded the metal to ignore Rose, Arcas, and the other grim.

Nothing else deserved her mercy.

Screeching echoed as Fae all around the courtyard were engulfed in iron. It scorched their skin, and the burning left nothing but silence and the tinkling of a hundred thousand bits of iron.

Joan exhaled, stumbling against Nick, and opened her eyes. Charred bodies lay strewn across the ground. Relief surged through her as she spotted Arcas and the others unharmed. Roars echoed over the courtyard as shadows passed overhead. Joan looked up, her heart racing.

Two of the three wyvern landed on the rooftop, sending Judith, Martin, and Roger scrambling to safety. They'd flown out of range of her attack. Her metal had done nothing against them.

She had to do it again. She raised her hands a second time to call the iron forth. Her knees buckled and she crashed to the ground as her vision went dark. She felt Nick pull her into his arms. She blinked hard, forcing her eyes to stay open.

"Stand down, Joan," Iya Mary said.

She stood over Joan, eyes locked on the two wyvern as Tobias closed the doorway behind them. He glanced over at Joan before he turned to Iya Mary. The old woman breathed deeply, then raised her hands. The ground at the base of the building bubbled and spewed forth a burst of wet clay. It slithered up the wall beneath the wyvern, forming into an enormous snake as it moved.

Iya Mary twisted her fingers. The clay construct wrapped around the body of one of the wyvern and squeezed. It screeched, the sound choked off by the pressure of Iya Mary's snake.

The other wyvern danced out of reach and a flurry of tiny iron needles shot into its tender belly. Blood gushed from a thousand small wounds. It gurgled out a scream as another set of spikes struck its throat. It dropped to the ground as dead as the first.

"Well done," Iya Mary said, sweat pouring down her face as she struggled to keep her clay snake intact. "Now do the other."

Joan shook her head, eyes wide as her heart thudded in her chest. She hadn't been the one to send the attack, even though she was the only one who could've commanded the metal in such a way.

"I recognize that . . ." Her mother glanced over, catching Joan's eye before they both spun in the direction from where the spikes had arced.

Joan's heart beat so fast that she thought it might stop. Baba Ben's thin form walked toward them, his hands still extended. He still wore the clothes from that last night in the Tower of London, though they hung looser on his frame.

"I feared I'd be too late," he said, his voice and cadence so blessedly himself that Joan wondered how she'd even believed Goodfellow's charade in the first place. Baba finally reached them, relief slipping over his haggard face. "But I see that I'm right on time."

Joan fought the urge to throw her arms around her godfather as tears sprang to her eyes. He seemed to sense it because he grabbed her first, tugging her close. She felt Ogun's presence within her and knew, without a single doubt, that *this* was truly her godfather before her.

"I thought you were dead," she whispered.

His arms tightened around her. "So did I, but Goodfellow protected me."

Joan pulled away, trying to find the lie in her godfather's face, but she found no signs of deception. She recalled the story that Goodfellow had told, about how her godfather had survived the attack in the tower. That tale had been the truth, but of course it was. Goodfellow was Fae, and the Fae couldn't lie.

Baba wiped the tears from her cheeks. "You're the only one who can reseal the Pact, Joan."

She shook her head. "It's impossible." The sick feeling in her stomach surged again. She tried to swallow it down. "I don't have the sword."

Baba pressed his hands together before spreading them apart again. A roughly formed sword hung in the air between them. Joan grabbed it, iron singing beneath her fingers. She refined its shape before slipping it around her wrist like Bia. She smiled up at Baba.

"You'll know what to do," he said fervently. "Now go. We have this in hand."

Joan nodded and raced toward the palace's main building. Titanea had disappeared early in the battle, and some part of Joan was sure that was where the Fae queen had gone.

She heard the wyvern shriek as clay clattered to the ground around her. It flew at her before an arrow struck it in the face, making it fall back.

Arcas and another grim dragged it to the ground by the joints at the top of its leathery wings.

Behind her, Joan could see more Fae making their way out into the courtyard, replacing their fallen fellows. An enormous white stag, its antlers draped with jewels, bounded into the courtyard from the road beyond the palace and snapped at Pearce. The old man dodged and swung his sword at it. James kept up his wind as Shakespeare's swell of river water whipped around them. Joan's mother battered creatures back with her iron cane, using her doorways to appear and disappear at will. Tobias used his own at Judith's command as she, Roger, and Martin shot a flurry of arrows through them. Baba Ben and Iya Mary focused on the wyvern, attacking it with clay and iron needles.

A six-armed Fae leapt at Joan as she reached the palace entrance. Rose's arm locked around the creature's neck, holding it in place as Nick sliced open its belly. Rose tossed the body out of Joan's way.

Joan whispered her thanks to both of them before shouldering through the door and into the darkness of Whitehall Palace.

CHAPTER FORTY-TWO
The Graceless Action of a Heavy Hand

hough her time in here hadn't been long, Joan could still remember her way through most of the palace hallways. For a moment, she wondered where Titanea might be hiding before heading directly for the main hall. She prayed her instinct would prove right.

Goodfellow appeared suddenly in her path, their face carefully blank.

"Turn around, Iron Blade," they said. "Take your people home and you might live."

Joan shook her head. "You know I can't do that."

"I gave you back Ben; isn't that enough?" Panic and rage shifted across their face. "What else matters when you have your loved ones? Take them home before you lose them."

She frowned, a sudden thought springing into her mind. "You wanted the Pact to be broken too. That's why you never offered to free Baba from the tower." She shook her head, pieces falling into place. "And you never wanted me to restore it."

"Why would I want to be sealed away again?" they sneered. "To only see my Rose if I carve out pieces of myself until I'm weak enough for that damned barrier to let me through." They glared at Joan. "You cannot fathom what that life is like."

Joan felt their words settle in her heart. She thought of Pearl caring for Baba Ben and his shop. She remembered Titanea defending her from the ladies at court and Arcas speaking mournfully about being trapped in one realm despite being a creature of two. She thought of Auberon, ready to die for his freedom, and she thought of Rose living the life of an orphan without her parent. She thought of Rufina and a love twisted even in death.

"That's not a world I want to return to either." She looked Goodfellow in the eye. "Believe me."

No, she had no desire for things to return to their old order. She wanted more, for all of them.

They searched her face frantically, trying to find the truth in her words. "You can't seal it as Rufina did," they said.

Joan shook her head and let the disgust she felt fill her words. "I won't build our safety on lies and betrayal."

"I knew it." Goodfellow laughed, tears springing to their eyes as hope bloomed across their face. "I knew you were made of different stuff, Iron Blade." They breathed deeply and turned their gaze to the ceiling. They glanced at her one last time, eyes shining. "Remember this: We can deceive without telling a lie."

And then she was alone in the hallway.

Joan shoved through the ornate wooden doors into the empty hall. The massive room was brightly lit, every candle around it flickering brilliantly and sending shadows dancing along the walls. The Fae queen watched from the far end as Joan approached. Titanea wore her own form now, her golden brown skin standing out against the cream of the king's jerkin and trousers.

"Make a deal with me, Titanea," Joan said, holding up her hands. "We've lost enough."

Titanea laughed. "Was any of it worth keeping?" She shifted into Lady Clifford, her face young and surrounded by blond curls. She laughed and her hair twisted itself up into an intricate style as she transformed into Queen Anne. She held that shape for a moment before her body twisted into King James's again. "Don't you think we were better royals than the ones you tried to protect?"

Joan frowned. She remembered how Queen Anne and her ladies treated her as an oddity, more of a pet than a person. She remembered how the king regarded each and every person around him as disposable, as if their only purpose was to fulfill his every whim.

Yes, Titanea had treated Joan as if she mattered, but she'd still allowed the innocent to be preyed upon. Though her hatred took a different form than the human rulers', it was no less dangerous.

"I don't want to fight you, Titanea." Joan let her resolve color her words, giving them force. "Help me seal a new Pact, something that will benefit all of our people."

The Fae queen scowled, her form shimmering to finally reveal her true self again. "You won't let this damned Pact go, will you?" She sighed and shook her head. "Shame, we truly did enjoy your company." She waved a hand in the air.

Goodfellow appeared out of thin air and swung at Joan. She twisted away as the blow split the tall candelabra near her in half. They struck

Joan across the chin with their elbow, knocking her backward. She tasted blood in her mouth as she dodged another hit. She caught their next punch and closed her fingers around their fist. Her feet slid across the floor.

"Why are you trying to kill me?" Joan hissed. She grabbed Goodfellow's other hand, twisting her arms around theirs to lock them in place.

Goodfellow leaned close. "We must give the queen a good show."

Joan felt the Fae press something into her palm. Bia vibrated as soon as the sword touched her fingers, and Joan's breath caught in her throat. She locked eyes with Goodfellow, saw the pleading in their gaze, and knew what she had to do.

She shoved her foot against Goodfellow's chest, sending the Fae stumbling backward before throwing herself at them with a primal scream. They both tumbled to the floor under her weight as Joan raised Bia in both hands. She drove it down with all her might, the blade's tip ringing against the stone floor beneath the reeds. Goodfellow gasped and twitched before laying still.

Joan looked down at where she'd curved the blade around the outside of their body, the deception hidden from Titanea by Joan's skirts.

She pulled the sword away slowly, straightening it as she moved so it looked like she drew it from Goodfellow's chest. She wiped it across their shirt, and crimson appeared where the blade touched the cloth, the illusory blood a gift of their magic. Joan hoped they felt her gratitude.

She turned slowly, Bia's vibrations sending a thrill through her.

The Fae queen snarled as she slowly stalked across the room, her eyes locked on Joan. "Will you send us back to our realm? Will you twist your words to beguile us with lies and promises like your ancestor? We will not have it!"

She leapt forward, knocking Joan to the ground with a shriek. Joan hit at her with Bia's pommel as they fell. Titanea caught her hand, squeezing until Joan's bones cracked. The sword clattered to the floor beside them.

Joan planted her feet and bucked Titanea off of her, scrambling over to Bia. She snatched it up and slammed the pommel into Titanea's face. Titanea tumbled backward. Joan jumped on top of her. She slid iron over her forearm and pressed it against the cloth covering the Fae queen's chest, pushing down with all her might. She grunted as the movement jarred her broken hand.

"I told you I want to make a deal," Joan huffed as Titanea struggled against her. "Give me your fair terms and I'll give you mine."

The Fae queen twisted an arm free before Joan trapped it under her leg.

"We'd rather die than make another deal with you or your Orisha," she spat. She stilled, then disappeared completely.

Joan scrambled to her feet and spun just as Titanea drove her sharp nails into Joan's shoulder. Joan gasped as burning pain shot through her body.

"She should've killed us instead of trapping us," Titanea whispered, rage rasping through her voice. "Then you wouldn't have to die for her mistakes." She withdrew her hand and slammed it into Joan's face, sending her tumbling across the floor.

"We offered you our affection, Joan!" Titanea called, then appeared suddenly in her face again. "But, of course, this is how you repay us."

She reached for Joan's throat, but Joan sliced out with Bia. The Fae queen screeched and stumbled away. Her severed hand dropped to the floor between them. Joan forced herself upright, her body aching and tired. But she couldn't stop, not now.

"I don't want to trap you and I don't want to betray you," she said.

Titanea sneered in response and disappeared. "You claim to want a deal, yet you cut off our hand." Her voice echoed in the room, coming from every direction.

"Because you're trying to kill me!" Joan shouted, searching the massive hall for any sign of her. "Please, Titanea, I swear I'm not trying to trick you or trap you. I want things fair for both sides, but I need your help to seal it."

Titanea's hand drove into Joan's side as her form shimmered to existence before her. "You mortals do nothing but lie."

Agony and rage overtook Joan's mind as she reacted, stabbing Bia into the Fae queen's chest.

Titanea's eyes widened as the blade burst out through her back in an explosion of blood. "You show your true self, Iron Blade."

"No," Joan said, her voice tight with horror and pain. "Titanea, no, I didn't . . ."

Titanea coughed, and crimson liquid stained her lips. "You'll have no new Pact if we die." She drew her hand from Joan's gut and dropped to her knees.

Joan went down with her, pulling Bia free. The Fae queen collapsed onto her side.

"Are you proud of yourself, Iron Blade?" The words came out hoarse, more blood splattering across Titanea's face.

Joan pressed her hands against the wound. "No. This isn't what I wanted at all." She hadn't meant to deal a mortal blow to the Fae queen, but in that moment of pain and fury, some instinct had taken over her. Despair pooled in her stomach. "I wanted to make a better agreement."

"You lie, just like your ancestor," Titanea spat, her eyes going glassy as they slid away from Joan's face. "She said she loved us and used our devotion as a trap." Rage contorted her face as she pushed at Joan's hands. "We hope she suffered."

"She did," Joan said. Titanea's gaze slid back to her. "She never forgave herself for hurting you, even in death."

Titanea's face twisted with disbelief. "Don't lie to me."

"She hated herself for what she did. It's why she let you control her."

"Don't lie!" She gripped the front of Joan's gown, her hold weak as blood pooled around them. "Don't lie about that."

A melancholy smile slid over Joan's face. "I only speak truth before you, remember?"

Realization dawned on the Fae queen as she recalled the final boon she'd forced on Joan. Her hand dropped to the floor, her eyes going distant again as they filled with sudden tears. "Then why..."

She didn't need to finish for Joan to understand. Even after more than a thousand years, Titanea wore her heartbreak as freshly as if it had happened yesterday. Joan could feel her own tears burning behind her eyes at the rawness of the Fae queen's pain.

"Love isn't always kind," Joan said softly. "Even when it's true."

The tears streamed down Titanea's face. "Damn you, Rufina." She coughed out the words, imbued with affection and despair as blood filled her mouth. "Damn you."

"There's still time. Help me seal a new Pact." Joan shook Titanea's shoulder as firmly as she dared. "Please."

Titanea wheezed, the sound rattling wetly in her chest. "No." Her gaze caught on something over Joan's shoulder. "Traitor," she hissed. "Puck... you traitor."

"I am." Goodfellow crouched on Titanea's other side, frowning down at the dying queen. "But you betrayed me first." They turned to Joan, their eyes sad. "It's too late for her. You struck true."

Panic pierced Joan's chest. She shook Titanea again, trying to catch her fading attention. As long as the Fae queen could speak, Joan could reseal the Pact. She only needed to make the vow.

Titanea glared at Joan and slapped her hand away. "Let us die. Please." The words were so faint, Joan could barely hear them. "Just let me rest ... after all this time." Her arm dropped to the ground limply as her head lolled to the side. Her eyes stared straight ahead, wide and unseeing.

The queen of the Fae was dead.

CHAPTER FORTY-THREE
Now Civil Wounds Are Stopped

"No," Joan whispered. She watched Goodfellow lean over to gently press Titanea's eyes closed. "No, no, no."

The building rattled around her as the fighting continued outside.

She'd come so far, they all had, and all for naught. Titanea was dead, and any hope of resealing the Pact perished along with her.

"I've failed," Joan whispered. Her head spun and she felt herself pitching to the side. She caught herself on clumsy hands before she could hit the floor and noticed crimson pooling beneath her, too far from Titanea's body to be hers. Joan touched her side, where Titanea had struck earlier. Hot blood gushed sluggishly over her fingers. A stark laugh burst from her lips as her elbow buckled and she slammed into the floor.

Goodfellow shouted her name, rushing to gather her in their arms.

"All this for nothing." The tears she'd held back until now flowed from her eyes, despair overruling the fear of feeling her body fail her.

"Not for nothing," Goodfellow said. They clasped her hand, bringing it up between them. "Make the Pact with me. I have the power to hold my people to our agreement." They shook her gently. "Don't give up yet, Iron Blade, we can do this together." Their gaze turned sad again. "I owe you a boon, remember."

Joan blinked, fighting to force her eyes open again as she held on to what Goodfellow offered. She could use that power she held over them to return things to the way they'd been before the Pact was broken. But then they'd find themselves here again, when the Fae grew so dissatisfied with their lot and tore the agreement asunder once more.

"What do you want, Joan?" Goodfellow said the words gently. They watched her calmly, but Joan could feel their hands shaking.

They feared her answer but still offered her the choice. Even after everything they'd said, the risk they'd taken to give her an advantage, Goodfellow didn't trust her completely. She felt the urge to prove herself to them, to offer more than she'd intended, but stopped herself. Goodfellow had broken her trust long ago; she didn't owe them assurances. She'd show them what she thought was a just Pact and see if their faith held.

She pulled her hand free of Goodfellow's and called Bia to her. The sword flew into her grip, blade held between them.

She'd been honest when she'd told Titanea that she wanted better for all of them.

"Peace," Joan said. She held Bia up, offering it to Goodfellow. "What I want is peace."

Goodfellow smiled and placed their hand against the blade. "Then peace we shall have, Iron Blade." They cut their palm on the sword.

Joan grabbed their hand, their blood mingling together. A sound like the clanging of a church bell echoed around them, and the sword vibrated so violently in Joan's weak grip, Goodfellow had to help her hold it. Joan's chest burned, the heady warmth of Ogun's presence flowing through her whole body before rushing down her arm and up along Bia. The metal turned red, the searing heat of it just on the edge of pain. Joan looked to Goodfellow and saw them watching the sword in awe.

"Speak these words," Joan said firmly, the magic of the boon flowing through her. She let her heart guide her, feeling Ogun's presence all around. Her Orisha knew justice; he wouldn't let her falter.

Goodfellow nodded, their body going tense with the power.

"With this agreement—"

"With this agreement—"

"—I vow to work alongside the children of the Orisha—"

Goodfellow's eyes shifted to her, another smile spreading over their face. "—I vow to work alongside the children of the Orisha—"

"—to maintain peace between the Fae and mortal realms," Joan finished, watching Goodfellow's face.

They grinned at her, smile radiant. "—to maintain *lasting* peace between the Fae and mortal realms."

The words seemed to ring in the air.

"For lasting peace." Ogun's voice thundered around them as the clang sounded again.

Goodfellow blinked at the sound. "Was that . . . ?"

"Meferefun, Ogun," Joan replied, knowing the Orisha heard the deep gratitude in her voice.

Well done, daughter, Ogun's voice whispered in her head.

Bia pulsed again and Joan could feel the force of it flow beyond them in this room. Then the sword went quiet, and Joan shrunk it around her wrist, the familiar weight comforting.

Her arm dropped to her side, Bia suddenly too heavy to hold. Panic slipped over Goodfellow's face.

"Hang on, Joan," they said firmly. "You're not done with this world yet." They gathered her up in their arms, pressing a hand against her wound as they stood.

Joan let her head rest against their chest, half annoyed by the exhaustion overtaking her. She blinked and they were outside, the bright sunlight stark against her eyes. They watered as she tried to survey the courtyard. The Fae and children of the Orisha all stared back at her.

"The fighting stopped," Joan whispered. She looked up at Goodfellow, who nodded.

"We have peace," they said, "thanks to you, Iron Blade."

"Joan, you did it!" James raced over to her, a wide smile on his face. "We all felt it when you sealed the new Pact." He finally seemed to take in her state because his eyes widened. "What happened . . ." He looked up at Goodfellow, eyes going dark. "What have you done to my sister?"

Joan held up her hand. "They didn't . . ." She squirmed out of Goodfellow's arms and tried to stand on her own. "Titanea stabbed—" She pitched forward into her brother's arms.

James cried out as Goodfellow steadied him and guided them all to the ground. Joan groaned, forcing her heavy eyes open again. Nick and Rose were standing over them. Rose's eyes darted between Joan and Goodfellow, her face pale.

"What's happened?" Shakespeare called as he approached.

He had Susanna draped across his back, blood running down the girl's face. Judith limped along behind them, a hand on Arcas to steady herself. She clutched her side but otherwise appeared to be unhurt. The grim whined when it saw Joan, and Judith let it bound over to her side. Joan tried to pat its head but couldn't force her arm to stretch far enough. It tucked itself under her falling palm and whined again.

"I'm glad you're all safe," she said, her voice too quiet. She saw Baba Ben approach and exchange a quick glance with Goodfellow. "You were right, Baba, I did it."

Tears sprang into her godfather's eyes. "Of course you did, Joan. Now lie still, your father's on his way."

She shivered, feeling cold all over, and James hugged her tighter. She moaned as he pressed against her wound. Someone shouted her name. Her father dropped to his knees beside her, opening his medicine case with shaking hands. Her mother crouched next to him and rubbed Joan's hair.

It felt nice. The quiet was nice. This was what they'd fought for, what she'd fought for, and it was done.

The Pact had been forged anew, fairly and without the bitter stain of betrayal.

Meferefun, Ogun, Joan thought and closed her eyes.

1 FEBRUARY

CHAPTER FORTY-FOUR
An Ever Fixéd Mark

he grave lay in a copse of trees outside of London's walls, its marker a sword entwined with stone lilies. Wildflowers already sprouted from the freshly turned earth, covering it with a carpet of bright blooms that defied the chill of winter. Joan thought it the appropriate place to lay Rufina's bones to rest again, and the flowers proved some part of Titanea's magic remained with her.

Joan hoped the two women could find each other in the space beyond life and release the wounds betrayal had left on them both. Despite all they'd done, they too deserved peace.

She touched Bia where it hung around her wrist once again. It sang back to her, and Joan smiled. She'd offered to bury the sword with its original mistress but had received a firm rebuke from Bia itself. It may have belonged to Rufina first, but it was Joan's now and it had no desire to rest in another's hands.

"Are you ready, love?" Joan's mother said. She stood a short distance away with Arcas at her feet, both watching intently but giving Joan her privacy.

Joan nodded and turned away from the grave. Her mother cut her magic through the air and a doorway opened before them. The three of them stepped through into the Sands house, the sounds of birdsong replaced by the clanging pans and plates in their kitchen.

"Finally!" James huffed as he bustled down the stairs. "You almost didn't have time to change." He shook his head as Joan glanced down at the red-and-rose-colored gown she'd put on that morning. "As if I'd let you wear *that* to the palace."

He had on a golden yellow jerkin and trousers, and Joan suspected that the matching dress waited for her in her room. She laughed as he dragged her upstairs.

Grace leaned out of the kitchen, wiping her hands on her apron. "Be quick, breakfast will be on the table soon." She patted Arcas's head when the grim padded past her to settle on its favorite velvet cushion.

"All right," they called back in unison.

Their father stepped out of his bedroom as they raced across the third-floor landing and Joan slowed down just enough to press a kiss against his cheek. He smiled at her before heading downstairs. They reached the top floor and James shoved her into her room.

"Hurry and change so Mother can redo your hair," he said, flapping his hands at her.

Joan frowned at him. "What's wrong with my hair?" She touched the twists she'd hastily wound together with red ribbon early this morning.

"You want to go to the royal palace," he said, "in a style that took as much thought as lacing a bodice?" He shook his head, walking out of the room as she flushed guiltily. "Don't speak, just change."

297

When Joan stepped through her mother's magical doorway into the palace, she found herself in the very rooms she'd used as Titanea's lady-in-waiting. She looked around in shock as James, their parents, Grace, and Arcas followed behind her. She'd been prepared to never see this space again and, even if she did, for everything to be covered in a month's worth of dust, but the entire room was immaculately clean. It looked as if she hadn't fled hastily almost a month ago. She turned to Grace, who went red.

"I wanted things to stay in their proper order," she said, "in case you returned."

Joan smiled back, gratitude warming her heart. She'd retained the title Baroness de Clifford and all that went with it, but she never expected that ownership to be honored still.

James flopped onto the enormous bed that stood against one wall of the room. "This is how you lived as the queen's lady?" He ran his fingers over the emerald velvet curtains draping the bed's four tall posts. "I might've hesitated over Titanea too."

Joan smacked him in the face with a pillow she snagged off the sofa. It only barely muffled his laughter.

"Enough, you two," their mother said, "we're already late."

She bustled them all out into the hallway and Grace took the lead. Joan felt a thousand things as they walked through Whitehall Palace, a mix of good and bad memories washing over her. She felt James take her hand and smiled at her brother as Arcas pressed against her side. Ahead of them, their parents had looped their arms together, her father whispering to Grace about venturing down to the ocean to show her other ways to wield her new magic.

When they reached the king's chambers, the doors swung open before they could knock.

"Finally," Baba Ben said as he waved them inside. He grinned as he saw Joan and James, recognizing the clothes he'd fashioned for them himself. "Excellent choice, James. This is some of my finest work."

Joan frowned. "How do you know I didn't choose this myself?"

James and Baba gave her twin looks of fond exasperation. Joan laughed. She shook her head and continued past as her godfather closed the door behind them. He pressed a kiss into her hair before crossing through into the king's inner bedroom. Joan watched him go; the reality of his presence still filled her with joy. She cleared her throat and tried to force the broad smile off her face.

The people who crowded the royal chamber wouldn't usually be in such intimate proximity to the king of England. Iya Mary and Sir Pearce talked with each other on the sofa nearest the large hearth. They both nodded cordially to Joan when they saw her. She did the same, determined not to be impolite but offered them no more than they did her. Iya Anne stood off in a corner, giggling and blushing as Aemilia Lanier whispered something in her ear. Susanna sat with Judith, Rose, and Dr. Hall, her hand on the doctor's leg. Arcas padded over to them and nudged against Judith's palm. She scratched behind the grim's ears without looking up. Rose turned, her expression brightening as she spotted Joan. Joan felt herself blush as Rose strode over to meet her.

"You look beautiful," Rose said. She touched Joan's hair, fingers tugging at the copper beads strung along the two long braids framing her face.

Joan smiled. "My mother's work."

She glanced over to see both her parents staring back, her mother's expression enough to make her put some distance between her and Rose.

The doors to the bedchamber swung open and Philip stepped out, his face slightly pink.

"The king needs a bit more time to prepare," he said, pulling the doors closed behind him. "We should proceed to the courtyard without them." A husky chuckle echoed from within the bedchamber and Philip cleared his throat. "With haste."

They all laughed but hurried out into the hallway to give the king, and his companion, some privacy.

"People of England, we have suffered through a harrowing time of dark days and things of nightmares. But, as I stand before you now, I promise you that there is light upon the path ahead for England."

The crowd roared as King James I held his arms open to them. The citizens of London had gathered in the courtyard of Whitehall Palace, their number so great they filled the streets as far as the eye could see. The energy of the moment pulsed through Joan, and as she stood near the royal dais, she could feel the presence of every person at her back. A hand slipped into hers as she twined her fingers with Rose's.

"Zaza plays the king well," Rose whispered, so close to Joan's ear that the words barely needed any volume.

Joan smiled but didn't respond. Iya Mary, Joan, Goodfellow, and Philip had landed on the unusual arrangement as the surest way to keep the peace. So few people had known that the true King James was dead. The complication of having the new ruler of the Fae also leading mortal England was far less daunting than it had seemed at first approach.

Goodfellow wouldn't rule unchecked. The children of the Orisha would keep watch as they always had, this time as true custodians instead of conduits. Nor would Goodfellow rule England eternally—they'd only stand in King James's place for the span of a mortal's lifetime before "dying" to let human rule return.

As proof of their agreement, and possibly something more, Baba Ben stood on the dais just behind the king. He was dressed in his finest clothes, his form still too thin but looking far healthier than he had when he'd returned to them. Goodfellow glanced back, catching Baba's eye and smiling with the king's face. Philip stood just over the king's other shoulder, his expression sly as he noticed the exchange. Rose tugged at Joan's hand, drawing her carefully through the crowd. The space they left behind was instantly filled by others, happy to hear their king speak for as long as he liked. A short way across the courtyard, Joan spotted the new red cap chieftain standing alongside the hag queen, their people spread out amongst the crowd. Their magic hid their true forms from the mortals around them. Both Fae nodded to her as she passed before turning their attention back to the king's speech. This wasn't Joan's first time encountering the chieftain or the queen since the forging of the new Pact, but receiving their respect like this still felt astounding.

She and Rose reached the edge of the crowd when the sire of the jack-in-irons stepped suddenly into their path. Joan inclined her head, pointedly ignoring his sash of severed heads as the sire nodded back. He patted her on the shoulder with one long-fingered hand; the gentle touch was still hard enough to make Joan stumble.

"Easy," Rose said with a good-natured smile as she steadied Joan.

The sire grinned back and ruffled Rose's hair before stepping aside so they could pass. Two more jacks-in-irons slipped into the crowd behind him with an ease belying their large forms. Joan watched for a moment, amazed at the strange accord she'd helped create, before Rose tugged at her hand again. She followed without protest. She knew exactly where they were going, and they were already behind schedule.

Rose guided her into a nearby alleyway before pulling Joan into her arms. The buildings around them faded away as Rose transported them to the tiring house of their new theatre. Blackfriars—an indoor playhouse—took some getting used to, but until their beloved Globe was rebuilt, it would do. Candlelight warmed the stage and the house beyond, the flames casting their own sort of shifting magic. None of them would complain about being protected from the elements either. Their Globe couldn't boast that feat.

"Damnation," Burbage shouted, clutching his chest as they appeared out of thin air. "Give a man some warning, will you?"

Rose laughed as Joan patted the man's arm. He shook his head before continuing to his dressing room. Rose just grinned and leaned in for a kiss. Joan obliged, slipping her hand around Rose's neck to deepen it. Someone cleared their throat aggressively, and Joan pulled away to see Shakespeare watching her with his arms folded.

"Isn't there work to be done, fight mistress?" He stared at her before looking pointedly at Rose. "Don't think because you're daughter to the king that you can disrupt our playhouse. This is a new play and I won't have you distracting Joan before rehearsal."

Rose laughed loudly, stepping away from Joan. "I wouldn't dream of doing such a thing." She grinned at Joan again. "Shall I bring your swords?"

"Thank you," Joan said. She leaned in for another kiss and Shakespeare placed his hand between their lips before they could touch. Joan blew a laugh against his palm.

He pushed his way between them, his glare aimed at Rose. "If you're bringing the swords, come this way."

Rose smiled sweetly at him and winked at Joan as she followed Shakespeare. Joan moved toward the stage when a hand grabbed hers. She turned to see Nick.

He pressed his lips against her knuckles. "You look beautiful," he whispered and leaned toward her.

"None of that!" Shakespeare shouted, flapping his hands at them. "Get onstage now, Nicholas Tooley."

Nick rolled his eyes so only Joan could see. "Later," he whispered in her ear before obeying Shakespeare's command. He stopped when he passed by Rose and kissed her softly.

Shakespeare screamed. "Enough! Enough! Separate them! Separate all three of them!" He rushed toward Nick and Rose, practically pushing the boy out onstage. "We have *work*."

Joan laughed so hard tears sprang to her eyes. How rich of Shakespeare, the most amorous of any in the playhouse, to be so disturbed by their show of affection. She'd hold off for now for the sake of the man's nerves. She'd bask in her loves' presence another time, but today, she had to ready the fights for Shakespeare's new play *King Lear*. They'd have an audience at two o'clock, and Joan refused to send any of the King's Men out if they weren't ready.

She moved toward the stage and felt her brother fall in step beside her. He'd proceeded to the theatre ahead of her and Rose by way of a magical doorway. She smiled at him as he elbowed her gently.

"You've managed quite the arrangement, dear sister."

Joan wasn't sure whether James spoke of the new Pact or her growing relationship with both Nick and Rose, but she enjoyed the praise nonetheless. She'd given both all the effort within her heart, and the results made her feel full of light.

This new Pact was far from perfect. There were negotiations to be made and violence was bound to happen amongst mortals, amongst the Fae, and between the two groups. The peace they had now would take effort to maintain, but that felt more just than the one that had come before it.

"Will you go back to the shop after our practice?" James asked the question without judgment, though she could tell which answer he hoped for by his furtive glances.

Joan shook her head. "No, I plan to watch from the house." She nudged him back, just hard enough to make him stumble a step. "None of the work Father has waiting for me would make me miss today's show."

James grinned at her, relief sweeping over his face as they stepped out onto the stage. Warmth spread through her, both Ogun's and her own happiness. She took a moment to breathe as the rest of the King's Men filed into the theatre. She thought of everything she'd been through, of all she'd wanted and all she'd brought to herself by her own hands. Of the loves she'd found, the peace she'd brokered. Of the people she'd protected and the ones she'd lost. Of her place within the King's Men and the goldsmith's shop waiting to bear her name. Of all that she'd fought and bled for and how it brought her to this precious moment.

Well done, child, Ogun whispered softly within her. Joan smiled and pressed a hand to her chest, filled with gratitude. Bia vibrated gently at her wrist. She discreetly grew it to its full size, hiding the magic in the folds of her skirt. It slipped happily into her hand. She raised it with a flourish and turned back to the gathered players. She dug Bia's point into the wooden floor of the stage, grinning at her company of actors.

"Now, sirs," she said, elation filling her in anticipation of the work. "Shall we begin?"

THE END

A Note on History

While this novel is a work of historical fiction, it was born from a place of historical fact. Several of the characters we meet were real people who were alive in 1606, and while there were narrative liberties taken with the timeline, most of it is true to life. While the existence of the Fae in England at this time is debatable, the presence of non-white citizens and queer people is not.

Real People

THE PLAYERS' FAMILIES

Anne Shakespeare (née Hathaway) was the wife of William Shakespeare and the mother of his three children: Susanna and the twins, Judith and Hamnet. Hamnet died when he and Judith were only eleven years old. Anne was listed as "Agnes Hathaway" in her father's will and was famously only left the "second-best bed" in her husband's will.

Susanna Shakespeare was the oldest child of William and Anne Shakespeare. She married the doctor John Hall in 1607.

Judith Shakespeare was the youngest daughter of William and Anne Shakespeare and the twin sister of Hamnet. She married Thomas Quiney in 1616.

John Hall was the husband of Susanna Shakespeare and Stratford-upon-Avon's sole physician.

Winifred Burbage (née Turner) was the wife of Richard Burbage. The two married in 1600 and had at least eight children.

Cuthbert Burbage was a theatre manager and the older brother of Richard Burbage. After the death of their father, James Burbage, he became the primary force behind the famous stealing of the Globe when he and fifteen others dismantled and moved the theatre across the Thames overnight due to a dispute with their landlord.

Ellen Burbage (née Brayne) was the wife of actor and theatre manager James Burbage and the mother of Cuthbert and Richard. They married in 1559 and had four children.

Henry Lanier was the son of Aemilia Lanier and Henry Carey—the 1st Baron Hunsdon, Queen Elizabeth's Lord Chamberlain (the courtier in charge of royal entertainments), and the patron of William Shakespeare's acting company until his death in 1596. Through his father, he was the grandson of Mary Boleyn and the great-nephew of Anne Boleyn.

Real Places

Stratford-upon-Avon is a small town in the West Midlands of England and the birthplace of William Shakespeare. It sits along the River Avon and was founded in 1196 through a charter granted by King Richard I. It is currently home to the Royal Shakespeare Company.

Oxford is a city about fifty-six miles north of London founded in the eighth century. It is also the home of Oxford University, where teaching has occurred since 1096.

New Place was William Shakespeare's home in Stratford-upon-Avon and the second-largest building in the town. While he spent most of his time in London, the rest of his family lived at New Place. It was given to Susanna and John after his death and is the only place on this list that you cannot see today as it was demolished fully in 1702, eighty-six years after Shakespeare's death. The Shakespeare Birth Trust has an exhibition on the land where the house once stood and continue to work to excavate its history.

Church of the Holy Trinity is the parish church of Stratford-upon-Avon. It was originally built in 1210 on the River Avon and rebuilt between 1465 and 1497. William Shakespeare was baptized, married, and buried here along with his wife, Anne.

The Orisha

This novel contains a fictionalized version of the very real tradition of Orisha veneration/worship, which was born in West Africa, mainly in the area we now know as Nigeria. While certain aspects may be familiar to practitioners, this is not a true reflection of the religion and should be taken as fantastical.

My personal knowledge of the Orisha is through Lucumí, commonly known as Santería—a branch of the practice from Cuba. It was born when enslaved African people blended their traditional religion with the Catholic practices forced on them by the Spanish. The cover of Catholicism helped them worship as they wanted without punishment.

For the religion as Joan and her family practice it, I asked myself what would things look like if it came to England without being shaped by the cruelties of the slave trade. I also added the idea that the Orisha give you magical powers.

If you'd like to know more about the Santería religion or the Orisha, I recommend *Black Gods: Òrìṣà Studies in the New World*, by John Mason, and *Finding Soul on the Path of Oriṣa: A West African Spiritual Tradition*, by Tone Melora Correal, but ultimately the best resource is an actual practitioner or priest.

Acknowledgements

The final book of the trilogy! We made it, y'all! Thank you to every last one of you for taking this ride with me and Joan. My gratitude is boundless and eternal. Thank you for picking up this niche-ass series and loving it as much as I do.

I want to start by thanking myself for staying the course and getting these books out year after year after year. Writing is hard, writing a trilogy is harder, and I made it on top of working my acting gigs and raising a whole kid. You did it, Britt, take a bow!

Maggie Lehrman, my wonderful editor, thank you for believing in Joan's story so hard and for not flinching when I sent you the roughest of rough drafts for this book. Thank you for your wonderful feedback and for seeking my input even when you didn't have to. I've said it before and I'll say it again, I can't imagine a better editor to take this ride with and I knew that from the first time we spoke. I can't believe we're at the end but I'm so glad we took this journey together.

To my fantastic team at Abrams and Amulet Books: Megan Carlson, Maggie Moore, Jenna Lisanti, Megan Evans, Trish McNamara O'Neill,

Kristen Luby, Beatriz Milander, Andrew Smith, and especially my publicist, Mary Marolla. Thank you for all your hard work bringing this series to readers. Every time I've felt the full force of Abrams behind me, I've felt invincible. Mary, thank you for championing these books and getting me opportunities I've only dreamed of in my journal. You are truly the best.

Thank you to my second editor, Claire Stetzer; my copy editor, Penny Cray; and my proofreader, Margo Winton Parodi, for helping me through all the things I forgot from English class and the details I forgot between chapters. Y'all have the eyes of eagles, and my chaotic, vibes-first drafting style thanks you for it. I will never forget the rules about "towards" and "backwards" for the rest of my life. There's one grammar issue resolved forever thanks to your efforts. Bless.

To my cover illustrator, Fernanda Suarez, thank you for every single stunning cover. I still can't believe I have these three beautiful pieces of art by one of my favorite digital artists! I was a fan before now and will forever stan your legendary skill.

To my cover designer, Micah Fleming, thank you for the way you bring these covers together and make serious magic. Outstanding. Incredible. Stunning.

To my map artist, Jamie Zollars, thank you for crafting a beautiful map for this final installment! I've dreamed of maps in my books and thank you for helping that come true.

Thank you to my beloved Carrie McClain for being my beta reader again and catching all the cultural bits I had to slide into this story. You always give such wonderful and encouraging notes. I've felt your love and support through the whole process of writing this series and I could not have finished it without you. I love you always, sis!

Thank you to everyone at my literary agency, Writers House, for always having my back. Special thanks to the foreign rights team: Cecilia de la Campa, Alessandra Birch, and Sofia Bolido for giving your best to this wild Shakespeare/Fae/Orisha mashup. Y'all are an incredible team!

To my incredible agent and friend, Alexandra Levick, thank you for being one of the first people to believe in and champion this series. Neither Joan nor I would've made it this far without your guidance, insights, business acumen, and friendship. Thank you for fielding my endless stream of questions, standing up for my mental and physical health, cheering me on, making me do the things I complain about because they're good for me, and not letting me settle for less than I deserve. I'm so glad these books brought us together and I can not fathom traversing this career with anyone else. Thank you, thank you, thank you, Allie!

Thank you to my wonderful friends who supported me through this process. Thank you to Baba Kevin for his incredible insights into Joan's magic and his generous support. To Tracy; Ayana; Amy and Paul; Leigh; Jalisa; Clinton; Ron and Leslie; Jonathan, Resse, Ashley, and my Arena Players family; Nicole, Leslie, Izetta, and Carrie, my Taco Tuesday, Womanism Everyday group chat; Will, Omar, and the rest of my Black Nerd Problems family; all my beautiful, chaotic geniuses in the Black Nerd Problems Discord; my hilarious and supportive D&D squad; to my 2023 debut babes Jade, Danielle, and Hannah; and Soni, Zoulfa, and the rest of my Agent Siblings. Thank you for making all the hard work a little bit easier on my heart and mind, for keeping me laughing, and for reminding me of my brilliance.

Thank you to my wonderful family. Thank you to the whole Williams/Johnson/Cook clan for all of your love and support. No matter where I am in the world, I feel it and I know y'all always have my back. To my brother, Eric, and his beautiful family, I love y'all so much! To my baby sister, Ericka, the flyest teen I know, I hope you find a beautiful reflection of the incredible Black girl you are in these books. To Mom and Dad Older for your boundless love and support and making room for me in your lives. To Malka, Lou, and the kids, thank you for loving me and welcoming me into the family with such warmth and generosity. To Grandma for being my number one forever cheerleader, my second mom, and my grandma in one. Thank you for supporting every wild and unusual thing I ever wanted to wade into and never pulling me back from being a Jack-of-All-Trades. Everything I am is because of you, and all of that fed into this series. I wouldn't be here without your love.

To my love, Daniel, thank you for being an incredible husband, partner, and dad. Thank you for pushing me and holding my hand through writing this series. Thank you for never placing us in competition with each other and cheering for my success just as hard as you root for your own. When I imagined what marriage would be like, I pictured something like this, and my imagination still fell short of the beautiful reality. I love you so much.

To my little Tito, who's grown alongside these books, thank you for being the brilliant, chaotic, loving kid you are. Thank you for making me slow down and for imitating me. Thank you for proudly pulling "Mommy's book" off the shelf whenever you see it and for always making me smile. I hope you too can find yourself beautifully reflected in these books. I love you always, my little bun.

Thank you to everyone who hosted me or invited me to an event. Thank you to every bookseller who stocked this series, to every reviewer who took the time to read and write such lovely things, to every writer who put these books on a list and got it in front of new readers. Thank you to everyone who came out to see me in person, I loved meeting each one of you. Thank you to all the authors and moderators I talked with on tour for your generosity and community. Thank you especially to the Folger Shakespeare Library and the Enoch Pratt Public Library. In my younger days, I dreamed of working with y'all, and I wish I could go back in time and share how incredibly generous you've all been in supporting me and this series.

Finally, thank you to Ogun, who has constantly guided my hands and laid his blessing over this series. Meferefun, Ogun and all the Orisha and ancestors behind me.

If you'd have talked to me when I started my YA Shakespearean fantasy back in 2018, I would've been unsure about finishing that book, let alone an entire trilogy. Now, we're on the other side and I'm just getting started. I hope you all can feel my overflowing gratitude as we finish this series together. I love you all and thank you from the bottom of my heart.